G R JORDAN

Death of the Witch

Siobhan Duffy Mysteries #2

There is no magic when one no longer believes.

Hilda Lewis, "The Ship That Flew"

Contents

Foreword

The events of this book, while based around real locations in Northern Ireland, are entirely fictional and all characters do not represent any living or deceased person. All companies are fictitious representations. Basically, it's a bit of blether!

Acknowledgement

To Ken, Jean, Colin, Evelyn, John and Rosemary for your work in bringing this novel to completion, your time and effort is deeply appreciated.

Novels by G R Jordan

Siobhan Duffy Mysteries

1. A Giant Killing
2. Death of the Witch
3. The Bloodied Hands

The Highlands and Islands Detective series (Crime)

1. Water's Edge
2. The Bothy
3. The Horror Weekend
4. The Small Ferry
5. Dead at Third Man
6. The Pirate Club
7. A Personal Agenda
8. A Just Punishment
9. The Numerous Deaths of Santa Claus
10. Our Gated Community
11. The Satchel
12. Culhwch Alpha
13. Fair Market Value
14. The Coach Bomber
15. The Culling at Singing Sands

Kirsten Stewart Thrillers (Thriller)

Jac Moonshine Thrillers

1. Jac's Revenge
2. Jac for the People
3. Jac the Pariah

The Contessa Munroe Mysteries (Cozy Mystery)

1. Corpse Reviver
2. Frostbite
3. Cobra's Fang

The Patrick Smythe Series (Crime)

1. The Disappearance of Russell Hadleigh
2. The Graves of Calgary Bay
3. The Fairy Pools Gathering

Austerley & Kirkgordon Series (Fantasy)

1. Crescendo!
2. The Darkness at Dillingham
3. Dagon's Revenge
4. Ship of Doom

Supernatural and Elder Threat Assessment Agency (SETAA) Series (Fantasy)

1. Scarlett O'Meara: Beastmaster

Island Adventures Series (Cosy Fantasy Adventure)

1. Surface Tensions

Dark Wen Series (Horror Fantasy)

1. The Blasphemous Welcome
2. The Demon's Chalice

Chapter 01

Lindsay McLaughlin swore under her breath as she walked along pushing the cart holding her cleaning materials. There were a couple of large brushes, one of those grabbers for picking litter off the ground so you didn't have to reach down, some shovels, and plenty of bags. There were always plenty of bags because there was always plenty of rubbish.

Lindsay had been told all her life to get qualifications, been told through her school days that if she didn't work harder, if she didn't give her exams a go, she'd end up with nothing. At nineteen years of age, she didn't think nothing would have happened so soon. She tried to get onto courses, well, the ones that were any use, but she'd been told that she needed a job, kicked out of the house by her father, until she ended up with this one.

The high street was frosty; the windows had a cold crisp glaze across them, as the day, which was still if bitterly cold, had begun. There were many that day, she thought, who would look over at the nearby castle with the red sky behind it, telling everyone how wonderful it looked. People would look to the Belfast Hills with the sun streaking across them, producing those browns of post-Christmas, held up at their best in the dim light of morning or the fading light of evening, but not Lindsay.

It was cold. Nothing else, just simply cold. Holding a brush with your mitts on as well was difficult. She tottered back and forth from her wagon, grabbing the odd bit of litter, bringing it over and dropping it into the central area of the device, the lid off because there was no one to complain about the smell. Lindsay wanted to do things the easy way, keep it simple. I mean, how difficult could it be? You picked up the litter; you put it into the bin; you wheeled on to the next place.

She'd endured several hours of training as they called it. Mind-numbing. Lindsay wasn't stupid. Academic? No. Inclined to academic activities, no. She'd been too busy. Too busy partying, too busy with boys. Blessed with a half-decent figure, she'd turned a few heads, enjoyed some good times. After all, that's what life was about, wasn't it? There was time enough later on to knuckle down. Why was she knuckling down at nineteen?

Lindsay took a moment to stare down at the grey flannel track bottoms she had on. They were some of the least attractive clothing she had in her wardrobe, but at least if they got dirty, she wouldn't care. Over her top, she wore a large fluorescent coat with a black beanie hat on her head. She also had a scarf around her neck these days because of the chill. It was almost a year since she stepped out to the clubs. It was harder to afford it these days because she was running her own budget.

Lindsay looked across the street at the clothes shop which she'd often gone into, buying nothing. Leaving her brush behind, she strode across the road, which was bereft of activity, and stood, looking through the window. She had to brush it slightly to get rid of that frosty glaze so she could see clearly. Here was a little top inside. She'd enjoy that one. She'd certainly be the centre of attention with it, dancing the night away, plenty of drink down her. Then off for a snog somewhere, maybe a bit more.

She needed to get out. She needed to get away from this crap. Yes, literally crap, the amount of dog doings she collected. Get a half decent job. She'd wanted nothing though. Her father talked about her being a good secretary, especially after the qualifications didn't come in but she didn't fancy that. Secretary at her age, she knew what that meant. Something to look at for the stressed-out individual who made his way into the morning office, no doubt harangued by his wife. Lindsay was worth more than that or this. She just needed to see it, to find where to go.

The one hope she had in her life was her volleyball. She remembered the poster back in her bedroom. Beach volleyball. They did it at the Olympics, but they did it all around the world as well. She had watched a lot. The idea of the sand, the sun, the surf beyond. Not that big here in Northern Ireland. Wasn't really the weather for beach volleyball. The beaches were here though. Some of the ones on the north coast were stunning. But, no, you'd probably have to play in a coat like she was wearing for the job.

She giggled and turned to walk back to the cart. She halted abruptly. While the sun was coming up and the tops of the buildings were emblazoned in an orange light, the alleyways beside the shops were still dark. Was that someone over there? She froze for a moment, peering. Or was it in her head there was someone about?

Lindsay didn't know where this paranoia came from. She was always afraid of something from the dark. An out-of-place figure that would kick off a wild terror. Too many horror films, she reckoned. It was always the case in the horror films, wasn't it? Young girl somewhere, all alone. Some mad guy chasing her or stalking her. She never fully understood it. Why? They always seemed to want to kill these young women that they were after. She'd never found that with the boys she'd been with. They all wanted something but not that.

Was she seriously reminiscing at nineteen? *What on earth, girl*, she thought to herself. *Come on.*

She moseyed across the road behind the cart and pushed it forward again. She halted. Not that far until the end of the street. Down at the far end, she saw that bit of history. Not a pleasant one. She remembered the first time she'd seen it, The Witches' Pillory. She'd seen it in some of the medieval horror films she had watched as a kid.

Some poor sod had been brought out and put in what most people called the stocks. Arms either side, head through a hole in the middle. They were forced to stand there while people threw rotten food at them. Cabbages, tomatoes. Tomatoes? Had they been a thing back then? She didn't know. She didn't know the genuine history, the truth of it. All she knew was of history was the horror films.

Except she had read about this one, because it was a replica and it had pleasant signs around it. It was a thing with her that she loved to tell people about the troubled times of where she lived. Well, the less paramilitary ones.

Carrickfergus had its marvellous castle, and it looked impressive. But here at the end of High Street, the corner of Antrim Street and Joymount, you weren't that far from the castle. It was here that they'd brought the witches, the last of which came from Island Magee, just up the road. Circa 1700 and something. Somebody had multiple fits. That was it. Because of objects hurled at them. She'd always thought it funny because the judge was going to let them off, but the jury had convicted them. Twelve months in prison, and time in the pillory, getting stuff thrown at them. One of the so-called witches had lost an eye.

The replica didn't have someone in the pillory, though. It wasn't like they had a grotesque figure there. No dungeon mock-up, some sort of horror-themed show. It was a good, clean history, at least good for the tourists. The trouble with history like this when you're in your own town, is you began to just pass it by. But not this.

Every day for the last three months, she'd struggled to clean the pillory, anywhere in and around it. It had always given her the shivers, as did the streets coming up to it in the pale morning light, the shadows creeping here and there. She was shivering now. *Come on, Lindsay. End of the street, we get our break; sit down with a cup of tea. People show up.*

Head down, she brushed up some rubbish before putting it into the middle of her device. Sauntering forward, she pushed the wagon, eyes peeled on the street until she came across it and swore loudly.

Nowadays, people with dogs should know better. They were all meant to carry those little green bags. Sitting in front of her on the pavement was the dog poo. She hated dog poo. Even if you picked it up inside the bag, it was squishy; it was yuck.

Lindsay took off her glove, reached into her cart, and picked up one of the little green bags. Rolling it inside out, she stepped forward and took a whiff. Oh, it was vile. What was it about dog poo? Most other things, rotten food, you could handle it. Dog poo was right up your nose instantly and it didn't disappear.

Right in front of her now was her life, in a metaphor. She hadn't done the time at school; she hadn't got herself to where she needed to be; and now it was just, well, poo, as her mum would say. Mum didn't like her using the other word.

Reaching down, Lindsay felt the squidginess of the poo as she picked it up. Quickly she rolled the bag round, tied it at the top, stepped quickly over to the wagon, and dropped it into the middle of the device. She turned away and breathed deeply.

If she found people with dogs who just left the poo lying around, she would shoot them. Some people might call it extreme, but really, she would shoot them. Dog poo was the worst, just the worst. She gave a sigh, turned back to her wagon and began pushing it down the street again, scanning left and right. She stopped a few more times, then looked up to see how far she'd left to go on the street. Far enough.

She knew, of course. She was opposite the organic food store. It was fairly new. She wasn't sure how well it was doing, but what she knew was she had probably another fifteen minutes at most down here if things were messy. Ten, maybe seven if they weren't. There was always the alley up ahead. She had to cover that off as well.

There was always glass in it. Idiots drinking through the night. Whoever they were, probably not much older than she, maybe younger. It was too cold to ask proper alcoholics to be out this time of night. Must have been young kids. Lindsay looked up to the opposite side at the end of the street and then stopped. The sun had risen a little more and the top of the Witches' Pillory was lit up. There was someone in the stalks. Someone was hanging in the pillory.

There was a shudder went down Lindsay's spine. It was like those horror movies. The good-looking girl, she would wander in, find somebody hanging there. Of course, she'd be in some scanty clothing for no real reason. She'd been chased out of bed, or they'd be on a camping trip. It was always something like that. Horror movies were so generic and yet Lindsay had imagined herself in one several times.

Right now, she didn't want to be in any because the hairs on her neck were rising. She left the cart and began walking towards the figure. Then she stopped. She turned back to the cart, took the long-handled brush and walked back towards the pillory. As she got closer, she could see it was definitely a human figure. Was that a woman? The head was hanging forward, and she was in what looked like a white sheet of some sort.

Could this be a prank? Could this really be a prank? It was extreme, but it must be a prank. Lindsay had fallen foul of pranks before at work. It was usually James. He was an older guy, and she thought he had a bit of a crush on her. He was in his thirties, and he was nice enough, quite funny in his own way.

She remembered the rat sitting on top of her locker. It was fake, of course. He'd also done that thing with the little alien jumping out of his belly. That was a good one. It didn't look that real, but it was a good one. This would be a cracker, though. He'd gone on about not getting her a Christmas present. Was this making up for it?

Lindsay eased a bit, and walked up towards the figure that was hanging in the pillory. It wasn't moving. The hands, however, were not hanging down from the wrists. If you were in a pillory and you'd been there a long time, you'd be tired, and the wrists would hang down. These were straight.

It must be somebody. It's not a dummy. Not a dummy because the wrists were straight. No, James would have been better than that, wouldn't he?

She held out the long-handled brush as she got closer. There were copious amounts of blood hanging off the white gown, or at least it looked like blood. The hair hung down over the face as she walked forward slowly. The handle of the brush ahead of her, gingerly, she poked the figure. It didn't move, not one inch. She poked it hard. Again, not a single movement.

Must be a mannequin of some sort, she thought, and put the brush down and walked closer. Up ahead to her left, she could see the main road. Some cars were on the move, but the frost on the High Street here said no one had been down in a car.

What time had they put the mannequin out for it not to have been spotted? Must be fairly recent. Although you'd do it in darkness, wouldn't you? There's no CCTV just at this bit.

At least, that's what she reckoned. James had given her a lecture once about if you're going to do something wrong, watch out for certain streets because they'd got CCTV. What on earth she'd be doing that was wrong while pushing around her little wagon and brushing the streets, she didn't know. James was paranoid as well.

Lindsay stepped up onto the little platform on which the pillory was set. She reached up and took hold of one hand. It was cold, so very cold. The flesh was incredibly realistic, peeling a little now. She was intrigued by it, truly intrigued.

She bent down, looking at the blood on the white gown. Right beside the chest, there was a hole where the heart would have been. It opened up into a cavity, made in fantastic detail. It was incredible. Too incredible. Lindsay put her hand forward, reaching into the gap where the heart would have been. She touched it, brought it back and looked at the blood on her fingers.

Shit, that was blood. It's blood, isn't it? She stumbled back, then stared up at the figure. *Isn't it? That is blood.*

Her heart thumped as her mind raced. Was she in the middle of a superb practical joke, or had somebody—no, somebody couldn't have taken the heart out of someone? They couldn't have!

Despite her terror, she stepped forward, feeling the hair. The hair would tell her, wouldn't it? Her hand went to the black hanging mess, to part of it clotted with blood. That felt like real hair. That was real hair. She shook uncontrollably, trembling inside. Despite this, something inside her was deeply intrigued.

Would this be a real person? The face would tell. The face didn't lie. If you saw those waxwork dummies, they weren't real, especially up close. You looked at the faces and the eyes were wrong. With a hand on either side of the face, she crouched down and then pushed back the hair, revealing the face.

Two empty eye sockets stared back at her. Blood was streaked across the face. The skin felt real. The face looked genuine. Lindsay fell backwards, shrieking. Her feet scrabbled on the ground, pushing her back, and she turned, running as hard as she could up High Street. After five steps, she kicked her own feet, falling over, scuffing her hand, but she didn't stop. Her long-handled brush was left behind on the street. The cart was abandoned as she tore up the street, screaming.

'No,' she yelled. 'No, it can't be.'

She turned round a corner and clattered straight into a man on his way to work. He looked bemused as she clung to him in tears. As he tried to pull her back off, she refused to move, shaking uncontrollably.

'What the hell's going on?' he said. 'Are you all right, love?'

'A witch. They killed a witch.'

Chapter 02

Siobahn Duffy sat in her small study, gazing out the window towards the sea. Life was good. Well, good enough. She was currently bogged down in paperwork, having set up her own small detective agency. Declan, her gardener, and Kylie, her housekeeper, would have to be put onto the books of the agency, but in what capacity? They'd insisted on joining her, but she couldn't pay them on a weekly basis if no cases were coming in.

It was different for Siobhan. She had money. Her deceased husband had left her so much from his window business that she didn't need a job anymore. She just needed something to fill in the time. Siobhan stared down at her hands, her nails cut trim. Not so that they didn't exist, but they weren't kept long like most women's. That had come from her days in the Service.

Long nails were awkward. You could always put some on if you had to disguise yourself. When she was young, she broke many a nail, clambering out of windows and doing other things, and then she'd got into the habit of keeping them short. She wasn't one for much makeup either. Touch of foundation if she was desperate. Siobhan thought beauty was in people's faces. She had studied them for most of her life, tried to guess what they were thinking. Tried to make sure that she was on the right side of them. She hated to see faces all dolled up. A load of slap-on, as one of her old aunts had called it.

Yes, she was happy enough now, but this morning, she'd been annoyed. Declan had kept interrupting her. He was young—youthful and restless. 'Come and see this plant. What are we going to do with this? What are we going to do here in the garden? You really should take more care of it.'

That's what I pay him for, she thought. *What's the point in a gardener if he's going to bring you out every two minutes to do everything with him?*

He was also on a drive to show Kylie how useful he was. Kylie was the dark-haired housekeeper in her mid-twenties and who, with a bit of effort, could certainly be a looker. She didn't fuss with that, however. The days of men long passed because of her trouble with the kid. Something Siobhan didn't bring up.

One day, she'd have to get past that. One day, she'd have to find the man that would help her do it. Not that everyone needed a man, but Kylie was one of those women who did. You could tell by the way she looked at them. Declan was someone she was interested in, despite how emphatically she denied it. He was a kind soul. Just very annoying this morning.

'Mrs D,' came the shout from the living room, 'you've got to see the news.'

Why, Declan? thought Siobhan. *Why'd I have to see the news? The news is repeated ad infinitum now for twenty-four hours a day. If you miss it, you can watch it in five minutes' time. They go over and over the same stuff. Over and over and over. Even the important stuff is analysed to death, so that after thirty minutes, you're bored with it, anyway. Why would you bother?*

There was a rap on the door. 'I don't need to see the news,' huffed Siobhan.

The door opened. It was Kylie. 'I'm sure you don't. I was just coming to ask if you wanted a cup of tea.'

Siobhan smiled. 'You're a godsend. Yes, the usual.'

Kylie held her nose and shut the door.

Lapsang Souchong was Siobhan's tea of choice, the smoky Chinese tea that Kylie hated. Every time she made it, she would make choking noises, as if the tea was strangling her. It wasn't Siobhan's fault she enjoyed tea with a bit of flavour.

'Mrs D, would you come in here?'

Siobhan ignored Declan, looking down at the form in front of her, displayed on the computer screen. She typed in some bank details and then there was a knock at the door. She looked up, smiling, and then thought that was quick for a cup of tea.

'Come in.'

The door opened, and Declan's face appeared. He looked like an excited child going to the Christmas party. 'Mrs D, you've got to come and see this on the telly. Something for us. Not that far away, either. It's Carrickfergus.'

'It's Carrickfergus. What about Carrickfergus?' asked Siobhan.

Carrickfergus was on the other side of Belfast Lough from Siobhan's house, but just out of view. If you carried on further towards Bangor, you could see over to the town and its castle, the most notable feature. She'd been there many a time, and it was quite outstanding. A highlight as you drove along the coast road before you wound further along and eventually came up to Ballylumford power station. A different sort of colossus and not quite the same grandeur as the castle. However, it still was imposing.

She remembered Sunday runs when she was young, driving out that direction. When you drove in Northern Ireland, town to country happened so quickly because of the smallness of the place. No, it wasn't small; it was just compact. Having been in so many parts of the world, Siobhan thought of how others drove for hours, sometimes for days, to get a change of scenery. The middle of Canada was so much the same. Northern Ireland, you had the town, mountains, shore, winding country lanes, all in the space of twenty minutes.

'I'm sure it can wait, Declan. I'm just getting a cup of tea from Kylie.'

'Come and see this before she gives you it. I'm telling you that you're going to like this.'

'Why?'

'Somebody's dead,' he said.

'Declan, I don't like things just because somebody's dead. What are you saying about me?'

'I mean, for the business. It's a chance for the business to show itself.'

'It's a body. I won't get hired by the police to investigate a body. Somebody has to come to us, remember? I'm sure if a loved one is dead, they will not be piling in first thing this morning. They're going to have a period of grief. Besides, I didn't think we'd be getting a murder case for our first one. We have to build up, start small. People have to get to know us. We couldn't make the last effort too public.'

Siobhan thought of how things had nearly gone wrong last time. There had been Russian hoodlums involved. Thankfully,

Julian had covered it all up. She smiled at the name 'Julian'. She was meeting him anyway in twenty minutes. Off to a small garden centre.

Julian Patterson was in the Service. Although he had said he was still working there and wouldn't be about, he seemed to be nearby a lot. Also, he was taking a great interest in her business and what she was doing. At her age, Siobhan wanted to settle down. Except she didn't. Siobhan didn't know what she wanted. The escapade with the Russian businessman and a man previously from the Service had given her a taste for the adventure again. Yet she also loved this home, out on the jokingly called *gold coast* between Bangor and Donaghadee.

Siobhan wasn't sure what she wanted, but having seen Julian again, she thought she might want him. He certainly gave every sign he wanted her. Having both been in the Service, Siobhan now retired, they talked with each other like they were still in it, feelings never showing. Siobhan was sure that Julian had a strong flame for her. Just what he wanted with life was another matter. What the pair of them wanted, how far they could make things work. All these ideas spun in her head.

It wasn't easy being in a relationship when you're in the Service, especially both being in the Service. Keeping secrets from someone you were married to if they didn't know your real occupation was one thing. It was worse if you both knew you were in it, as you knew the secrets were there. She gave her head a shake.

'Mrs D, stop drifting away and come and look at this.'

He was like a child, and like children, Declan never gave up. Siobhan stood up, pointed out the door, and followed Declan into the living room.

There was a man on the TV holding a microphone and talking away about one of the worst scenes in Carrickfergus's history. Siobhan wasn't that au fait with the town's history, but she didn't think it was that bad. There was a large tarpaulin draped across where one of those historical recreation things had been. She'd wandered past it. Stocks, that was it.

'Are those the stocks, Declan? Just at the end of the high street?'

'It's the Witches' Pillory,' said Declan excitedly. 'There's been a body found in it. Street cleaner found it. Look, she's on now.'

The wide-eyed face of Lindsay McLaughlin stared back from the TV screen. She was blurting out about approaching the body, saying how horrific it was, but before she could describe it in detail, the image cut away to a police inspector who calmly said investigations were going on, but how it was such a shocking crime.

'Could be one for us,' said Declan.

'How?' asked Siobhan. 'We don't just look at the news and weigh in on anything that's going on. People have to come to us. It's a business, Declan. Last time I got involved was because my friend was dead. Now, we have to wait for people to come to us. We need a reason to be involved. It's a business. It's why I'm filling in the forms, getting an account for it, so we can do expenses and stuff properly and I'll be able to bill people properly. We don't just get in a camper van and drive around. Do you want me to get a dog with us, and do some sort of mystery reveal at the end of it?'

'A dog would be good,' said Declan. 'Especially if you got one of those trained ones, which could sniff stuff out.'

'Declan, behave,' said Siobhan. 'Anyway, I'm off out.'

'Not before you drink your tea. I've just made it,' said Kylie, walking in the door of the living room. 'Here.'

Siobhan took it. It was extremely hot. Still, she wouldn't be going for at least another ten minutes. She plonked herself down on the sofa and Declan sat down beside her.

'You sure there aren't any plants you can have a look at?' Siobhan asked.

'I feel like I've done something wrong,' said Declan.

'Do you?' said Siobhan. 'Do you really?'

'Are you okay, Mrs D? I'm just sensing a wee bit of hostility.'

'Declan,' said Kylie, 'look at some plants.'

Kylie handed over a mug. It was a thermal one which kept the liquid hot that Declan used outside. He cast a glance at Kylie, and Siobhan noticed she gave him a smile. Off he toddled. The boy was smitten. She wasn't yet, but the boy was smitten. She had a couple of years on him. Some women didn't like that, although today, age didn't matter. At least, that's what they always said.

'So,' said Kylie, 'Julian, again.'

'Stop it,' said Siobhan.

'What?'

'Stop it. I don't talk to you about Julian.'

'Who are you going to talk to about Julian then, if you don't talk to me about him? You have got nobody else to talk to about him, have you?'

'Who says I want to talk to you about Julian, or to anyone else, for that matter? I can talk to Julian about Julian.'

'Oh, right, it's going that well.'

'Enough,' said Siobhan. She put the cup to her lips and tried to take a larger gulp than normal. She forced the liquid down, hot as it was, desperate enough to show Kylie she hadn't taken too much of a drink.

'He's still about quite a bit, isn't he?'

'That's it. Your tea's not getting drunk.'

'Then I'll put it in the microwave next time and you can have that.'

'Don't you dare,' said Siobhan, placing the cup on the coffee table and jumping up. She got to the door of the living room and turned around to Kylie. 'Okay,' she said, 'I'm not too casual, am I? Blue jeans, jumper.'

'You look great,' said Kylie. 'You always look great.'

'Thanks,' said Siobhan. 'Just a bit nervous.'

'Nervous?' queried Kylie. 'Why are you nervous?'

'This is Julian, and I don't know where we're going to go with it. We haven't even gone anywhere yet, but you just don't know.'

'Why do you have to go anywhere? Just enjoy it,' said Kylie. 'Maybe you need him; maybe you don't. He certainly does you good, though.'

'Thanks,' said Siobhan. 'I won't be that long. He's got to be somewhere. Maybe an hour and a half, two at the most.'

'You said that last time and you were three.'

'No. This time, he has to be somewhere,' said Siobhan. 'He told me with that manner of his. The official voice.'

'That's fine. I'll have dinner on for you then.'

Siobhan drove out to the garden centre on the outskirts of Donaghadee, and as she parked up, she felt the butterflies in her stomach. She didn't even look at the plants as she made her way to the café.

Standing at the window, staring out onto the green countryside with its rolling hills, was Julian. He was looking dapper in a suit. He could do that. Julian came from a posh background, and he could dress the part, but at heart, he wasn't stuck up. He could be with the lowest of the low and not put them on edge, not seem above them. He was just too decent, too kind-hearted, despite his Service days. Siobhan had not come through as unscathed as he. She corrected herself. No, he wasn't unscathed; he just carried it better.

'You've really got to try the little croissants,' said Julian.

'It's good to see you.' Siobhan stepped forward, putting her hand up, as if to shake his as he turned to face her.

'Is that where we're at?' asked Julian. 'A handshake.' He stood up, put his arms wide, and together they hugged. It was going to be a brief one, except Siobhan hung on just that bit longer. When they sat down, she saw the smile on his face.

'I'll get tea and that.' He raised his hand towards a waitress.

'I think you have to go up,' said Siobhan. She'd always gone up.

'They know what we want already. I took the liberty,' said Julian.

'Am I late?'

'You're a touch late,' he said, 'but you're worth waiting for.'

Many men saying that would've sounded corny, but not from Julian. Julian didn't do corny. Julian said things with heart. He meant what he said.

'How's the agency going?' he asked, after a woman had acknowledged his request.

'Getting there, all signed up. Just need a case.'

'Well, there seems to be plenty going about.'

'Look, don't. Declan's been on at me about that thing over in Carrickfergus. Says we could leap in and investigate.' Julian raised an eyebrow. 'Oh, I told him,' said Siobhan. 'I've explained that we have to wait for people to come to us. It might take a while. I'm in no rush. It's good to be thinking about something, though. About doing something. '

'It's good to see you enlivened and in one piece,' said Julian. 'Last time was close. You don't want to be going through stuff like that again.'

She saw the concern in his eyes. 'I don't need to be told what to take on and what not.'

'Sorry,' he said, but she waved her hand at him.

'I know you're only concerned. I know . . .'

'I just want you to be safe while you're doing all this.'

'Do you ever think,' she said, 'that we should meet up somewhere other than a garden centre?'

'Is there's something wrong with it?' he asked. 'I thought it was quaint, informal. I didn't think we were—'

'What?' she said.

'Well, with my work . . . being called away, well, I didn't want to—'

'Julian,' she said, 'I've known you for a while and I've never known you lost for words. What are you trying to say?'

'I didn't think we were going into a relationship. I didn't think you wanted to push it that way.'

'Who said I didn't?'

'Just awkward,' said Julian. 'With my work in—'

'It's not your work. I've been in that line of work,' she said suddenly, reducing the level of her voice. 'I know the risks. Know all the rest of it, too. I just thought that maybe next time, a bottle of wine in a restaurant somewhere. I could get dressed up in a bit more than jeans and a jumper.'

'There's nothing wrong with your jeans and jumper. I've seen you for most of your life in jeans and a jumper,' said Julian.

'I know,' she said, 'but I'm fifty. Sometimes I might want to get dressed up and feel glamorous.'

'Fine,' said Julian. 'We'll get dressed up, but don't feel that you're not.'

'Feel what?' asked Siobhan, suddenly.

'Beautiful unless you're dressed up.'

Siobhan gave a smile, and sat back, much more relaxed.

By the time they left the garden centre, Julian had promised that next time they'd be somewhere with a bottle of wine. He escorted her to her car, put his arms around and gave her a tight hug. They said goodbye, and Julian turned to walk to his car. As he reached it, Siobhan marched over towards him and he looked a little shocked. She threw her arms around him, planted a kiss on his lips, long and deep, before breaking off.

'Just in case you've any doubts.'

'I think that was more to reassure your doubts,' said Julian. 'I have no doubts.'

She gave a smile and walked back to her car. As she did so, she knew Julian knew her better than she knew herself. The short drive back to the house seemed to disappear without her realising where the time had gone on. When she parked up in the driveway, she was suddenly jolted out of her happy place, seeing another car there. Opening her car door, she walked down the driveway before Declan rushed up to her.

'Mrs D, Kylie's got a woman in there.'

'Okay. Over excited about it, aren't we?' said Siobhan.

'It's the sister of the dead witch.'

'Come again?'

'Carrickfergus, the pillory, the witch they found dead. Her sister's in your living room.' The first thought that ran through Siobhan's mind was, 'How do I explain this one to Julian?'

Chapter 03

Siobhan stopped in her hallway and checked herself in the mirror to make sure that she was presentable for meeting her first client. Having pulled down her jumper somewhat and adjusted her jeans, she walked into the living room. Kylie was sitting beside a woman in her thirties.

'Siobhan, this is Angela Lynch,' said Kylie, standing up. 'Angela, this is Siobhan Duffy, our lead investigator.'

Our lead investigator? No! The boss, the complete boss, thought Siobhan, *not just the lead investigator.* She couldn't think about it for too long, for Angela Lynch was an interesting character.

The woman's hair had clearly not been brushed that day and it was black and long, fighting a losing battle to keep clear of her face. A face that was pale, white like only redheads can be, with eyes that were sunken. The woman's limbs were bony, as if they lacked any muscle or fat around them. She was sitting in black. This wasn't unusual, for after all, her sister had died, if Declan was to be believed. The overall demeanour of the woman gave the impression of a person who struggled to look after herself.

'Mrs Lynch, Siobhan Duffy,' said Siobhan, stepping forward and putting her hand out. 'I hear you've had some bad news.'

'They killed her,' said Angela.

'Just to clarify, killed who?'

'They killed my sister, Deborah. Part of the coven. You see, the coven killed her.'

'Just a moment,' said Siobhan, and turned to Kylie. 'Can you get me a cup of tea, please? Would you like something, Angela?' Siobhan needed to slow down and process this. *A coven?*

The woman shook her head, and Kylie raised her eyebrows at Siobhan. Clearly, Kylie had wanted to stay for this, but Siobhan was worried that the woman might be a fraud. For the moment, she looked just a little too strange to be believable.

'The usual tea, Kylie,' said Siobhan, moving past Kylie to sit down beside Angela. The closer she got to Angela Lynch, the more haunted she looked. Her eyes were almost soulless, never looking at her, always beyond. She was never quite sure where they were looking to.

'They killed my sister, Deborah. We grew up and lived together until they took her. Worked for them for a while. You don't think of them round here, but they lurk everywhere. They're in every corner controlling it. That's the thing. They control everything and yet nobody knows who they are. Nobody knows they exist.'

Siobhan took a deep breath. Was the woman a crackpot? She didn't know. Had she just jumped on board the strange death in Carrickfergus? Again, she didn't know. Siobhan would be professional about this. She would hear the story. She would look at the evidence and decide if the woman should get help herself rather than approaching an investigator. Maybe there'd be nothing to explain to Julian after all. It was too much of a coincidence for her to believe that the sister of the murdered woman in the pillory had simply walked into her home.

'Tell me a little about yourself,' said Siobhan, 'and your sister.'

'We lived near Carrickfergus, on the outskirts. We lived together, you see, but Deborah, Deborah's not who she was. She got involved with the occult. She's always been fascinated by the occult, always wanted to be part of it, and then she joined them. Deborah joined them and she was never the same.'

'Just to be sure of who we're talking about, she joined who?'

'The witch's coven,' said Angela, almost as if it was a matter of fact. 'This is her, there,' she said, reaching inside her black top and pulling out a handful of photographs. She placed them on the table in front of her and Siobhan could recognise they were from probably the last ten years. Angela was looking decidedly better, it had to be said, in most of the photographs than she probably did right now. Beside her was a woman who had long black hair and was dressed, most times, in something that resembled a witch's outfit. Possibly a wizard.

'She used to go to their meetings. They dance naked sometimes. Disappear off to go to different places. That's the thing. You don't see them. Middle of the night, mixing up their potions and their brew, getting together for their meetings. But she must have crossed one of them. She must have crossed one, because they killed her. They put her in the pillory. Do you hear me? They put her in the pillory.'

'I hear you,' said Siobhan. 'Slow down. Slow down. You live outside Carrickfergus. Where does the coven meet?'

'I don't know. I don't know that. Why would I know that? They're not going to tell me. I'm not part of the coven.'

'Okay,' said Siobhan, trying to be as delicate as possible.

'How do you know, then, that your sister was a witch?'

'When she first joined, she changed. At least, I think that was when she first joined. I don't know dates and that. They made her do things. Things she wasn't happy about. She would talk in her sleep about how she'd betrayed herself, had betrayed her family, betrayed decency. Had to do things that weren't right. I would listen to her at night. Her room was beside mine. She'd thrash in bed. I think she was taking things as well. I saw needle marks.'

'Could it be that your sister was just, excuse my expression, a junkie? She just got into drugs?'

'No,' said Angela. 'No,' she pulled her arms around her. 'If only. Because they see things, don't they? Witches. They know things. Maybe they know me. Maybe they know I'm here. I should have met somewhere private. I didn't want to use the phone. The phone and the messages.'

Siobhan sat back, staring at the woman. She was clearly troubled. Clearly believed that something had happened to her sister. Siobhan would have to ring. She'd have to talk to someone about this. If this was indeed the sister of a murder victim coming to speak to her, she'd have to talk to the police just to clarify who the woman was.

'You still haven't said why you think she was more than a junkie. Everything you've said to me could just be her being a junkie.'

'No,' said Angela, and she stood up and walked over to the window, looking around the garden. Kylie walked back into the room at that moment, placing Siobhan's cup down, and then started to walk over to Angela. Siobhan waved her off.

'Go on,' said Siobhan, not unkindly.

'We were drunk, or at least she was very drunk. I hadn't

had much. She broke down, crying, telling me she needed to tell me something. Told me about how she'd got to be a witch within the group.'

'She certainly dressed up as a witch, didn't she?' said Kylie, looking down at the photographs. Siobhan put her finger to her lips.

'She said to me she regretted getting into the group. She talked about their dancing, but that she didn't regret that. It was part of the occult idea, wasn't it? Jumping around, dancing naked. Just larks. What she regretted was having to kill them. Having to commit the crimes. Controlled everything, she said. Controlled everybody. They were on top of it all. Knew too much about everyone, everywhere. Pulling the money in. Witches in control.'

Angela paused for a moment, breathing deeply. 'You don't think that, do you? You don't think it. She never showed me her proper outfit. The ones in the photographs are all the pretend ones. I think they call it cosplay. I think that's what drew her in. She thought it would be like that. Fun. Just a group, a little society. She found the real thing and went downhill. Worried about it for the last few years. She said she couldn't take it anymore. Said what they'd asked her to do, she couldn't follow through with.'

'What did they ask her to do?' said Siobhan.

'She didn't say. Then they killed her. They put her in the stocks. Heart torn out. Eyes no longer there. Can't come back when you can't see and you've no heart. Heart is kept. Eyes are kept. Witch stays dead then, don't they?'

Siobhan stood up, looking past Angela, and saw the wintry day outside, the beauty of her garden and the clear blue water beyond it. The weirdness of her situation did not escape her.

'Just a moment,' said Siobhan. 'I need to make a call.'

Kylie looked over at her, and Siobhan waved her out through the door into the hallway.

'What are you doing?' asked Kylie.

'We've either got someone who's playing me along, or someone that's deluded, or someone who's in complete shock. I need to know she's Angela Lynch.'

Siobhan picked up the phone and dialled into the police station at Carrickfergus. She announced who she was as a private investigator and said she believed that Angela Lynch had just walked through her door. Detailing the situation, she said that she felt that the woman may need medical care, if indeed, it was the woman.

'I'm not sure I can help you,' said a police officer on the other end of the phone.

'Well, it's quite serious,' said Siobhan. 'If it is the sister of the deceased woman, I'm sure your officers will need to speak to her. Especially if she's going off kilter like this. If it's not, we need to nip this in the bud. I was wondering, could we get someone on the team to speak to her just now? They could ask her about something, but only she would know. I don't need to know, but I'll come back on the phone after, and they can tell me if it's a case, or if I'll take this one down to the local police station to have a word. Frankly, none of us need this if it's a prank.'

The officer agreed, and Siobhan waited a few moments while he called up the team who were investigating. It was a junior level officer and Siobhan took the phone through to Angela Lynch before stepping out of the room. Angela called for her a few minutes later and Siobhan took the phone back, stepping back into the hall.

'Hello, Mrs Duffy. Yes, that is Angela Lynch. How is she?'

'Rather strange and going on about witches.'

'We think she's had a shock. Not convinced that what she's saying is true. There's certainly no evidence around it. I'd be very gentle in how you deal with her, and I'd be surprised if you have anything here to deal with. Obviously, we can't tell you about any of our investigations, but a coven of witches is not a line of inquiry.'

Siobhan thanked the man, put the phone down and re-entered the room.

'Angela, I'm going to be frank with you,' said Siobhan, 'at the moment you're talking to me about a coven of witches. The police officer I spoke to doesn't believe there's any evidence for them. What I have at the moment is you, in shock at your sister's death and a sister who liked to get involved in cosplay. You've seen her go downhill, and she's talked about it as being part of a coven. At this time, it would be remiss of me to take any money off you, or to say I will investigate.'

'It might not be the first death,' said Angela suddenly. 'This is a long-forgotten order of women, a long-forgotten order of witches. They had trials back then for reasons, because they existed. Then they got smart. The rumour is they've always been there. There's always been things happening. People watching and controlling things up and above. I want you to investigate.

'I want you to take this on. I want you to find this coven. Do I think that they're controlling people? Well, they controlled my sister. How did they do that? I don't know. She talked about them like they were genuine witches. If the effect's the same, does it matter?

'Deborah always wanted to be a witch. She was easily taken

in. All I want you to do is start and put together what you can. I'll pay you for a couple of weeks,' said Angela. 'If you turn round and tell me there's no evidence of witches and whoever was talking to my sister is somebody completely different, then fine. But I need somebody to explain to me why she was hanging in a pillory with her heart and eyes cut out.'

That detail wasn't put on the TV, thought Siobhan. *If that detail's correct, it seems a rather brutal killing and a weird one. There are ways to kill people if you were hoodlums, if you were from some of the bad elements in the province.* This was weird.

Angela turned round and stared at Siobhan, the eyes sunken and hollow. No longer were they void looking off beyond Siobhan. Instead, they were looking at her and she could feel the haunted presence inside the woman.

'Help me,' said Angela. 'Help me.'

'Okay,' said Siobhan, 'I'll help you. But I won't get too carried away. I'll go through this as I would investigate anything. This is not a look for the occult. This is to find out who affected your sister. The police are investigating as well. I must ask you to tell them everything you tell me. They're on a murder enquiry.'

'The coven has control,' said Angela. 'It's what I've been trying to tell you. They don't control all the police force, but they control people. They have their hands everywhere.'

'You're talking like it's a society, like a bad version of the masons for women,' said Siobhan.

'A coven. If the effects are the same, what does it matter whether it's magical or not?'

'I'll take the work,' said Siobhan. 'No promises.

Angela Lynch nodded, turned, handing Siobhan a piece of paper.

'That's my address.'

'Don't you want to know my rates? How much it would cost?'

'No. This needs done,' said the woman. Without another word, she left the living room. Siobhan watched her through the window as she walked up the driveway, out to her car.

Declan barged in. 'Well?' he said. Siobhan reached into her pocket and threw her car keys at him. 'Go move my car. I've blocked the woman in.'

'Okay,' said Declan, catching them, 'but are we on? Are we?'

Siobhan nodded. She should've been happy. This was her first case. Something inside her was gnawing at her about it. Gouged out eyes, heart missing. The Service had seen little like this. This might be different. Very different.

Chapter 04

Where do we start?' asked Declan, having returned from moving the car for Siobhan.

'We start by having dinner because I'm starving, and then tonight we'll plan out what we're going to do. First thing in the morning, we get onto it.'

'Do we get to make a big board and write everything down?'

'No, Declan, we don't. We didn't do that for the last one either. What we need to do is find out about Deborah and Angela Lynch's friends, Deborah's especially. See if we can come up with any potential leads there. If she's working within a coven, maybe she was friends with some of them.'

'Do they all know each other in these covens?' asked Kylie. 'I'm not so sure they do.'

'We're dealing with covens,' said Siobhan. 'It might not be a coven. It might just be a group of people getting together. A group of women. If she's talking about them controlling in the way she says, they might operate more like a criminal gang. Maybe they keep themselves separate. Keep their identities quiet, known only to a few so that if things come back at them, they can soon cut off a limb and save the body. That's if this is what it is. I am not sold that there are witches about. I mean, are you sure that witchcraft exists?'

'Witches existed,' said Declan.

'I didn't ask that,' said Siobhan. 'We know historically there were women perceived as witches. Whether they're proper witches, people who can do such strange things, is what I'm asking. Or are they just people who can coerce along with the best of them? People who can coerce others; I know them. I've worked among them for a long time. The Service taught me how to do that.'

'Taught you how to do it? Have you been coercing us?' asked Declan.

'Of course, she has,' said Kylie, causing Siobhan to give her an angry stare.

'I don't coerce. You're my staff. I'm not allowed to. That would be irresponsible.'

'You get your way, though. That's coercion, isn't it?'

'No, that's just psychological know-how. It's not coercion. You just do it because you think it's the best for you, not because I've forced you to do it.'

'Great,' said Kylie.

'And speaking of which, it's teatime. I'm now going to coerce you to make the dinner.'

'There's no need for that. You pay me for that. That's the proper form of coercion.'

Kylie disappeared off while Siobhan retreated into her study. She wasn't totally convinced of what would come up. She'd give it a week, tops, to see if they dug up anything that was useful. If they hadn't, tell Angela Lynch it was better left to the police. She wouldn't charge her much anyway. The poor woman had just lost her sister in horrific terms. Siobhan sat back in her office chair, spun it around and stared out of the window. She loved this part of the world. Even as the sun was descending, the thick caramel-like waves just off the end of her garden made her smile.

I wonder if Julian would like that, too. What would it be like to sit together over an evening, maybe a glass of wine here? Then he wouldn't have to think he was coming back. We'd just be here. We'd just . . .

I'm getting ahead of myself, am I not? After all, is that what I want? The trouble is that once I start down that line with Julian, if it goes wrong, will I lose that friendship, that closeness? At the moment, we are good friends. Very good friends to become . . . What do you call it at fifty? Lovers? Partners? People in a relationship? Better friends?

She wasn't sure. It was easier when you were younger. Lovers was definitely the term for back then. You were off and running like rabbits. She laughed at the terminology she was throwing out, but now at fifty, they certainly wouldn't be like rabbits. Special friends. Oh, this was rubbish. Just together. Yes. That's better.

Siobhan put a piece of paper in front of her. *Deborah, friends, family, need to find out who they are. Angela—you need to get an assessment of her. Places, where did Deborah go? Where did she go that she told people about? Where was she seen that she didn't tell people about? Start there. The building that Deborah inhabited, her room, she needed to go through it, see if there was anything in there that would give her some clues. The photographs that Angela had brought had shown Deborah dressed up in witches' outfits. Who made them? Where did she buy them from? Did she buy at all? Was there anything special about them?*

The thoughts raced through Siobhan's mind and she wrote them down on a piece of paper while she waited for tea to be made. There came a rap on the door and Siobhan realised she was staring blankly at the paper in front of her. Not bamboozled by the case, but her mind had been on choosing a bottle of wine and what sort Julian would like. She was too distracted. She needed to put him to one side at the moment, for she was working. Well, no, she was going to have dinner; then she'd be working.

'Tea's ready. Declan's staying.'

'Good,' said Siobhan. 'Then we can sit and talk about what we do. I can lay down a few ground rules, explain how I am not just simply the lead investigator.'

'Well, what do I describe you as? This is Siobhan. She used to be in the secret service. I can't say that. Can I?'

'No, you darn well can't.'

'So, what do I say? We never talked about that,' said Kylie.

'But I didn't think you'd have to say anything. I thought I'd be the first person people would speak to.'

'Well, there you go. Let's get some dinner,' said Kylie. 'It's salmon.'

'I hope you haven't . . .'

'No, I haven't overdone it. Just about cooked. Didn't take long. It was the potatoes that took the time.'

'Good,' said Siobhan. 'Sorry, I shouldn't question your cooking skills.' As she went to stand up, Kylie was still in the doorway. 'What?' asked Siobhan.

'How did it go with Julian?'

'Good,' said Siobhan.

'That's it? I get "good"?'

'I'm not talking about it in front of Declan. Okay? Really good.'

'Really good?' said Kylie. 'Like, fantastic or just really good?'

'I kissed him, all right? Now, can I eat my salmon?'

'Oh, you've got to tell me more details than that.'

'No, I don't. Now get through to the kitchen and get me my salmon.'

As Kylie turned to walk away to the kitchen, Siobhan smiled. It was refreshing having the young ones about. It made her feel young. Nobody her age would have asked her that sort of question. Not at the age she was now. Back in the day, she'd have gossiped like that with the best of them. Well, at least to a point. It was sweet that Kylie was interested, like the daughter she had never had.

Siobhan stopped herself there. *She's an employee, maybe a friend. She's not that. Be careful.'* The Service had taught Siobhan not to be too close to people. They could feel like they were your friend. You could feel you cared for them and maybe she did, to a degree, but don't get too close because things change. They always did.

That evening, the three of them planned out their first moves. The next morning, they would interview Angela Lynch in the house that she shared with her sister. From that, they would find out Deborah's haunts. Where she was known to have gone and do a quick run through those. They'd also search the house.

With everything planned, Siobhan was happy and went to bed that night, content that tomorrow would be a good day. As she lay in bed, she heard the phone ring. It was late. Eleven o'clock and she was going to leave it until the answer machine played Julian's voice. She jumped out of bed, opening the door and bolting for the phone in the hall. Picking it up, she pressed it, but just too late.

Damn it, she thought. *Could she ring him back? No, that would sound keen, wouldn't it? Not like she'd just been up.* She played back the message. Just calling to say how much he enjoyed the day. Also, to see how she'd got on with the rest of her day.

Siobhan was fifty and she shouldn't feel giddy, but she did. Why? Why was she this giddy? No. Julian would have to wait. She was approaching her work head on in the morning, so she was going to get a good night's sleep. If she called him now, she might not put the phone back down. She returned to her bed and took another hour before she fell asleep.

The following morning, everyone was up early, and after Kylie had made them breakfast, they drove off from Donaghadee. The car swept through Belfast and out along the other side of the Belfast Lough, towards Carrickfergus. They stopped briefly, passing by the pillory where the body had been found. Except they couldn't get close because it was still cordoned off.

Siobhan had already decided that she couldn't pull in Julian to get her details of what the police had found. Her business would be run as her business. Getting favours like that from him would be unfair. The police would soon get gnarled the Service was calling in on every two-bit problem that had cropped up. That was if a murder could be described as a two-bit problem. Well, the Service could do that sometimes.

She rapped on the door of Angela Lynch's cottage. At half-past nine, the woman was already up, but the eyes looked no less haunted than before. Again, she was dressed in black and ushered the three of them through to her sitting room.

'Do you have any parents?'

'Dead, unfortunately,' said Angela. 'Well, thankfully because I don't think they'd have worn this. My sister would have driven them into the grave if they hadn't had gone before.'

'Any other extended family?'

'Not really. Just the two of us. We have got aunts and uncles, but they don't live local. We have a few friends. I can give you a list of Deborah's, although none of them are in the coven as far as I can make out. If they are, it's been done very well.'

'Did Deborah ever go anywhere?' asked Siobhan. 'Anywhere that you wouldn't have thought of her going to.'

'She was seen once up near the Gobbins.'

'Islandmagee? That's that cliff path, isn't it?' said Siobhan. She'd never walked it, but it was a treacherous cliff path that went round the side of the cliffs hanging out over the top end of what was the extreme end of Belfast Lock. 'Did she like outside? Out and about?'

'No. She wasn't one for the wild. She wouldn't be going up there to have a look at nature. That wasn't her. When she dealt with occult things, she was interested in the power from them. She was interested in strange artefacts. Not like some witches you hear about who are getting back to nature.'

'We'll take a trip up there,' said Siobhan.

'Do we want to check her room?' asked Kylie.

'Could we?' asked Siobhan.

'Of course,' said Angela. 'You can look through her room. I want to take a shower. I probably need to sleep too. You see, I haven't slept.'

'Of course.'

Siobhan looked outside at the weather and then checked the forecast on her phone. 'We'll go up now,' she said to Angela. 'Have a look up towards the Gobbins to see what may be up there and then we'll come back. I think it's going to rain this afternoon. I'd rather not be stuck out in the rain. It'll give you a chance to go to sleep as well. Have the police wanted to talk to you any more?'

'They want to speak to me again, but they're leaving me alone for a bit. I had one of those counsellor people come. Special officers. I'm Deborah's next of kin, you see? They want to go through where she's been, but I don't know outside of here.'

'Well, make sure you tell them what you've told us. Hide nothing,' said Siobhan.

Half an hour later, the small team was leaving the car up by the Gobbins. There was a centre for the cliff path and Siobhan was able to get close to have a look at where the path would lead. However, you had to book tours and at this time of the year, they were scarce.

'We can book you a tour if you want, but it's a path, and it's three hours of a walk and there's lots of ups and downs,' said the man on the information desk.

'There're no areas to break out into?' asked Siobhan.

'No,' said the man. 'We don't get people coming up here on their own. You're not meant to. We close it off. It's dangerous. You can get a rockfall.'

Siobhan thought about what the man said and made her way back towards the team.

'Maybe it's not what they came up here for. I mean, we've come to the Gobbins because she said the Gobbins, but it's not the only thing here, is it? It's the landmark, yes, but people don't always go for landmarks,' said Kylie.

'Let's take a tour of the area,' said Siobhan. 'If she's been up here and she's not a hiking junkie, there must be a reason.'

The team got into the car, and Declan drove, Siobhan scouting around her. It was all small country roads. They had farmhouses and other small houses off them. *Here on this spit of land with Ballylumford power station at the end, Islandmagee in the middle,* Siobhan thought, *if you needed a space to do something, you could do it here.*

You'd be away from prying eyes. Did they meet here? Angela had talked about the witches coming together, dancing naked. Why would you do that? You couldn't do that somewhere close to a town. You'd have to be hidden away. And here, there were certainly fields where you could do it. At four in the morning, when everything was dark, you could find places here, couldn't you? Would you be seen?

Everything was too much up in the air for Siobhan's liking. Everything she was talking about seemed to hinge on the idea of a coven being real. Why would you do things like that? Dance in the buff out here? It would be cold. Siobhan felt a shiver.

'Declan, if you were going to do some nude ritual where you had to dance about naked, would you do it out in these fields?'

'I would do it somewhere warm,' said Declan.

'I think the point Siobhan's making is, would there be enough privacy?' said Kylie.

'Well, some of these fields are quite hard to see from different places, aren't they?' said Declan. 'I guess you could get away with it. Would you have to have flaming torches?'

'I don't know,' said Siobhan. 'I've never joined a coven and danced naked with them.'

'It's all a little surreal,' said Kylie. If you didn't have the dead woman at the end with her eyes gouged out and heart missing, I think we'd be laughing at the moment.'

'Very much,' said Siobhan. 'But that's the problem. We've got a dead body and a person who's dead in such a way that there must be meaning behind it. By the sounds of her, she wouldn't be out on that cliff path. What could you do out there? We need to find out more about covens and witches in the local area, but first, we get back and we search her room. See what we can dig up about Deborah. Honestly, her sister doesn't seem to know that much, considering she lived with her. That bothers me.'

'You think Angela is not very with it?' queried Declan.

'No, that's not it,' said Siobhan. 'I don't think Angela is that far off the mark. If she doesn't know that much about her sister living with her, it's usually because the other person is hiding. Hiding something from her.'

'The coven,' said Kylie.

'I think it's a bit early to say that, but something, something doesn't feel right,' said Siobhan. 'Let's go see what her room holds.'

Chapter 05

Siobhan returned to the house of Angela and Deborah Lynch to find a police team not long after leaving. Angela was standing at the front door, watching the police as they disappeared. Siobhan pulled up. Angela remained at the door, still dressed in black, eyes looking sullen.

'Here to interview, were they?'

'No, they've just gone through her room. Said to me they found nothing. At least, nothing obvious. They have taken nothing away, either.'

'We'll see how good their search has been,' said Siobhan. 'Do you mind if we look now?'

'No,' said Angela, 'but I am going to go back to sleep, so please keep it quiet.'

Siobhan nodded and turned and looked at Declan. He shrugged his shoulders. Together with Kylie, they traipsed up the small stairs and into Deborah's room. Angela followed them briefly, but finding nothing to say, withdrew, going to her own room.

The room was simple. A double bed in one corner, a wardrobe in another, and a desk with a mirror above it.

Around the mirror were several photographs, mostly showing Angela and Deborah. The room, however, had a darker spin to it. Painted with purple walls, the ceiling had stars and the moon on it, as well as various images of cats, witches' hats, and other strange symbols around the room. Before she started searching, Siobhan stood in the middle, turning round and round, trying to gauge a feel for the room.

'It's like being in the room of a child,' said Kylie.'

'You're right,' said Siobhan. 'It's not like an adult obsession, isn't it? It's more like a child's. All witches, all that sort of old folklore feel to it.'

Declan had ignored the walls completely and was staring at the photographs surrounding the mirror.

'Certainly keen on her sister, anyway. There are photographs of them all the time. They're not that similar, really, are they?'

'Voice down,' said Siobhan. 'She might not be asleep in the other room, and that sort of comment can upset people, especially at this sort of time.'

Declan nodded. Siobhan went to the wardrobe and opened it. She found several costumes. There were some ordinary clothes, jeans, dresses, and blouses. Over half the wardrobe were dark outfits.

'Declan, come over here a minute,' said Siobhan. 'I want you to take out each of these dresses for me.'

'And do what with them?' asked Declan. 'Try them on?'

'No, just hold them up,' said Siobhan. 'I want to take a photograph of everything in here. We don't want to be running back and forward. These dresses, these witches' outfits, so to speak, well, they meant a lot to her, so they could be important. I don't want to be trying to remember what they look like.'

Declan took each of them out and turned, holding them up as Siobhan photographed them. Then he went to put them back in.

'Before you put them all away, that other one, the one towards the end.'

'What? With all the symbols?'

'That one. Put it out a minute on the bed.' Declan laid down a black dress that was covered with symbols.

'You recognise any of those symbols?'

'No,' said Kylie. 'I'm no symbologist. I wouldn't know what most symbols I see mean.'

'I don't think that's what she's getting at,' said Declan. 'I think what Siobhan's saying is, we don't really see many of those symbols.'

'No,' said Siobhan, pointing to one that has a curved end and a circle towards the top. 'I don't think I've ever seen that one before.'

'I think you're right,' said Declan. 'It certainly doesn't look like something I've seen.'

'Why would you?' said Kylie. 'If it's meant to do with the occult and it's meant to do with witches, why would you?'

Declan put the dress away and Siobhan started going through other drawers within the room. First, she found underwear and then some small tops and some tracksuit bottoms. She then came across a drawer that had a lot of knickknacks in it. Many of them were strange. There were candles as well, lots of them. None of them were good fragrances, and some of them looked positively unholy.

'Not seen anything like that either,' said Kylie. 'I'm more of a dance chick.'

Siobhan frowned. She didn't want to believe the coven idea, or anything about witchcraft. She wondered more and more, because everything that Angela Lynch had said, Deborah was seeming to live up to. How the police would take it. Was it just a daft cosplay that had gone wrong? Why was she out there? The symbology struck her. Siobhan looked down and under the bed, finding a stuffed cat. She pulled it out and noted that the eyes hadn't been done particularly well.

'Why would you keep that under your bed?' said Declan. 'Horrific looking.'

Again, Siobhan put her finger up to her lips. 'Maybe it was part of being the witch,' said Siobhan softly. If you can't keep a cat, maybe that's the best you're going to get. You could take it out, stroke it at night, talk to it.

'Are you thinking she's delusional? Are you thinking that Deborah is not the full shilling?'

'It's a possibility we have to entertain,' said Siobhan. 'If she isn't, she's gone the whole hog into this. What I know is we're going to have to get deeper into researching witches properly.'

Siobhan scanned the room, trying to find any crevices or spots where something could be hidden. Her fingers found a loose patch in the wall. As she pushed her fingers at it, it twisted, allowing someone to put their hand through into a tiny area. The area at this time was empty.

'That's ingenious,' said Declan.

'Maybe,' said Siobhan. 'There's nothing in here, though. Angela said she was worried Deborah had been forced to take part in something she didn't want to. She was also talking about other murders. We need to look into the possibility of a coven. Not that it will look anything like that of a horror film. Maybe more like a very close-knit secret society. Given that someone's dead, we need to do it quietly, too.'

'Let's get home,' said Declan. 'Think about where we go next.'

'That's not a bad idea,' said Siobhan. 'I'll just speak to Angela first.'

Siobhan looked for Angela in her bedroom but found that she was fast asleep on her bed. Walking over to the bedside table, she found some sleeping tablets. Siobhan left a note beside the woman's bed, advising that she'd be back in touch and that she'd got what she needed from the room. On the way back in the car, Siobhan sat looking out of the window while Declan's mind was churning as he drove.

'How would she keep a coven secret?' asked Declan.

'That's the whole point, isn't it?' said Kylie. 'Big secret. How do you know someone's a witch unless they tell you or unless you see them?'

'Secret society in control, dominating, affecting the local landscape,' said Siobhan. 'That's what we're being told. That's what Angela said. Stop seeing it as something from the movies. As far as I'm aware, witches don't exist. As far as I'm aware, magic doesn't exist. Whatever they're doing, how are they doing it? What way are they doing it? Why are they doing it? What's the important thing to find out? What's the key to all this? There might be some dress up around it.'

'Dress up?' queried Declan.

'Imagine,' said Siobhan, 'that you are running one of these secret societies. That you have your fingers in so many pies. If you get discovered, you want to pass it off as something innocuous, ridiculous, so you can move elsewhere. Be another group. Another innocuous group, even though what you're doing, is running a proper organisation underneath. That's maybe how we need to think about what's going on here?

'I don't know for sure,' said Siobhan. 'I'm just postulating. We've got to think about all the different options why people would do such things. Why things are as they are. We'll head back and get the whiteboard out. See what we can come up with. Also get a hold of her friends soon. Find out if they knew anything.'

Within an hour, they were sitting in the living room of Siobhan's house with a small whiteboard stuck up in front of them. Having served drinks, Kylie sat down beside Declan as Siobhan stood beside the whiteboard.

'What do we know? We know Deborah Lynch died. We don't know if she died in the pillory or away from the pillory and how she was put there.'

'How are we going to find that out?'

'I don't know,' said Siobhan. 'What is significant about the pillory? Maybe a point's being made.'

'A point?' said Kylie.

'If you're a coven and you're trying to keep under the radar, why would you kill someone and stick them in a Witches' Pillory? Raising up the notion of witches again? Why not put a bullet in the back of their head and dispose of them?'

'Because this is important,' said Declan. 'They're sending a message. That's what they're doing, isn't it? Angela said Deborah was having problems, regretting stuff. You can't have that sort of thing in a coven. It has to be dealt with. One deals with it more visibly, like this. Plenty of signals sent out. Plenty of warning given to people.

'What else do we know then?' asked Kylie.

'Well, Deborah liked the dresses. She was into the occult,' said Declan.

Siobhan wrote the word down. 'We've also got a lot of dresses, but we've got one we don't recognise the symbols on,' said Siobhan. 'We've got to identify the symbols. It might tell us where it's come from. We've also got the costume. Did Deborah make it herself? I didn't see any sign she was capable of that. We find out what places can make these outfits. See if we can get a hint. We're also going to need to go to the library and find out about witches in the area. Trace back. Angela said they were coming from a long line. Things in the past and that's when the coven was known. Let's find out what that's all about. Who did what? Maybe it has a bearing on today. Maybe it doesn't.'

'Who's going to do what, then?' asked Kylie.

'In the morning, I'm going to find a folklore lecturer or rather I'll find him tonight and talk to him in the morning. See if I can get these symbols identified. I'm feeling that there might be a symbolist somewhere. We might have to re-go over what Angela's saying, see if there's any other areas we can look into.'

'The other side is the dress, of course. The cat being stuffed. Anything to the occult we've got to track down,' said Kylie.

'Good thinking,' said Siobhan. 'Absolutely. Anything tied in at all. I'll get on to finding my folklore lecturer. Kylie, you get ready to visit the library tomorrow. Declan, I guess you can drive me.'

Kylie smiled. Clearly, being trusted to go off on her own suited her.

'Early start, Declan,' said Siobhan to him. 'Off you go. See if you can think of anything else by the morning.'

Declan got up to get his coat, then waved goodbye. 'See you in the morning, Mrs D. I can take you up the path,' he said to

Kylie, 'if you're going to your house.'

'Thanks, Declan, but unnecessary. I want to make sure Siobhan's all right before I go to bed.'

Declan nodded. He exited out the front door, closing it behind him.

'I think I can find my bed all right,' said Siobhan.

'You left me hanging last time. Julian, what happened?'

'What I told you happened. I planted a kiss on him.'

Siobhan could feel excitement building in her stomach, especially the way Kylie was teasing her, wanting to know more. She'd shut out Julian from her mind when she'd been at work. Now they were relaxing again, slowing down. The thoughts of the previous day come back to her.

'You told me you kissed him. In what way did you kiss him? What was he like?' said Kylie.

'I'm fifty,' said Siobhan. 'I just kissed him. You get to my age, you don't want to hang about. You don't sit there and analyse it all. I kissed him; he kissed back. It's all good.'

'Good?' said Kylie. 'That is a bland word. You were off out for lunch.'

'Yes, we were off for lunch at a garden centre. Not exactly the most romantic.'

'I thought that's what you oldies did. I thought that's the only place you got to.'

'How dare you!' said Siobhan suddenly. She walked over and sat down beside Kylie on the sofa. She elbowed her in the side. 'That's cheeky.'

'Well, that's what I'm here for, isn't it? I'm your rude friend. I'm able to prompt you. I feel we've got past the boss-employee stage.'

'I wasn't aware we had a boss-employee stage,' said Siobhan.

It had been nice, though. Having Kylie about had brought back a young streak. She saw the world through their eyes. Not just the old, embittered ones that she now had. Did you good to surround yourself with younger people. They took you to task a lot more than your peer group would.

'If we're talking about me,' said Siobhan, 'what about you? '

'What about me?'

'Walk you back up to the house?'

'Don't,' she said. 'Don't!' There was a sudden finality in the way she said it.

'Something wrong?' asked Siobhan.

'Last time I got close to someone, we created someone. Someone who then died. Who died without his dad being around. I don't want to go through that again.'

'Declan's not like that, though. He's a good sort. He's a rascal, but he's a good sort.'

'So you say. You never know people until you live with them, do you?'

That stopped Siobhan in her tracks. She thought about Julian. It was a risk. Then again, it was all a risk. The question was, was he a risk she was prepared to take? Siobhan had seen enough and lived enough to know that she should take this risk now. She only hoped that Kylie might do too. That she hadn't become too battle-hardened, to know an excellent opportunity when she saw one.

Chapter 06

Armed with photographs of the witch's outfit found in Deborah's room, Siobhan sought someone who could explain the symbology on it. She needed someone who wasn't a crackpot, someone who wasn't simply into dressing up and having fun with it. Rather, someone who could be a cross between a historian and an occultist. Someone steeped enough in the lore, but who could also provide a reasonable idea of what was true—not caught up in lots of paranormal mumbo-jumbo. Bringing witches into the investigation caused people to think about abilities beyond the ordinary.

Siobhan was seeing the coven as a secret society, if it indeed existed. Lots of secret societies had existed with a strange aura around them, something to ward people off. Yet at heart, they were simply gangsters. Gangsters carried an aura with them, sometimes well deserved, sometimes not. You had to get beyond that to see their actions, to see how to close them down. As part of the Service, Siobhan had dealt with organised crime before. This felt like organised crime, but organised from a distance. It certainly didn't feel like paranormal beings were back to avenge those who had slighted them or whom they'd fallen out with.

Siobhan first tried looking at the university to see if there were any folklorists. Despite the many departments, including the history department, Siobhan couldn't find the right type of person. She knew also that marching into the university could be highlighted by certain people. So far, she wanted to stay under the radar.

Siobhan went online and tried to look up books about witches, to see if any of the authors lived in the province. After a couple of hours of investigating, she pulled out a name: Ciaran McGee. During her online search about Ciaran, she discovered that he regularly gives presentations to small communities, focusing on the history and various folklore. Most of it seemed to harken back to occult activity.

A picture of him showed a long, pointed beard and bushy eyebrows. A man probably in his sixties. Whether that was part of the act to look impressive and dramatically wise was another matter. Siobhan felt he might be a good start. There was a number to call to hire Ciaran to come and do a talk, and Siobhan called it. The hour was now getting late, just passing eight o'clock. She hoped to catch him for the following morning.

'Hello. You've got through to Ciaran. How can I help you?'

'Mr McGee, my name is Siobhan Duffy. I'm a private investigator, and I've currently got an issue that surrounds certain occult activity. I'd like to come and chat with you to find out a bit of history and background about certain symbols I've got to deal with.'

'Extremely busy,' said Ciaran. 'Extremely busy at the moment. I could probably book you in a couple of weeks, maybe for an hour.'

'I was hoping for quicker for that. It involves murder, the current investigation, and the possibility of witchcraft.'

'I'll try to do what I can over the phone,' said Ciaran. 'Have you got any detail?'

'I'm trying to identify some symbols,' said Siobhan. 'Hang on, and I'll send you one by text.'

Siobhan closed down the call, pulled up a photograph of one symbol, and texted it to Ciaran McGee. As she stood in her front living room before the fire, Siobhan toasted her backside, wondering if she'd made the right call with this man. One symbol would be enough. She would not show him everything until she'd met him.

Her mobile rang. *That was quick.* 'Hello, Mr McGee,' said Siobhan.

'I'll meet you tonight,' he said straight away. 'Where are you?'

'I'm on the far side of Bangor. Where are you?'

'Currently up in Belfast. We could meet.'

'Where would you suggest a meeting?' asked Siobhan.

'Well, I'm a strange man to you, so it'd probably be best if we do somewhere public. Maybe one of the friendly pubs. We might haul up in one of the snugs, maybe Mulligan's. You know where it is?'

Siobhan did. It was quite upmarket, but it had a very cosy feel to it, with wooden floors and an old-style bar.

'What time are you thinking?' she asked.

'As soon as you can, I'll head there directly. I'll meet you.'

He seems very keen, thought Siobhan, and tried to work out if that was a good or a bad sign. If he was completely disinterested, she guessed, the symbols would mean nothing.

Declan had gone home for the day, so Siobhan dropped into

the small lodge at the front of Siobhan's house where Kylie lived, and advised her what she was going to do.

'Can I come with you?'

'You're out and about to Belfast Library tomorrow. Why don't you get some rest?'

'Cramping your style, am I? Thought I could be a chaperone, just in case Julian hears you've been out with strange men.'

Siobhan raised her eyebrows. 'Enough of that,' she said. 'This is work. It needs done. No, you'll be better getting some sleep. Besides, I don't know this guy. It could be two minutes and back out the door, because he's some sort of nut job. Best I see him first.'

Kylie gave up fighting and turned around to watch the television programme on her TV. Siobhan left the house, wondering just what on earth the new generation was coming to. She hated soaps. There was enough going on in real life.

Siobhan parked in one of Belfast's many multi-storeys and walked in her blue jeans and jumper until she got to Mulligan's. She didn't feel overly dressed, which was good, because Mulligan's was not the most formal of places. Rather, it was somewhere that people went for a good evening of craic and alcohol.

Walking into the establishment, which was reasonably full despite it being a weeknight, Siobhan coasted through the bar, looking this way and that, until she spotted a man in a tweed jacket in one of the snugs towards the rear. He stood up, his brown pointed beard highlighted against a white t-shirt underneath the tweed jacket. *He has every look of a dotty professor*, she thought. She watched as he raised his hand and Siobhan came over.

'Would you be Mrs Duffy?' he said rather hesitantly.

'Siobhan. You must be Mr McGee. Can I call you Ciaran?'

'Absolutely. Can I get you a drink?' Siobhan glanced down at the pint of Guinness in front of him.

'I've got the car,' she said.

'They do the alcohol-free stuff now,' he said. She nodded.

Really? She should buy him a drink, for he was going to be giving her information. He looked like an older sort of man who would take care of a lady. Siobhan hoped she didn't look like the older sort of lady. She was only fifty, after all.

Having got Siobhan's pint, Ciaran set it down before her and slipped in on the opposite side of the table.

'Tell me you've got more of these symbols,' he said enthusiastically.

'I've got a whole horde sewn on an outfit. The outfit of a deceased woman.'

He looked up at her. 'Deceased? How?'

'As far as I can make out, she was possibly held while her heart was removed.'

The man's face went pale.

'Anything else? Was her body affected in any other way?'

'Her eyes were . . .'

'Gouged out,' he finished. He leaned forward, staring down at the symbols. 'How involved are you with these people?' he asked.

'I don't know who these people are,' said Siobhan. 'I have taken on an investigation, because a relative of the dead woman wants me to find out who killed her.'

'Was the woman presented in her death throes?'

'Was the woman what?' asked Siobhan.

'Was she put in front of people? Was she in any way . . .'

'She was put in . . .'

'Stocks. The Witches' Pillory,' said the man. 'It's the woman from the Witches' Pillory, isn't it? They never said how she died. Never said about the heart or the eyes. They thought it was just a prank. The papers are running a line of something weird. Tittle-tattle. Talking about witches, but there was no evidence. Just somebody dumped in the stocks.'

The man took a large drink of his Guinness and when he put it back, a third of it had already disappeared.

'Are you okay?' asked Siobhan.

The man nodded. 'You're looking potentially at witches.'

'Easy,' said Siobhan. 'The next part of your conversation is going to be very measured. If you're going to talk to me about supernatural beings, about chanting and dancing, then you and I might part company quickly.'

'We're talking about witches,' said the man. 'When you get to Halloween, everybody talks about broomsticks and people flying here, there, wherever. Witches were seen as powerful, because they knew how to use herbs, other plants to cause death, to cause healing. They understood childbirth. What changed some of them from being mere midwives into witches or just simple killers, or expert herbalists, was the fact that they could gang together.

'Some did indeed do pacts with the devil. There was talk of tongues and people speaking in certain ways. I'm not getting ahead of myself here,' he said to Siobhan. 'The church will tell you people talk in tongues. Good tongues, they say. Witches talk in wicked tongues. Depending on what type of witches they may be, some were more naturalists of a rather superstitious sort.'

'Tell me,' said Siobhan, 'what sort is associated with this death?'

The man went quiet for a moment, and she looked at his ruddy cheeks, which had gone red underneath his beard. It was thin in places, which meant she could see that he was affected by what he was talking about. Was there a sweat over him?

'A long time ago, near here, witchcraft was said to be rife. There were several trials; that's why we have the pillory or rather the mock-up of the pillory in Carrickfergus. Witchcraft, whether it be actual or the feared reasonable activities of certain women, is a historical fact. It was persecuted. There are also stories from the time, not attributed or rather not substantiated, that talk of societies of women. Women didn't get to vote for a long time. Women were pushed out of major decisions.

'The capacity of women to influence and to take charge is no different today than back then. The rules, the regulations, society may change, but women are as capable as men. They have an ability to get together and orchestrate, the same as any group of men can.'

Some would say better, thought Siobhan. She liked the cut of his jib. He talked methodically. He talked about people, not about the weird and the wonderful spirits that lay beyond the world.

'Sometimes in the past, you controlled the society with talk of things that were beyond comprehension. We still do nowadays. Although science tries to debunk myths much more. But think about it. Our science is rather lacking. We can neither prove nor disprove God. That's because we instantly are talking about something that is beyond our comprehension. If it's beyond our comprehension, how do we prove it? How do we get on top of it?

'Back then, lots more things were beyond comprehension. Why somebody would just die suddenly when they'd been simply poisoned with a herb mixed into their food. There was all the paraphernalia that went with it. The symbology that set who was who in an order. These symbols here,' he said, pointing to the photographs that were on Siobhan's phone in front of him. 'This is a new initiate. I have only read of symbols like this. I have never seen them. To have them on a garment, though, is quite remarkable.'

'Could it just be that somebody else has read it? Somebody else has randomly come across these symbols and stuck them on an outfit?' asked Siobhan.

'They're not randomly stuck on. The placing of them is very specific. You have someone at the lower level of a coven. You would say second order. They're not a novice just in, rather they have been in for a little while.'

'So far I've got no evidence that these people actually exist,' said Siobhan and then lowered her voice. 'All I've got is a dead body. You could fill in the blanks.'

'This is a very specific order of witches,' said the man. 'The coven name, I can't even pronounce. It's written in an ancient script. They talk in a language that I don't understand. Not that much is known about them, but there are tales where those who betrayed the order were presented so that the villagers around would understand. One of the ways of presenting them would be with the heart missing and the eyes gouged out.'

He took another large drink of his Guinness, this time draining it. 'I warn you to be very careful,' he said.

'You'd think they actually have some influence.'

'When this order was about, they controlled a lot of what

was going on. At least that's what the books say, those books that remain. Handwritten accounts from the lords of the land, so to speak, of how they appeased them, of how certain things were brought together. You had women then with enormous wealth, but they could hide it and be in the background, controlling the men and the power makers in front of them.

'I do not know how that would work today. Maybe somebody has taken on the mantle, maybe somebody has read up on them,' said Ciaran. 'What I do know is the stories I've read from back then are horrific, terrifying. They are quick, they are deadly, they are brutal. There's an evil in it too.'

'Did they engage in any other activity, any ritualistic type of activity, things that we would say are more sort of . . .'

'Paranormal based, weird? Totally,' said Ciaran. 'They still did all the "let's dance naked under the moonlight witch stuff." That's keeping your people on their toes. Some witches believed they had powers, because not all of them understood what was handed down to them. They just knew you mixed in certain things; you handed people different potions. Hypnosis was taught without being understood— the power of suggestion. There are many techniques that are not paranormal but would be viewed as such back in the day, and may even be seen now by some people.'

'Thank you,' said Siobhan. 'Am I able to contact you again if I need you?'

The man looked left and right suddenly. 'I'd rather you didn't, unless you truly need me. I don't wish to be involved. This is an amazing find, but it's a terrifying one. For this to have kept going, the order, the coven, is amazing. I fear it may have been dormant, lying there, being worked on. To come to the fore after all this time, I don't wish to discover it.'

'Thank you for your time. I'll call you only if absolutely necessary, life and death,' said Siobhan. The man swallowed hard and nodded. 'Thank you for your time. Please bill me for it.'

'No,' he said. 'No traces, no connections. I've been watching around us. I don't think anyone is observing us.'

Siobhan agreed. On the way in, she'd noticed no one, and sitting now, she had seen no one watching. She would look on the way out, though.

'Well, that's good,' said Siobhan. 'Thank you again.'

Ciaran stood up, gave her a nod, and wished her all the best. He shuffled off back out of the bar, leaving Siobhan with a dilemma. Did she believe these tales of witches, or were they just mere folklore? Was somebody digging up the past to pretend to be something or had a society continued for that long?

As she stood up to leave the bar, there was a slight shiver that ran through her from top to bottom. Looking around, she could see no one watching. If someone was tailing her in here, they were doing a great job. When she reached the car, she turned on the radio, putting it up loud, for some reason requiring some company on the trip home.

Chapter 07

The following morning, Siobhan was up early, still feeling somewhat agitated by the previous night's meeting. As she stood in the shower, she couldn't help but feel a little uneasy. She was used to the idea of murder, of killings. She'd worked in the Service after all. Her former lover and service colleague was killed at the Giant's Boot up at the causeway. She'd seen other people die while out on service duty in Russia and other places, but this felt strange.

She remembered touring up by Ballylumford power station around Islandmagee. That there was a coven of some sort, even if it was maintaining political and economic influence as opposed to some sort of magical control, still got to her.

Northern Ireland's history always had people being pushed and pulled here and there. As she grew up, she'd been told what to believe, which part of the divide you stood on. Throughout it all, she'd felt a level of coercion put upon her by different people. Some were even well-meaning, but she thought that a new age was coming. A time when the province was more like other places and for the better. You could have a society that wasn't divided. But this was division, and this was control. This was people steering things.

Drying herself down, Siobhan heard Kylie coming through the front door. She always shouted when she did so. Siobhan thought Kylie was simply scared that if she didn't, Siobhan would assume it was an intruder and possibly end up taking her out. Although fifty, she still had some skills of an operative. Although they were nowhere near as honed as they'd been before, they were a match for anyone like Kylie or Declan. Siobhan changed in her bedroom.

'What time are you heading up to the library?' Siobhan shouted through to Kylie.

'We'll get your breakfast done and then I'll get the bus.'

'I don't mind Declan dropping you off if you wish. It's on business time after all.'

Siobhan came out of her room and marched into the kitchen to find scrambled eggs sitting on a plate with some generously buttered toast around them.

'Brilliant, Kylie,' she said. A cup of Lapsang Souchong tea came along with the plate.

'This all looks good,' she said. 'Have you had your own?'

'Yes, I've had my own. I haven't seen Declan yet.'

There was a loud bang on the front door, which then opened. That's me, Mrs D. Morning. I don't think Kylie's up at the lodge. Is she down here?'

'Yes, Kylie's here.'

'Okay. You might want to tell her that there's a woman standing outside her door.'

'What?' blurted Kylie.

'There's a woman standing outside her door.'

'Who is it?' asked Siobhan.

'That woman that was here before.'

'Well, get her, Declan.'

'I didn't want to come down and intrude. You're having your breakfast and that.'

Siobhan started piling her scrambled eggs into her and got through a piece of the toast by the time Declan had returned with Angela Lynch. Siobhan wiped a bit of egg off her mouth before approaching the front door and putting her hand out to Angela.

'Sorry for leaving you up there. I don't know what Declan was thinking.'

'I didn't want to come down,' said Angela. 'It seemed a bit early. I was going to wait ten minutes.'

'Why are you here, though?' asked Siobhan. 'You could have rung. I'd have come up to see you.'

'No,' she said. 'It's the lake.'

'Cup of tea, Kylie, please, and refresh mine. I think I've drunk half of it.' Kylie nodded and Siobhan led Angela Lynch through to the sitting room.

'Get a fire on, Declan,' said Siobhan, and sat down beside Angela Lynch. 'What's the matter? What's brought you down here at this time?'

'It's the lake. The lake, you see. The lake's a problem. I remembered. I remembered talking about it with her. We were all pretty drunk. Most of us didn't know what was going on, but I remembered she talked about the lake. Dancing at the lake.'

'Dancing to do what?' asked Siobhan.

'It's where they dance. Their rites must be satanic rites.'

The woman was incredibly distracted, and Siobhan was wondering if this was normal for her or if her sister's death had sent her over the limit. Angela was her client though, so she tried to be sympathetic and bring out what was really troubling the woman and where exactly this lake was.

'You mentioned the lake,' said Siobhan. 'Whereabouts is the lake?'

'Ballylone.'

'Ballylone?' queried Siobhan. 'Anything better than that? Anything more?'

'Saintfield. Near to Saintfield. You go out from Saintfield, there's a lake.'

'And the lake's important, is it?' asked Siobhan. 'Why do they need the lake?'

'Lake's not important. Lake's just a lake.'

Kylie put her cup of tea down and showed it was heavily sugared before placing another cup of Lapsang Souchong in front of Siobhan. As the cup touched the table, Angela Lynch reached forward, grabbed Siobhan's cup, and started sniffing. 'Smoke,' she said. 'Smokey. They do smoke too, there's always smoke. When they dance, you get smoke.'

'When they dance. Did they dance at the lake?'

Angela Lynch stood up, walked over to the window, and looked out. She went silent. Siobhan turned and looked over at Kylie, who shrugged her shoulders. *What was going on with the woman?* Siobhan walked over to Kylie and whispered in her ear.

'Get Declan to take you up to the library. Find out about local covens in the area. I spoke last night with Ciaran McGee. Don't mention his name to anyone. He said there was a coven in the area. I want to cross-reference what he said because if it's true, we may begin to understand what's going on.'

'Where do I get the information?'

'I wrote it down when I came in last night. It's on a piece of paper in my study. Photocopy it. Take it. I'll see you later.'

Siobhan watched Kylie disappear, and as she walked past the front window, along with Declan, out to the car, Siobhan saw that Angela Lynch never moved. Her head never turned to watch them. She just stared off.

'Where's this lake, Angela?'

'Ballylone. Ballylone.'

'Did you tell the police about Ballylone?'

The woman nodded her head.

'Do you know exactly where it is?'

She now shook her head in the negative. 'Maybe we could find it,' said Siobhan. It had to be better than sitting here with Angela Lynch, looking out of her front room. Yes, the fire might go to waste, for Declan had only just started it, but that would have to do. 'I'll get my coat,' said Siobhan. 'We'll take a little trip.'

It took Siobhan ten minutes to get Angela Lynch into Siobhan's car. She sat in silence. Siobhan drove out from Bangor towards Newtownards and Comber. Then she went towards Saintfield, following the Ballylone Road towards Ballynahinch. It wasn't the main road, breaking off from the A21, otherwise known to the locals as the Ballynahinch Road.

Siobhan laughed about that. Everywhere in Northern Ireland, people didn't refer to the numbers of the road. Those who had moved over in recent years, especially the English, would always refer to road numbers. They were used to motorways, or the A this, the B that. Not for Northern Irish people, it was the Ballynahinch Road. Why? Because at one end it went to Ballynahinch. The Bangor Road or it was the Belfast Road? The Belfast Road was the one that got Siobhan because there were loads of roads into Belfast. It was utterly confusing. And yet it worked. People from home didn't use numbers to describe their roads. They were only just getting the hang of motorway names.

Siobhan followed the Ballynahinch Road down, past a warehouse. On either side, there were country fields. The roads meandered up and down. Outside of Belfast, the further you got away from it, these small hills would drop in size. They were called drumlins, something that was a unique feature around Belfast. Something that made every road seem quainter as you went up and down hills. You never saw what was so close by until you reached the peak of the next small hill.

As they went past a crossroads, Siobhan thought she could see something up ahead. There was a lake out in the fields, or it might be a lake, for there was definitely a dip with trees around it. The lake was behind a couple of houses, and. Siobhan was not wanting to go up their driveway to look at the lake. After all, if things were happening here, maybe the people in the houses were involved.

She drove a little further up and found a road—more of a tractor path than a road— that broke off there to access the fields. She followed it, parked up towards the end, just across from the lake. There were a few scattered trees towards the lake. Siobhan reckoned you could dance in and amongst them, probably without being seen from the road. The lake may have been deep in the middle, she couldn't tell. It had a lot of greenery, soft floating plant life around the edges. Keeping up with Declan's assessment of her complete lack of green fingers, Siobhan couldn't tell you what the plant life was.

'Is this the lake?' Siobhan asked Angela. The woman had accompanied her, but her head had been down the whole time they'd walked across to the lake. Now she looked up, looking left and right.

'Maybe. I've not been here,' said Angela. 'She just said Ballylone Road. Out on the Ballylone Road where they danced. Rites, she talked about rites.'

'What sort of rites?'

'Murderous rites.'

Siobhan stopped for a moment. 'Murderous?'

'Not sacrifice. Not sacrifice, it was someone else. Someone had done wrong. Somebody wasn't—I don't know. She was drunk,' said Angela, 'but she described . . .' Angela nearly broke down. Siobhan walked over and put her arm around the woman. She could feel her shiver.

'What happened to the liaison officer?' asked Siobhan, wondering how this rather confused woman was not being better looked after.

'Sent away,' said Angela. 'No use. Better on my own. Hired you. You do more. Cleverer. You seem to understand.'

Let's hope the police see it that way, thought Siobhan. 'Best we get back,' Siobhan said to Angela. 'You need to have a rest. You need a cup of something. Maybe we'll stop off somewhere, yes?'

She put her arms on the woman's shoulder to turn, but Angela Lynch wasn't for moving. Angela stared at the water. 'Deborah said she had to lift out her heart.'

Siobhan froze. 'She had to do what?'

'Remove the heart. Deborah removed the heart.'

'No,' said Siobhan. 'Deborah's heart was removed. Deborah died because they removed her heart, and they . . .'

'Gouged out the eyes,' said Angela.

'That's right,' said Siobhan, 'horrible. They gouged out

Deborah's eyes.'

'No,' said Angela. She slapped Siobhan hard on her thigh. 'Don't put words in my mouth. I'm telling you something. You need to understand. The water. The water. Eyes. Deborah took out the eyes. Deborah had to. They had a knife. She told me about a knife. A handle and markings on the knife. They killed. They—no. Not killed, purified. Purified . . .' Angela drifted, her mind suddenly elsewhere.

'Angela. Angela,' said Siobhan. The woman looked back at her, eyes hollow. 'Are you telling me that your sister killed someone how she was killed?'

'Drunk,' said Angela suddenly. 'Totally drunk. We just talked. Talked and drunk. The Ballylone Road.'

Angela fell silent. Siobhan tried to shake her, tried to get her to talk more, but there was nothing. Siobhan walked Angela back to the car before returning to the lake. Did Deborah do something? Was Deborah not the first? Was this something that went on? Why was Deborah telling her sister? Why was . . . Siobhan was stumped.

You would show someone the punishment so people would understand for a reason. Was she missing a trick with this? Deborah was in the pillory for a reason. Was there somebody around here to be found? If Deborah did to somebody, did she do it out here? 'Dancing at the lake,' that's what she'd said. Angela talked about dancing. She talked about Deborah killing someone, rites as well. No wonder the woman is messed up, if that's where her mind was.

'Focus,' said Siobhan to herself, placing her hands inside her jacket pocket. It was cold even with a jumper underneath, but more and more Siobhan realised there was a shiver there that wasn't just the elements. She hoped Kylie was getting on well because she needed more information. She needed to know where to start.

Chapter 08

Kylie hopped out of the car and gave Declan a wave, telling him she'd meet him for lunch. She wasn't sure how useful Declan would be in the library. He was more of a hands-on person, not a research person.

Not that Kylie thought of herself as a research person. She had no formal training, but she did like to learn things. Whenever Siobhan pulled out any facts or any details about people, Kylie would sit and read them. They churned through her memory, and she produced ideas and thoughts about different situations. She could then find suspects. Suspects—she chewed the word over. It sounded good.

Belfast Central Library had a classical orange tint to the front of it because of the stone that was built in. There were several archways to enter through, and the floor above had rectangular windows set in line with the archways. It was far from the largest building, but Kylie hoped she might find something of use.

Inside was rather plain. Many white pillars, wooden shelves with books, and occasional seating areas. It was an old building that had been converted or at least had been changed to allow a modern library to exist within it. It was quiet which

Kylie didn't see as a bad thing.

Quiet was good, especially when thoughts ran through your head. Sometimes it did her good to let them have an airing. If you put music on, or you watched television, your thoughts got pushed out. Then they came back to you in the middle of the night when you weren't awake, you weren't responsive; you weren't there to realise the brilliance that you could come up with.

Yes, thought Kylie. *Brilliant, that's what I'm going to be today, a source of brilliance for Siobhan.* Looking around her, Kylie could see several librarians behind the main enquiries desk and wandered over. She didn't understand library systems. Having not used them that often, she thought it best to use the knowledge of other people there rather than waste the next two hours being unable to locate any books.

'Hello,' said Kylie, approaching the desk.

'Hello,' said a rather dour-faced woman.

'I'm wondering if you could help me. I'm looking for books on witches.'

'Okay,' said the woman. 'Children's books on witches or adult books on witches?'

'Adult,' said Kylie. The woman raised an eyebrow but nodded, and then led Kylie along several rows of books until coming to a small section.

'This is our collection on the occult. Several books about witches within it. You're free, of course, to take them out if you have an account with us. Otherwise, please feel free to sit down and browse them. Just pop them back in the same place. You can see from the numbered system where they go.'

Kylie looked at the numbers on the edges of the books. She'd have to remember where they had come from. Kylie sat down with several books which had witches on the cover. Some had them in rather provocative poses, but always with some horned man running around behind them. Kylie supposed that was the devil.

One book seemed to be pro-witch, discussing how they were simply like modern-day druids. Kylie did not know there were so many types involved in so many other things. The trouble with the books, though, was that everything was incredibly general. Kylie didn't need that. Kylie needed something more specific. Placing the books back carefully in case she caused offence, Kylie made her way back to the front desk again.

'Oh, it's you again,' said the woman. The face hadn't brightened up at all. Maybe she was having a bad day.

'Thank you for that earlier,' said Kylie, 'but I'm looking for something about witches locally. Maybe some local history?'

'Right, I'll need to get someone else if that's all right. I'm afraid I'm not so good in the local section. Just a moment.'

The woman turned and walked away as Kylie looked around her. The library wasn't that busy. Some people had obviously come in to get out of the cold, sitting and reading newspapers in one corner. There were a few students working with books open beside them. There was an occasional child with mother, walking towards the kids' section. *At least it is warm, though,* thought Kylie.

'I hear you're looking for some detail,' said a man with glasses. He had black hair and a greying beard.

'Yes, thank you,' said Kylie. 'I'm wanting to know more about witches in the local area.'

'When you say local area, what do you mean?'

'Northern Ireland, Ireland, really. Preferably Northern

Ireland.'

'Okay,' said the man. 'There are the odd couple of history books, but I think we have some archived books. Let me have a look for a second.'

The man disappeared off to another room. When he came back, he had a smile on his face.

'I think I might have something for you. I'm going to have to come with you, though. Bring a pen as they're all on old microfiche. We've been updating these, trying to get them all on the computer system, but it takes time. These few haven't. You can't walk away with them. You'll have to copy down notes from what you're looking at, but I've got a minute or two. Probably more like ten or fifteen. Yes, let's pop through, see what we can find.'

'Great,' said Kylie. 'But there's nothing I can take away.'

'There's the odd history book that mentions witches, but to be honest, I don't think they say much. Nothing that you couldn't read by walking down to Carrickfergus and having a look at that pillory or some of the other historical areas around. Or you could search on the internet, and you'll find it. No, these books that are in the microfiches, they're quite old. Some of them are tales from long ago, handed down, written into old books, but best I show you.'

Kylie followed the man through to another room, where he told her to sit down in front of a large screen. He produced several slides that he placed into the machine and then scrolled through them.

'Here we go,' he said. 'This book here has a section on it. Let's have a look. It's about superstitions in the local area. Quite an old book, pre-1900s. Yes, here it is. A couple of pages and sections.'

'Do you mind if I photograph it with my . . .'

'No, I'm afraid not. It's held by the collection here. I'm happy for you to write down any information you need from it. Sorry. Once we get it all up, and put it under our own network, you'll be able to come in and browse it, but then some of these books are quite old. They're going to be stored away and these are the only bits that we have that anyone's going to see of them, even when we get them up on the computer.'

'Right,' said Kylie. She looked up. 'I noticed that there was a mention of Islandmagee. It says there is a witches' coven there.'

'It does,' said the man. 'Imagine that.'

Kylie scanned the information in front of her. The author seemed to believe that the witches' coven controlled a lot of what went on in the land. It mentioned various landlords and how they were in the grasp of this witches' coven. Various names were mentioned, as was the demise of several people who seemed to have gone against the plans of the witches.

'Do you think any of these people would have surviving descendants?'

'I doubt it,' said the man. 'They killed off a lot of the witches prior to that time, but who knows. I'm not an expert in these things.'

Kylie wrote the names of various witches. Then there came a picture. She drew one symbol on her pad of paper.

'That's different, that one, isn't it?' said the man beside her. 'I just find it weird. You'd think we'd have seen most symbols by now. The hook at the top, the roundness in that bit at the bottom. I haven't seen that one before.'

I have, thought Kylie. *That was on the dress. That was on Deborah Lynch's witch's dress.*

The man swished through the fiche and took her to another book. 'There we go,' said the man. 'I thought there was something about this. I remember going through these and there were confessions made. This is a witch's confession. It differs from a lot of the others because most of the others didn't confess. They just made it up after.

'This one, it says how she was taken in by the group and it says that the group has lots of power over the land. It's naming lots of different men that the group has influenced. Lots of different transactions and goings on. Quite interesting that, isn't it?' said the man. That they were toying with everyone else, pulling the strings behind the scene. Not really the image you get of a witch, is it?'

'No,' said Kylie, but she was too busy writing the confession.

'Shall I move on?' said the man.

'No,' said Kylie. 'Just wait a second. I need to get this down. This is great.'

'Excellent,' said the man. 'What are you using it for?'

'Research for a book,' said Kylie quickly.

'Oh, you're a writer, are you?'

'No, I'm just the researcher. I dig out a lot of the information for my writer. She makes it all add up in the end.'

The door opened and the original librarian stepped in. 'You not done yet, John? Taking up an awful lot of time, this.'

'I'll be through soon. We've been finding some things, some good things. Just helping the customer out. Don't worry, I'll cover your lunch. It won't be a problem.'

The woman stepped out, and John turned to Kylie. 'They're always worried about their lunch, aren't they? I have a young woman here,' he said, pointing to Kylie, 'fascinated by all this old material. Well, it's why we're here. I'm a librarian. I'm here to open up the world of books, old books at that. It's an absolute delight to have you here.'

'Thank you,' said Kylie. 'What else have you got?'

The next few books seemed to be copies of what had already been written, but the details had been dumbed-down somewhat. The detail level was not the same. Then they found a different book. There was a hand-drawn picture which showed large robes, symbols interwoven, and Kylie copied it all down. The woman there had a large bun of what presumably was white or grey hair tied up behind her head. From her hands, what looked like electricity or something else was flowing.

'That's some picture, isn't it? For back in the day,' said John. 'You've got to admit, some of them had some talent. Wild assertion, though, for someone to be like that.'

John moved the old microfiche through another couple of turns. Then another picture was there.

'Oh, that's gross,' said John. 'The things people did to each other back then.'

There was a picture of a pillory and a woman getting pelted. One eye was hanging out.

'I know that story. That's about the witches that were on the Carrickfergus pillory. It's said that one of them had the eye fall out after they were hit with many things. You wouldn't get away with that today, would you?' said Kylie. 'Makes you glad we've got a proper justice system.'

'People are never happy, are they?' said John. 'Even today, there's always something wrong with it. At least that's what they say.'

The door of the room opened again and the initial librarian stepped in.

'What's up, Anne?' said John. 'I told you I'm with a customer here. I'll be there. I won't forget your lunch.'

'It's getting busy outside.' John leaned backwards so he could look past Anne.

'Nonsense. There's nothing the rest of you can't handle. I'm doing this. Now, go on. I'll be there to cover you.'

The woman turned and stared at Kylie, who felt a shiver go down her spine. What was the woman's problem?

The door closed and John shifted a little uncomfortably in his seat. 'I'm afraid I have to apologise for Anne. She's a bit highly strung. She knows her stuff well enough, but not always the best demeanour to a person who's so interested in books.'

John moved the microfiche before Kylie could reply, and her jaw nearly dropped at the picture in front of her. It was a hand drawing again, but this time the image was of one witch holding a heart. Before her, a woman dressed in white, to whom the heart had previously belonged, was being held up by the arms. Her eyes had been gouged out, too.

'Dear God,' said John. 'That's disgusting.'

'Are there any words with it?' asked Kylie.

'You find that interesting?' said John. 'Must be a rather strange book. That's probably a bit much for general consumption.'

'Oh, very much,' said Kylie, 'but easier to get the entire story and then pare it back and you can then present it to people in a more palatable form. We don't always have to show what happens, but you could always explain it to a point that you can understand it without being too repulsed by it.'

'Of course,' said John, and moved the microfiche onto the next page.

'*Purity of the Coven*,' said Kylie out loud, reading. 'The heart removed, the eyes so they may no longer look and they may no longer come back.'

'Come back from the dead,' said John. 'There's only one person allowed to do that. Until we all get to the end.'

'Indeed,' said Kylie. 'They obviously thought that with the heart still there, you could raise the witch.'

'Bizarre,' said John.

'Indeed.' Kylie wrote it down, every detail, lapping up what was in front of her.

'It is getting close to lunchtime,' said John suddenly. 'I am going to have to cover. I think I may have raised their hackles a bit. Hopefully, you've got enough. If not, you are always welcome to come back after lunch and see some more.'

'No, no, this is fascinating, and it's all from the local area. Most of it up from just to the northeast of here.'

'Yes,' said John. 'These are local books. They aren't in a wonderful state—ancient, a lot of them. Some of them have been translated from copies of books that came before. Few copies made of them, but an interesting insight of the times.'

John switched off the microfiche, put away the various records, and then showed Kylie out of the door of the room. The lights of the library caused her to blink, but then she clocked the initial librarian over by the welcome desk. She thought that an irony. The woman had been nothing like welcoming. She positively seemed hostile now.

'I've got your break covered, Ann. Away you go,' said John. Kylie followed him over to the desk and thanked him. She was going to leave, but she noticed Ann was watching her. Kylie remained, going over to a random section and pulling out a book. She began looking at it. Ann looked back and then, as it was clear that Kylie was going to stay, and John was looking at Ann wondering why she hadn't left, departed the room.

Kylie turned the book over and realised that *Clay Pipe Making for Beginners* may have been a bit too much for her and put it back on the shelf. She walked away, gave John a wave and thanked him again before heading out into Belfast and finding the small cafe she was going to meet Declan in.

'Anything of use?' asked Declan as she sat down beside him.

'A lot of use. You won't believe what goes on in this place. I grew up my whole life here. I didn't realise there was juicy enough stuff like this in the past.'

'Well, where's the books then?' said Declan.

'On old microfiche, likely to go on computer, so I had to copy a lot down. Siobhan's going to love this. She really is.' Sitting back with a cup of tea, Kylie smiled to herself. She was good at this investigating lark.

Chapter 09

Siobhan sat in her kitchen thinking through what they'd learnt so far. She'd come back from the lake where Deborah Lynch had described strange goings-on. A place that might be at the centre of the mystery, but Siobhan had found nothing. But that didn't mean that it wasn't important. It just meant there was nothing there at the moment.

The wintry weather outside made her glad to be inside her own kitchen. The cup of lapsang souchong in front of her, made by her own fair hand, was comforting. But Siobhan was agitated. Something was up here. Something wasn't right. There'd been a coven in the area. That seemed to be true, at least in the past. Could it have continued? Was it still about? Did it matter if it was about? Were tales of witches just enough to cover up whatever else was going on?

Deborah Lynch was dead, and Angela was deeply affected. Siobhan knew people could be haunted by siblings that had died. They could be in a different state of mind from what was healthy. But she thought Angela was sound, if somewhat scared.

'Think, Siobhan,' she said. 'Think. What have we got that's

concrete? What can I go to that I can actually investigate? That I can actually look at?' This was to be her first case. Her first actual case, as a proper independent detective. A private investigator. She needed to get somewhere with it. Needed to come through.

What did Deborah have that was unusual? The witch's costume. The tales of the coven. Follow the coven. Follow the witch. Follow what was being portrayed. Then you might just find out why and what the real reason was for what had happened.

She'd been left in a Witches' Pillory. The costume would be important. It was handmade and very detailed. It was a work of art. Siobhan wondered just how many people in the province could make that. How many people in the local area would be willing to make it? It wasn't simply some sort of fancy dress outfit.

She picked up her cup of tea and took it towards the window, looking out to the sea beyond. It was calm today for the overall weather system was a high, maintaining a very steady weather pattern. Cold and crisp, but blue skies with the occasional wispy cloud.

Siobhan didn't mind the winter if it was like this. She minded if it was raining. You would get warm winters, winters that didn't freeze you. But it made you go cold when you got wet and the wind hit you. Winters like this were beautiful. You could see the browns left by the death of all the leaves. The trees with their intricate patchwork of branches. The occasional evergreen interspersed between them reminding you that at some point spring would come again.

That was the thing about death. In nature, it was always to do with rebirth. Siobhan stopped for a moment. Did that mean that in a coven, death didn't mean the end? Did it mean replacement? Had Deborah been a replacement for someone else? And had the coven just kept going all those years without people realising? If so, was she seriously up against something that was supernatural?

Siobhan doubted it. She had seen nothing supernatural in her life. She'd seen plenty of things purporting to be that which manipulated other people. Siobhan saw superstitions and old customs being used to fuel something in the future. Usually something that would be criminal but disguised with ceremony and palaver.

A coven's not that. Of course, that's if they were bad. Nowadays people talk about white witches and being at one with nature.

Siobhan pulled her arms in close as she held the cup, looking outside at the wintry weather. Well, she didn't want to be too close to nature. She was happier in front of her fire. When you turned fifty, you felt it more. She was sure of that. Or did she just happen to have lived in much warmer countries when she was younger? Well, she said lived but in truth, she flitted between them.

She'd lived in cold ones too. Moscow was never warm. Even in the summer, it never truly got warm. In the winter, it certainly was cold. Siobhan *caught herself on* from her daydreaming and turned back to look at various paperwork she had lying on the table.

'The dress,' she said. 'The dress.' She opened up her laptop and began typing in costume designers, looking for them within a locale outside of Carrickfergus. One by one she went through them, noting the different ones, noting the style of what they did. She wondered how discreet some of them were. It took her all afternoon, but she came up with a full list.

* * *

That evening, returning from Belfast and her visit to the library, Kylie entered the kitchen to make the dinner. She started chopping up vegetables as Siobhan asked her how she got on.

'Good,' she said. 'The coven had a lot of influence. It was certainly a long time ago. I reckon they've died out, but I don't know. I was looking at a microfiche because it was all stored in the old style while they wait to get it across to the new systems. There was a librarian there that didn't seem to like what I was doing, but the chief man, he was good. He helped me.'

'So, we've got what?' asked Siobhan.

'A coven that had influence over the place, but the story seems to be that they've died out.'

'Were they well known at the time, though?' asked Siobhan.

'Very much so. People were scared,' said Kylie. 'But like I say, the story is that they've died out.'

Siobhan sat down. Kylie continued to make the dinner. *Died out or just gone on to the quiet? Maybe in a new world, they decided it was better to work even more from the shadows.* Siobhan was going to get up the next day and go round all of the costumers she had on her list. Yet Kylie had been out there, and somebody hadn't been happy about what she was doing. Siobhan had an idea.

'I've got a list here, Kylie,' she said. 'Tomorrow, how do you fancy going out around all the costume shops, all the independents? See if they made Deborah's witch's outfit for her.'

'Well, it's better than cleaning up your house.'

'Good. Don't let Declan drive you. I want you to go on your own.'

'You want me to go on my own? Is this a new level of trust? Is this a . . .'

'No. Don't take it that way. You've done well with the library. Head out, see what you can find at the costumers. I've got a little more research to do and I might try to contact the police.'

Siobhan gave a smile, but inside the cogs were turning. Maybe the woman in the library was just a busybody. Maybe she actually had reason to not be happy at Kylie asking these questions. It seemed extreme. Over the top.

The following morning, Siobhan was up early and let Kylie take her car, disappearing off as Siobhan remained at the house. Siobhan called the police trying to make discreet enquiries, but they were tight-lipped about what was going on. There could be two reasons behind this.

Maybe the investigation was going well, and they just didn't want anybody to know. Or the other one. They didn't have a clue. Saying nothing meant nobody found out you didn't have a clue. They'd be busy though, trying to work out Deborah's circle, the surrounding people, who would want to kill her. It was unlikely the police were going to be thinking about a witch's coven. They would check for routine contacts, not a coven. They wouldn't follow that line of enquiry, and they sure as heck wouldn't mention it. It was a bit of a long shot, but Siobhan always believed in following what you had, and this is what they had for now. She'd see that evening how Kylie would get on.

When that evening came around and Declan had disappeared home for the day, Siobhan saw the lights of her car in the driveway. She was glad that Kylie was back, but she was keen to know how the woman had got on. Kylie bustled in and Siobhan looked at the clock showing seven o'clock. It was completely dark outside, and Siobhan had some dinner a while ago.

The door opened and Kylie rushed in, meeting Siobhan in the hallway.

'Do you want some dinner? You've had a long day,' she said.

'No, no. No, no. See, look what I've got.' Kylie held two small packages wrapped up in paper. 'Fish suppers. I popped in to get them on the way back, thought you probably wouldn't have eaten since I hadn't cooked for you.'

'I'm not completely useless,' said Siobhan. *I'm only fifty, not in a care home here*, thought Siobhan, but she smiled and wondered if she could stomach a full fish supper after her own dinner.

'Take them into the living room. We'll sit in front of the fire and eat. Declan's built it up nice,' said Siobhan.

A few minutes later, the women were sitting on either side of the fire with their fish suppers open in front of them. Vinegar and salt were liberally poured across them and Siobhan had opened up a bottle of wine, pouring Kylie some and some for herself. It wasn't her habit to have wine with chips, but she wanted a convivial atmosphere. Let Kylie talk about her day.

There was two reasons for this. She wanted all the information, but she also wanted to know how Kylie had got on her own. If they were to run this detective agency, Siobhan would need help, and she wanted to know Kylie and Declan were really up to the task. Last time, the time that caused the idea for a private investigator firm, they'd nearly got caught out. Siobhan had done well to rescue them, done well to make things happen. That meant the right guys got caught, but it still had taken Julian to come in and help. He had tidied up the loose ends. He wouldn't be able to do that all the time.

'How did you get on?' asked Siobhan.

Kylie was wolfing chips into her, and she spat the words out in a most unladylike fashion. Siobhan didn't care, as long as she didn't drop any of the chips on the floor.

'All morning traipsing round. Absolutely nobody doing witch's outfits. Nobody had them and I just kept going. Oh, I stopped for a cup of coffee and a bun. I'm putting that on expenses. Is that all right?'

Siobhan waved her hand.

'Well, then in the afternoon I started going round some others. There was one that did witch's costumes, but they looked like Halloween outfits. They didn't look like a serious outfit. Deborah's outfit was serious, heavy material, well made. Most of the Halloween costumes, they're lightweight.'

Siobhan shook her head, wishing that Kylie would just get to the point, because she was obviously excited about something.

'Then I went into this one shop. It's just outside Carrickfergus. I say shop. It's more like a wee setup in the garage of a house. I went in and the woman there, she was about sixty. She was almost annoyed that I'd come in. I started asking about a witch's outfit and she went cold on me, really cold. I said to her, did she do witch's outfits, and she said no. And I'm looking around and I'm thinking, well, actually, I don't see why not because a lot of the clothing is very heavy.

'There's gowns; there's material there that would fit for a costume. She's making proper dresses, but they were very ornate, stylish. Looks like gowns, almost old style. And that's the thing,' said Kylie. 'I said to her "Could you make me a witch's costume?" I was grabbing some of the material and rubbing it, showing I was interested and said I was happy to pay. I don't look like I don't have any money, do I?'

Siobhan looked at Kylie and maybe the woman was wondering why somebody of her age would want a witch's costume made of superb material. Siobhan shook her head instead and let Kylie continue.

'I kept going and kept asking her and then she got really annoyed with me. She stood up, and she had this stare. I swear to you, it reminded me of school, where teachers used to look at you over the top of their glasses. Some of the really nasty ones, they used to stare, and they could freeze you. This woman was like that, only it was more sinister. The teachers, you knew why you were being looked at, you were misbehaving. I was just asking about costumes. The woman looked like she was near ready to kill me.'

'What did you do?' asked Siobhan, trying not to influence Kylie's story.

'Well, I thought I needed to find out why she was annoyed, but asking her would be pretty unsubtle, wouldn't it?' Siobhan nodded. 'So, what I did,' said Kylie, 'was I kept pushing. That's what they do, isn't it? That guy on the telly, that old detective. What do you call him? In America. He just keeps going and pressing and pressing and eventually winds people up and they end up telling you stuff, don't they?' I thought I could do it like him.

Siobhan wanted to roll her eyes. This was an investigation, not a TV show.

'Well, anyway, she then mutters under her breath. But it's not like expletives. I'm sort of expecting her to be swearing at me under her breath. She was speaking . . . well, I don't know what she was speaking. Latin? Maybe Latin.'

'How much Latin have you heard in your life?' asked Siobhan.

'A wee bit, maybe. Some of those Catholic priests do it, don't they? Yeah?'

'So, you don't know what she was saying?'

'No. But she was staring at me. It was like the evil eye. And then, well, she practically threw me out. But I could have sworn she cursed me. It's like she was trying to cast some sort of spell.'

'Are you not getting a bit carried away here? We're talking about a costume for a witch. You haven't just put this . . . '

'No,' said Kylie. 'No, she was definitely saying something against me. I wouldn't have been surprised if she'd picked up a doll and started sticking pins in it. Her house was pretty dark as well.'

'Anything else about her?'

'Well, she had a cat.'

Siobhan didn't want to look disappointed, but she put her head down, staring at her chips, and sat for the next minute eating them. The woman had a cat; therefore, she must be a witch. Is that seriously what Kylie was saying? A sharp rebuttal seemed too much.

'Did you do anything else after that?'

'Checked off all the others on your list. I have got nobody who's saying they do witch's costumes. Well, a couple of them did, but not like Deborah's witch's costumes. They were very simple fabric. Stuff that would fall apart pretty quickly. It wasn't the right thing.'

Siobhan trusted Kylie on this, but she was intrigued by the rebuttal the woman had given her.

'Did the woman follow you outside?'

'She did.'

'And what did she do when she did that?'

'She followed me all the way out to the car.'

Number plate, thought Siobhan. 'I wonder.'

'Wonder what?'

'Nothing,' said Siobhan. But she'd made up in her mind that Kylie would not be left too much on our own. She certainly wouldn't be sending her back out to those shops.

'Did you get bread, by the way?' asked Kylie.

'No,' said Siobhan. 'You didn't tell me to get bread.'

'We're out of bread. We'll need it for the morning. I'll just pop out in the car.'

'But the wine,' said Siobhan. 'You've been drinking wine. You shouldn't drive.'

'You're not much of a detective, are you? I haven't touched that yet,' said Kylie. 'I'll finish it off, don't worry. Don't put your hands on it. I'm going out to get some bread, though.'

'Finish your chips first,' said Siobhan. 'Plenty of time to get that.'

Kylie nodded and smiled. She seemed happy to Siobhan. Happy that she was making a difference. Happy that she'd been trusted by Siobhan to complete this task. But Siobhan was more worried than anything. She laughed about the cat. Maybe there was something here. People don't throw you out like that. Not unless something is truly up.

Chapter 10

Siobhan cleared up the wrappers from the fish suppers that Kylie had bought and sipped on the red wine again. The young woman was taking a while to get the bread. Standing up, Siobhan walked out to the kitchen, put the wrappers away and thought about heading to bed soon. She felt like this sometimes. She'd been working long hours, so maybe an early night was required. Sometimes the brain needed to reset.

She wouldn't go to bed until Kylie came back. Kylie stayed up in the lodge, but the car hadn't returned and it was normal for Kylie to pop her head in at the very least and say she'd returned. Also, Siobhan didn't feel their conversation had finished. Kylie would want to talk about what came next, what to do if she could get another chance out there.

Siobhan finished her glass of wine and thought about pouring another one. Then she thought, *No, where is Kylie? Surely, she was okay. Maybe she'd just bumped into someone and was having a chat, but it didn't take you this long to pop out for bread. 'At the moment, I'll be legal in a car. Best not have any more until she's back.*

As Siobhan waited, she fielded a text from Declan asking

what was happening the next day. Siobhan fobbed him off with more words about the garden and what would need done, but in truth she didn't know. She wasn't sure how to play it. Then a text came in from Kylie.

Being followed. Recognise the woman. Red hair. Saw her in the store. When I came out, her car followed mine. I took a couple of turns around one of the Donaghadee estates and she followed me the entire way. Not sure what I do. Driving at present as I text this.

Siobhan was impressed. If Siobhan was driving, she couldn't have texted that much information.

'Go to the front at Donaghadee,' Siobhan wrote in her text message. 'Park up the car and walk down along the front. I'll be there soon. Don't acknowledge me. Don't say you recognise me. I'll bump into you and tell you exactly what to do.'

Siobhan slipped the phone inside her jeans pocket, walked to the coat rack, slipped on a large dark coat, and put a hat on her head. It was a fedora, and yes, she looked ridiculous. Almost like a spy, but in truth, it was a classy-looking number. If she was wearing an evening dress underneath, most people wouldn't have bothered to even acknowledge her. The key thing about it was, it was a black coat and a black hat.

Siobhan's jeans were also black. She did, however, have her trusty white jumper underneath. The one that went right up to her neck, with a rolled-over collar. It would be bitter out tonight. She'd take gloves as well.

Siobhan kept telling herself this information to stop her from thinking about what was happening with Kylie. She needed to get there quickly. While Kylie was driving the car, she was probably safe. Probably, not definitely. Last time they'd encountered Russian mobsters trying to make their way in Northern Ireland and buy into things. Who knew what this was about, but it seemed extreme to be followed simply by asking about witches' outfits in a dress shop.

Siobhan walked out and realised that Kylie had the car. She must have been tired, for she'd even thought about staying off the wine. She stood outside on the road looking up and down. Should she call a taxi? What would be next? There was a bus going the other way, heading into Bangor, not out towards Donaghadee.

She reached down and grabbed her phone while racing across the road. Siobhan was still texting as she stepped onboard the bus, tapping her card before sitting down. Her text message told Kylie to drive to Bangor and park up by the marina.

Siobhan sat on the bus. She thought about how she would play this. Bangor was a seaside town, a place that had developed into a commuter town for Belfast. But it now had so many people in it, it could rightly be called a city of its own. At least, that's what it was deemed to be now. There were many satellite estates all around, but the core of the town was still on the seafront. In previous times there was a small beach over a wall, but now that had been taken away for a car park and a marina beyond it with numerous yachts.

Alongside it, Pickie Pool, which previously had been a pool, albeit an outdoor one, was now a place of family entertainment. There were swans on a small lake, pedalos you could go out in. There was a small gauge railway. A crazy golf course, but still, there was a path that ran around it and then up Belfast Lough, heading out towards Crawfordsburn and the small beaches out there.

Bangor would have some people about it. You could duck in and out. Siobhan knew it well. She'd lived, well at least her home had been, near to Bangor and she'd visited the now city frequently. Siobhan knew the back roads. She wondered if the red-headed woman tailing Kylie did as well.

Siobhan jumped off the bus and made her way to the car park beside the marina. It was large, and beyond it was a walkway where you could look at the boats. Siobhan texted Kylie that she was to park up in the car park and then walk around the Pickie family area. The attractions would be closed at this time of night and if someone was following her through there, it would be pretty obvious.

Siobhan wondered how good a tail the woman was. If Kylie had picked up that she was tailing her, she couldn't have been that good. Kylie had no training, no expertise. Siobhan stood in the shadows under a tree and watched her own car come in and park up in the car park. Straight behind her was a BMW. It parked maybe six spaces away and waited while Kylie got out. Kylie looked around her, clearly trying to spot Siobhan, but she couldn't. Regardless, she walked off towards the Pickie Fun area.

Less than thirty seconds later, a red-headed woman stepped out of the BMW. She had a large bubble jacket on that looked like a duvet. It was certainly not something you would tail somebody in. The woman was middle-aged, as far as Siobhan could tell in the light, and she certainly wasn't looking for anyone checking on her. Instead, she followed Kylie, less than one hundred yards behind. Siobhan tore off by a slightly different route into the Pickie Fun park.

Kylie had walked along the main path to the entrance of the Pickie Fun park and then started wandering through.

Scooting around the outside, Siobhan was now waiting inside, hidden behind an ice cream booth. As she saw Kylie walk across the miniature railway track lines, Siobhan realised she would be out of sight for maybe twenty seconds from the red-headed woman following her.

Siobhan stepped forward out of the shadows and had to slap her hand over Kylie's mouth as Kylie nearly jumped out of her skin.

'Don't say a word. With me now.' Siobhan pulled Kylie into the shadows, hiding in between the ice cream booth and changing rooms beyond. In front of her, the path that Kylie had followed would sweep by, trailing out of the Pickie Fun park. It would join up with a path that led out around the coastal walk towards Crawfordsburn. Siobhan held Kylie close, hand over her mouth, in case she blurted anything out.

A clip of heels was heard when a red-headed woman walked past. In the dim streetlights that lit up the area, Siobhan could see a woman who was intent on catching her prey. However, with her prey not there, she suddenly sped up, rushing out on the path towards Crawfordsburn. Siobhan whispered to Kylie that she should stay put until Siobhan came back for her.

Then Siobhan made her way out through the darkness, keeping off the path and remaining in the cover of bushes, watching the woman search here and there for Kylie. Siobhan moved as quick as she could, silently out of sight, back to Kylie.

'With me, now,' she said quietly but fervently. 'We need to get back to the car. It needs to be gone when she gets back.'

Taking the more circuitous route, Siobhan ran as hard as she could, breathing deeply as she did so. Kylie was as fit as her and kept up well as they reached the car park.

Siobhan said to her, 'Get in the car, drive. That street over there, take a left, park up. I'll tell you when I want you.'

Kylie ran forward, getting into the car as quickly as she could, while Siobhan looked back along the path. Kylie was out of there and gone as the red-headed woman arrived back in the car park. Siobhan watched her staring at the empty space. She took out her phone and called someone.

There seemed to be a brief discussion, and then she placed the phone back inside. She took off the large bubble coat, wrapping it up like someone would a duvet. Siobhan hated those coats. They may have been warm, but there was no class about them and everyone in them looked enormous. Why, when you were older, did you want to do that? It's like you were giving up the ghost. You needed a bit of class about you.

Siobhan watched the woman get into the car and called Kylie on the phone from the shadows.

'Start the car, Kylie. Get ready to go. Turn it around in that street, ready to come back out the way you came.'

Siobhan watched the BMW reverse. It left the car park and took a right up a hill, heading away from the seafront.

'Out now, Kylie. Out now. I will meet you. Be ready to slip over.'

Siobhan sprinted from her cover, watching the car disappear up the hill. It was dark for it was nighttime. She had the number plate, however, memorised in her head. If she could pick it up quickly, she may find out where the car is going.

Kylie had pulled the car out and had slipped over into the passenger seat, parked on the side of the road. Siobhan jumped in, dropped the handbrake, and got the car moving before she'd even put her seatbelt on. The BMW was at the top of the hill going over a small roundabout.

This was the back way out of Bangor. The redhead could have cut left, headed up into the town centre, and then gone out onto the road to the Belfast Road. Instead, she was taking the road out through Carnalea, towards Crawfordsburn. Siobhan picked up the trail and stayed a respectful distance back.

'Who is she?' asked Kylie, as they drove along.

'No idea,' said Siobhan. 'But we're going to find out where she lives. Only fair, since she was trying to find out about you.'

Kylie smiled, but then Siobhan caught a look of apprehension. Siobhan settled in for the drive as the BMW went out through Crawfordsburn before joining up on the main Belfast road. As the vehicle headed towards Belfast, it followed the M3, passing the ice rink where the Giants played their matches. They were a new introduction to Siobhan, although they'd been here now for several years. Back in the day, there was no team in Belfast. There was no such ice hockey league, and yet now they seemed to be an integral part of the city.

Siobhan continued across the M3 out to the M5, a motorway that ran beside the M2. It was a wonder the province could handle all the numbers. She was heading back towards Carrickfergus. Sure enough, as the M5 broke away from the M2, the car then took the coast road. It continued out towards Carrickfergus, driving past the castle, and then made its way out towards Green Island. Stopping just short, it turned off at a house that looked like the owner had money.

It was impressive. A bungalow, but it was expansive, and there was a heck of a garden with it. Siobhan drove straight past, turned around about four hundred yards up the road, came back again, and watched as the woman got into the house.

'So that's where she lives,' said Kylie.

Siobhan drove back then towards Carrickfergus and stopped at a petrol station. She picked up a cup of hot water, along with a cup of tea for Kylie. When they got back inside the car, she dropped a bag of lapsang souchong into hers from the glove box compartment. Siobhan took a sip before heading back on the road where they spent the next half an hour going backwards and forwards in front of the house. Convinced that this was where the redhead lived, Siobhan headed for home.

'Why were they after me, though? Just for asking those questions?' said Kylie.

'Presumably, but we don't know. It may have been your trip to the library. However, somebody tailed my car and followed it. Maybe they know my name by now. Maybe they think you're me. I don't know. I don't know what they know, but I'm going to find out. There's too much talk in this about witches and covens and yet it's a good old-fashioned tailing that happens. You ask questions, they come after you. They see what's going on. I think they were looking to see where you lived. I don't think they intended to cause harm to you yet.'

'Harm?' queried Kylie.

'Harm. I'll tell you something though,' said Siobhan. 'That person's not an operator. She couldn't put a tail on the donkey!'

'What makes you say that?' said Kylie.

'Well, for one, you spotted her. Two, when she was tailing you, she was rubbish at it, and three, she lost you easily. Anybody worth their salt wouldn't have got back in the car like that. They'd have realised where people could have gone. Reaching there, they wouldn't have followed. You'd have had to come back to the car. You would go nowhere else, would you? At some point, you would have picked up the car and gone home. That was the point. They didn't know what you were doing there. There was no reason for them to follow you.'

'That's right,' said Kylie. 'You know what you're on about with this, don't you, Siobhan?'

Siobhan nearly rolled her eyes, but she would take the credit when she got it. 'Don't you worry about that,' said Siobhan. 'I know my stuff. I know what I'm doing. This person doesn't. But still, they were following you, and I want to know why.'

Chapter 11

'Declan, get your arse up. We need to get out this morning.'

'What do you mean?' spat Declan. 'It's 5:00 a.m. Why are you calling me at 5:00 a.m.? Mrs D, you're not serious. This is a wind-up.'

'It's not a wind-up, Declan. It's 5:00 a.m. Get your backside out of bed, get some breakfast, and get over here with your car. I need to be on the road at a quarter to six.'

'Why? Where are we going? Who's died?'

'We've got a job on. Kylie got tailed last night. I tailed the tailer, and I now know where they live, and we're going to tail them today. You and me.'

'Wow,' said Declan, and then suddenly he stopped because he must have thought of something.

'Are you there, Declan?'

'Yes, but why didn't you call me last night? If she got tailed, it could have been difficult. There could have been trouble. You might have needed me to sort these people out.'

'Declan, I'm fifty, and I can sort more people out than you ever could. Let's not get overexcited. Let's not be thinking that we can do more than we can. Your job today will be driving a car which I'll be in. Focus on what I said to you. Get your bum out of bed, get some breakfast, and get the car over here. Understood?'

'Mrs D, you really need to speak better to your employees,' said Declan.

Siobhan put down the phone. *He'll be busting to get here though*, she thought. *He'll be absolutely desperate to get out here.* She had told Kylie the previous night after she'd come back that she was not going out. Kylie would remain at Siobhan's house and was to be careful answering the door.

Siobhan had taken the car and parked it a little distance away so that it couldn't be identified with the house. However, if somebody could get records that the government had, it would be easy enough to trace the car to the house. She would, however, leave it there for the meantime.

Siobhan was up and into the shower, running through her plan of action for the day as she washed herself. She would take up a position in the field opposite, watching the redhead's house. Declan would be nearby in the car. When the woman went out, Siobhan would follow. She'd check at some point today the number plate of the car as well and the address, to see if she could put a name to the woman. She'd also need to find out how the woman was connected.

Was she part of this cult that may exist? Did she know Deborah? Where would she go first? What was her daily life? What was she doing?

Siobhan didn't like to step in until she understood just who this woman was. It wasn't like when she worked in the Service, and there was a ton of backup to come running to her. She'd have to be more careful.

When she stepped out of the shower, Siobhan dressed in

green fatigues. She put on a large camouflage jacket and a hat, too. She packed a bag with a change of clothes good enough for the street, along with a third change. If she was tailing today, she might have to keep changing jackets. The one she had thrown in the bag was reversible, showing a different colour. She had a couple of wigs as well. Always good to make yourself look different as long as you didn't look like a bad pantomime actor with how you dressed yourself.

Declan arrived bang on a quarter to six, and Siobhan didn't let him get out of the car before she jumped in beside him. Her bag was thrown into the back seat, and she told him to drive out to Carrickfergus. She had a small pair of binoculars with her, a mobile phone, and a small rucksack containing some tea and some food. There were also a couple of heat pads which she'd have to crush to release the heat within. She was going to be out in the field in the early part of this morning. She didn't want to freeze while she was out there.

Declan took the road back out to Carrickfergus that Siobhan had driven the previous night. He stopped about half a mile away from the house that the redhead lived in. Siobhan got out and started running through fields in the dark until she was across from the house.

The BMW was still in the driveway. The house lights were not on, and Siobhan hoped that she'd arrived in time. Taking up a position, she lay down on her front, binoculars in hand, watching the house.

A light came on around around seven o'clock. Siobhan watched more lights coming on. She glimpsed the woman passing by her kitchen. Siobhan couldn't see anyone else in there, and it wasn't long before the woman made her way out to the BMW dressed in a short jacket. She had a skirt that went down to her knees but there was bare leg below that until some ankle boots. She'd clearly worked on her hair and for going out that early, she looked very impressive.

Siobhan messaged Declan, telling him to bring the car along. The BMW turned, left the driveway, and started back towards Carrickfergus. Once it had disappeared far enough up the road, she saw Declan arriving. She leapt over a barbed wire fence before jumping into the front seat of the car beside him.

'Along the road now. Go,' she said. Declan drove along. Siobhan started stripping off her camouflaged coat. She threw it into the back and slipped off her camouflaged leggings.

'Don't look at me,' said Siobhan. 'I need to get changed. You need to watch the road. You're too close to her. Drop back. Drop back.'

Declan clearly felt uncomfortable, his boss changing beside him. Siobhan found it funny and as she turned, just in her jumper and her underwear, to reach into the bag at the back, she heard Declan swear.

'Bloody hell, Mrs D. I can see your arse there.'

'If it's too much for you, Declan, you can get out of the car now. Some men have reacted in the extreme at seeing my backside.'

She turned and saw Declan's face. Did he really think she was being serious? She grabbed her trousers, putting them on in the front seat while Declan stared intently out through the front windscreen. He wasn't horrified by her, was he? He didn't seriously dislike what he saw.

Siobhan shook her head, and concentrated on the car ahead. They drove down the Shore Road into Belfast, then cut up towards the north of the city. There, they moved out onto an estate that looked rough.

'Easy round here, Declan,' she said. 'Drop back. I think she's going to park up soon. You don't come in here unless you're actually looking for something.'

The walls were daubed with propaganda, and some houses were boarded up. This was not a place that Siobhan would want to live. On some walls were paramilitary murals. Siobhan always thought the artwork was stunning, though she never approved of either side displaying these. In some ways, Siobhan was apolitical. She just wanted the wee country to get on, to do all right for itself.

Siobhan watched the BMW stop, and the woman stepped out of the car. She'd lost her jacket, now wearing a tight-fitting blouse. *For her age,* Siobhan thought, *she looked the part. Stunning in some ways.* The red hair cascaded down around her shoulders.

'Don't slow down too much, Declan,' she said, telling him to drive on past. Siobhan looked back out of the car. The front door of a house opened, a man stepping out. He was a lot younger, quite gruff in his appearance, but he clearly was eyeing the woman up.

'Keep driving,' said Siobhan as the woman stepped inside. As they drove on along the estate, Siobhan wanted to get out, to run round to the house, to watch in through the window. She didn't know how long the woman would be there. Quickly she worked out how to get back out of the estate. What were the roads she needed to cover to make sure the BMW didn't leave without her knowing?

'Park up over here, Declan,' she said. This road would be needed to get back out of the estate. They wouldn't move. They wouldn't do anything. Movement could cause attention. It was bright; now the sun had started to rise. People were coming out to go on their way to work. This was a bad time to watch, a bad time to sneak up. You'd only do it if you really had to.

It was an hour and a half before the BMW trundled past them. Siobhan told Declan to follow it. It headed out of this estate and then over to another estate. The estate was similar except for the colours. She'd been visiting a loyalist and a republican estate. *Strange*, Siobhan thought.

In almost identical fashion, the woman had parked up, walked over to one house where the door had opened, and she'd been brought inside. In similar fashion, Siobhan got Declan to park the car up, and they waited until another hour and a half later, when the woman departed again.

At the fourth estate they visited, Siobhan decided she needed to see what was going on. At each house so far, of the three that she'd gone to, the door had been opened by a man. Some people in these estates were not good people and ran various parts of organisations that in other countries would be called hoodlums or gangsters. On the other hand, some people here were not that. Maybe she was just an expensive call girl for men who liked the older woman.

Siobhan found that unlikely. After all, why would she be tailing Kylie if the cult was some sort of sexual services provider? Nothing indicated that Deborah had been part of that type of thing. Your family noticed, so they said.

When they reached the fourth estate and the woman got out to visit another house, Siobhan got Declan to park up at another opportune road. But she got out and walked back towards the house.

This particular one was a terrace, and the terrace had a square in front of it. Another terrace was opposite, along with one at the far end, the road passing by the open end of the enclosed area. Down the back, though, was an alleyway to the house.

Siobhan walked along with her handbag as if she was just disappearing off to work. She didn't look classy, just a woman walking about on her business. She cut up the alleyway. Looking behind her, she saw no one and ran along, counting the houses. When she reached the rear entry for the house, she stopped.

She tried to peer in, to see if she could find any gaps in the small wooden gate that was there. It was over a person high, made entirely of wood but with sectional parts, some of which were not that strong. Siobhan was able to glance through a tiny hole and saw a house that had a conservatory at the back. Siobhan decided she needed a better look, but found the gate was locked.

Reaching into her bag, she found her lock picks. After thirty seconds of working on what was a rather simple lock, she could turn the handle. Slowly, ever so slowly, she pushed open the gate, peering round to see if the conservatory was empty. Before the gate had been opened much, Siobhan could spot that the red-headed woman was in the conservatory, sitting opposite a man. She looked flirtatious, but then she looked angry.

She was railing at him. Then she stepped across and slapped him hard across the face. The man looked terrified, trembling. She was pointing to him, saying something, something about disappointment, something about next time. It was hard to read her lips because she kept turning away from Siobhan. Thankfully, she didn't look too hard towards the gate.

Siobhan pulled the gate til it was almost closed, reached

inside her bag and took out a mirror. Carefully, she positioned it just inside the gate and was able to see the conservatory with the gate barely open. Because it was a mirror reflection, she kept trying to reorientate in her head what was really going on.

The man was slapped again, but he didn't react. He didn't strike back. He just took it. The woman didn't look that powerful. If Siobhan hit a man like that, she'd expect him to come after her, but he didn't. Who was she? Who was this woman that was stepping on both sides of the paramilitary line, if that's indeed who these people were?

She'd maybe write down the addresses and find out, see what was going on, see if she knew who lived there. The woman then stormed out of the conservatory to the front of the house, and Siobhan quickly closed the gate. She locked it again, put the mirror back in her handbag along with her little pick tools, and walked back out to where Declan was sitting in the car. As Siobhan got into it, the BMW passed him by and Declan rolled out, following it.

'Any ideas what's going on?' Declan asked. He'd been very patient and hadn't bothered Siobhan that much. Even when they were just sitting in the car, he said very little, for it was clear that Siobhan was working.

'No, Declan. She's meeting people I think are gangsters, hoods, both sides of the paramilitary divide. I don't understand how she's working both. They wouldn't like each other. I don't know if she's a supplier for them. In that house, she slapped a guy, hard, several times. She was raging with him. I don't know if she's a player in that or what's going on. It makes little sense to me. We're going to have to work on this. You're going to be busy for the next day or two with me because we're going to watch her and we're going to find out who she is and where she's going and why.'

'All right, Mrs D. No problem,' said Declan.

He continued to follow the redheaded woman in the car. Siobhan wrote down, on a pad of paper, the addresses they'd visited so far. She'd write more that day. She knew she would. This woman was making calls, house calls to people who were working for her or who owed her something. How on earth Deborah fitted in with all of this, she didn't know, but maybe there was a good reason she tailed Kylie. If she was messing these people about, though, Siobhan needed to be careful. She may not be a woman to take it lightly.

Chapter 12

Siobhan sat in the car, staring at her phone, but she'd heard nothing from Declan. They had trailed the red-headed woman for the last three days and Siobhan now had a name to put to the face.

Lorraine Campbell was a woman who was hard to identify. There were no pictures of her just about anywhere. She didn't seem to work for anyone, and yet, clearly, she did, and probably some hardhead. A clever one who seemed to work both sides of the paramilitary equation.

Campbell had a house that was in her name. Siobhan had struggled to find out how she'd paid for it. Using some of her old spy methods, Siobhan had tracked down what apparently was Lorraine's bank account. There was barely a couple of grand moving in and out of it every month. It wasn't enough to pay for her clothes, car, and the house that she owned.

Siobhan was interested enough to keep following the woman, but frustrated because she was a nobody, a ghost. The woman went nowhere. Well, at least not in these last couple of days. She only travelled to estates that she shouldn't have been on, not coming from the area she lived in. There was nothing classist about it. Siobhan wasn't making any social commentary. She was just observing that the people from the type of house that Lorraine Campbell lived in didn't visit the type of estates that she was going to. Especially not on their own, and not to the doors she was knocking on. And certainly, they didn't give a hard time to the men that had answered it.

Siobhan thought the woman was formidable, doing all of this. When she watched her, Siobhan reckoned she didn't have any guns. She didn't think that Lorraine posed an obvious threat, and yet clearly, she did. For the men that she intimidated were truly rattled, and these men didn't scare easy. Siobhan tried a few police contacts, but they didn't know about Lorraine Campbell. As far as Siobhan could make out, she wasn't part of the investigation into Deborah Lynch's death.

The stories had been that the witches operated on the quiet. The stories had said that the group hadn't stopped. This Lorraine Campbell certainly fitted the bill, but she could be something quite else, although Siobhan was struggling to see what. No, there was no evidence she was a witch, but was there a gang influencing others over and above those with paramilitary intent?

As much as there were romantic ideals of defending your country, whatever side that may be, there was always the undercurrent of extortion. Lorraine Campbell seemed to be part of that, although Siobhan couldn't work out why, or how. But the woman was interesting enough that she was sitting here at two in the morning on what felt like a cold start to the day.

Siobhan had taken the first watch of the night, sitting out in the field, until approximately one when she had changed position with Declan. Declan was now clothed in a camouflage jacket and told to sit down quietly, simply watch the house, and text Siobhan if anything was happening.

She was literally three minutes up the road in the car. As she yawned, Siobhan wondered if tonight was going to be like last night, when nothing happened, except Declan and she got exhausted. Siobhan had managed about four hours' sleep the previous night, Declan the same. And when they'd followed Lorraine Campbell that day, there had been little chat or banter in the car. The frustration was growing. The feeling that they needed to do something, to find out more about this woman, to see who she really was. Yet all they could do at the moment was watch.

Siobhan missed the old days. She'd have been straight into that house trying to dig things up. She'd have a surveillance team that could listen in properly. People who could get close, infiltrate or put pressure on those that Lorraine Campbell was clearly extorting. It was easier than this detective work, a private investigator out on your own with only two amateurs to help.

She'd also taken it in the neck from Kylie. Fed up being stuck back at the house, she complained to Siobhan. Kylie had planned dinners, and they were well appreciated whenever Siobhan reached them, usually sticking them in a microwave to heat them up. But this was work. This was what she wanted to do now. Kylie would have to wait her turn.

Until Siobhan knew who this woman was, she would not put Kylie back in the field. This could have nothing to do with the investigation and she could be dealing with some very bad people. Kylie wasn't ready for that, but Siobhan would know how to extract herself from it.

Siobhan's phone beeped, and she looked down to see a text from Declan. *On the move*, it said, *with a big cloak.*

Siobhan thought to herself. *What on earth is he on about? A big cloak? Can't he be more descriptive?* She turned on the car engine, thankful that the heat was now going to come back into the car. Throwing off the blanket that was around her, she drove the three minutes down to the house of Lorraine Campbell. She spotted the woman going the other way in her car approximately a minute from her house. And Siobhan, once she'd passed her, put the foot down, raced to pick up Declan, and then turned to catch her back up.

Lorraine Campbell wasn't driving quickly, doing the forty-mile-an-hour that people who really can't drive do along sixty-mile-an-hour roads. But Siobhan thought this wasn't her trying to be careful, a woman who feared the road, for she'd handled the car in the daylight fine. This was a woman who was trying to arrive at a particular time or someone who really wasn't wanting to attract attention in the middle of the night.

Siobhan stayed a reasonable distance back as the car drove into Greenisland, the small spit of land with Ballylumford power station at the end. But as she drove on to the Isle, Lorraine Campbell turned off to one side down a dirt track. Siobhan drove quickly past, taking the car off to one side when she saw a farm track. She parked.

Siobhan told Declan to get his gear together. Declan had a small infrared camera, and as he got out of the car, he threw the rucksack over his shoulder. The pair disappeared off in camouflage fatigues.

Siobhan may have been fifty, but she was still fit, and easily outpaced Declan. They made their way back along the road, remaining off it, and racing through the fields beside. They were low cut, the type that sheep would graze in. As they got to the track where Lorraine Campbell had pulled off, Siobhan could see several car rear lights about a thousand yards away.

'That's it,' she said to Declan. 'That'll be it.'

'What?' said Declan. 'Why are people meeting in the middle of the night? It's freezing. What are you going to do here in the middle of the night? Why wouldn't you meet in a house?'

Declan has an excellent point, thought Siobhan. *Why wouldn't you meet in a house? Surely, above all things, the last thing you would want is to be standing out here talking. Nothing Lorraine Campbell has done over the previous days meant she's met in any discomfort with anyone. She went to their houses.* Siobhan was intrigued.

'Stay close to me. Everything quiet. If you want to speak, tap me on the shoulder so I can lean in close,' said Siobhan, 'and we whisper, speaking only if we have to.'

Siobhan crouched down, following the track over towards the sea and an extensive field that lay in something of a hollow. The car rear lights were all out and as Siobhan reached the end of the track, she could see them all parked. She counted them: twelve.

Looking to her left, she could see the sea beyond, but couldn't see the field that led to that sea. It was in such a hollow that sight was impossible from either the road or from the track. It was as secluded a place as you could get here and yet was completely open. Maybe you could see them from the sea, Siobhan wondered. She indicated to Declan that they needed to creep up towards the top of the hill at the side of the field. The rise was giving cover to whatever was going on in the field.

Carefully, Siobhan crept up before eventually lying down,

thankful that she had a large jacket on, keeping the chill off her body. She pulled out her infrared binoculars, scanning in front of her.

Siobhan was bemused at the sight. Although she was looking at lots of green because of the infrared sight, she could see figures dressed in large cloaks. The figures were clearly female, for when the cloaks were pushed aside, the curves could definitely not be male. She scanned the crowd of women and counted twelve. *Twelve women had come in their own cars. Twelve women were now standing, dressed . . . well, as witches*, she thought, *in a heavy garment. Then again, if you were going to meet like this, you'd have to be in a heavy garment, wouldn't you? Something to keep the heat in.*

Siobhan reached over to Declan, lying beside her, tapped him on the shoulder. He put down his own pair of infrared glasses and leaned into Siobhan, who whispered to him.

'What do you make of that?' she asked.

'Witches,' he said simply. 'Twelve witches? They must be frozen,' said Declan.

'But what are they doing?' said Siobhan.

'Ritual, probably. We'll find out.'

Siobhan turned the glasses back and saw that a small brazier had been placed in the middle of the field. Inside of it was wood and then someone had a small petrol can pouring it over the wood. There was a sudden spark, and the fire came to light. It wasn't enormous, but through the infrared goggles it sent a green cloud obscuring Siobhan's vision.

For a moment, she was in disbelief. The women seemed to step back, and they dropped their cloaks. They dropped everything. Siobhan dropped her glasses and looked with her naked eyes. The twelve women were dancing around the flame and although the light wasn't incredibly bright, Siobhan could see the curves of exposed flesh. She shivered involuntarily, wondering how they could do that in this current cold. She tapped Declan on the side, leaning into him. 'Are you getting this on the camera?'

'Damn right,' said Declan.

Oh, for goodness' sake, thought Siobhan. 'Stay professional, Declan,' she said. 'This is not one for your private collection.'

'Who said I have a private collection?'

Siobhan waved her hand at him. This wasn't the time to be discussing anything like that. Siobhan trained her eyes on Lorraine Campbell. She seemed to dance just like the other women. There didn't seem to be anyone in particular who was in charge. Instead, they were all together until they stopped. Each woman was taking up a specific place around the fire, a fire that was now slowly dying. Except there was clearly someone missing.

'How many witches in a coven?' asked Siobhan to Declan.

'How the hell would I know? Could be anything, couldn't it?'

Maybe it would be thirteen, thought Siobhan. *It's a wrong number, isn't it? It's not right; it's the number of people at the last supper. Especially if it's a nasty coven. Especially if it's not white witches. If it's there to do harm, to do evil.*

Siobhan watched as the women there stood motionless as a bitter wind swept across and eventually put the fire out in the brazier. Siobhan reached down for her infrared glasses and by the time she'd put them back up, the women were dressing again, their rather strange dance over.

Declan tapped her on the side. 'Shall I keep filming?' he said.

'Yes,' said Siobhan quietly.

'Even though the erotic bit's over?'

'Just film,' said Siobhan, wondering how the guy couldn't just get on with it.

Siobhan watched as the women, now having dressed, didn't speak to each other. Instead, they walked back towards their cars. Siobhan and Declan lay in the grass waiting until the last car had disappeared, the red rear lights disappearing out to the road.

'Bloody hell,' said Declan. 'Can you imagine that? Did you see them? There wasn't . . .'

'There weren't any clothes on them, Declan. I know,' said Siobhan. 'Would you stop thinking like that and start thinking like a detective?'

'Sorry,' he said. 'If there had have been a group of men doing that, you'd be thinking like I'm thinking.'

'No, I wouldn't,' said Siobhan, but part of her thought maybe she would. No, she wouldn't.

Siobhan slowly stood up, and packed up her gear, indicating Declan should do the same. They didn't speak as they made their way back to the car.

'Do we stake them out again? Do you want me to go back to the field?' said Declan. He seemed incredibly keen. Maybe he hoped the women had all gone back to Lorraine Campbell's house. Who knew?

'No, we don't. We're going back home. You can kip on my sofa or something until morning.'

'Why? Have you worked something out?' asked Declan.

'No. The thing is, we've now got a few faces. I need to identify these people.'

'Well, Mrs D, all that stuff about the witches—it looks like it's true. It looks like there is a witches' coven here.'

Siobhan drove the car off Greenisland back towards Belfast. It was around three in the morning and the roads were quiet. *How was there a witches' coven?* she thought to herself. *How does nobody know about these people? Would that fire have been seen? Is that hollow deep enough? Surely, you'd see it from the water. That time of the day as well, police would be up, helicopters would be up, wouldn't they?*

That time of night only if there were operations on the go. Did they know when things were up? Did they have contacts? Siobhan was doing her best to not use any mystical ideas. The very idea of a coven of witches gave rise to all thoughts about supernatural things. She stopped herself and turned to Declan, not so much as to inform him, but as to get off her chest what she needed to do.

'Declan, this is just a group of women. They're gathering together. The one we have followed has been intimidating men on both sides of the political divide. Nasty men, using them, somehow, instructing them. This is not a group of witches; this is a group of women who clearly are in charge. The only way that this actually is a group of witches is in the old sense. Kylie said back then they were dominating what was happening in the area or certain aspects of it. That's what we've got, isn't it?'

'Don't look at me, Mrs D. I know little about witches, but they were all dancing in the nude. Few of the women I know do that on a frosty morning like this. It sounds more like witches to me.'

'Well, I'll go through the tape in the morning,' said Siobhan, 'see if I can identify any of the faces.'

'If you need . . .'

'I don't need help with it,' said Siobhan suddenly. Next time she was bringing Kylie, especially if there was going to be a next time like this. A man in his early twenties was not what she needed right now to assist her.

Chapter 13

'Julian,' said Siobhan, 'good of you to come.' It was seven in the morning and Julian was on her doorstep. She'd barely got back to the house when she'd phoned him, asking for his help. He'd sounded intrigued by what had happened, but not how Declan was intrigued. Julian wondered who the women were, why they were there. He felt that the idea of twelve was worrying, especially when there was a thirteenth, clearly not there.

Siobhan had just showered half an hour ago, and was eating a piece of toast when Julian rang the front doorbell. Now she'd opened the door to him. She ushered him through, avoiding the living room, which had a sleeping Declan in it.

'We can watch the video in my office. I was out with Declan, so he's in the front lounge, sleeping.'

'Well, you phoned me at, what was it, four? Three, four?' asked Julian. 'You can't have got much sleep.'

'I didn't get any,' said Siobhan. 'Just thinking about it. I wasn't expecting you until later.'

'Really?' said Julian. 'You didn't sleep? You're buzzing about this. I know we've got this whole idea of witches, but you're seeing the other side of it? Yes? How does someone deal with the paramilitaries in that fashion and then turn up with a group of women like this? This has got your hackles up. Also, the missing woman.'

'The missing woman,' said Siobhan. 'Deborah had a witch's outfit. The ones we were watching, none of them were exactly the same, but they were all thick and heavyset, the same as Deborah's was. I think Deborah's the missing woman. I think Deborah was part of this group.'

'Not a hard conclusion to jump to even at seven o'clock,' said Julian. 'If we've got people influencing those who do such damage around this community, we're not talking about any old weird people. I'll need to know about it. This is going beyond even murder.'

'Indeed,' said Siobhan. 'Do you want to get straight to the film?'

'No. Let's have breakfast.'

'Come on in then. I'll make you something,' she said.

'You sit down,' said Julian. He took off the suit jacket he was wearing. He also had a clip-on tie, which was then hung over one of the kitchen seats, and he undid the top button of his collar. 'Have you got eggs?'

Siobhan nodded, pointing to a rack at the end of the kitchen.

'Scrambled fine for you? I'd like to say I can do something a bit more exciting, but . . .'

'Scrambled's fine,' said Siobhan.

She may have been tired. Well, no, she was exhausted, but as she sat watching Julian cook, there was a warmth inside of Siobhan. She felt comfortable when he was here. Kylie and Declan were fine, but they were amateurs. Julian understood the score, understood what Siobhan had looked at. Kylie didn't even know about last night yet. As for Declan, well, Siobhan was feeling a little more forgiving now. At his age, seeing a field of women like that must have been like his dreams had come true, and he was sitting with a camera, able to capture it all. Siobhan chuckled to herself.

'What's so funny?' said Julian, turning round with the pan, working the eggs inside with the beater.

'Just thinking about last night. Declan's face. All these women just started stripping off and then dancing. I was intrigued, wondering what was going on. All I could think of was how cold it was. You must be an idiot to be doing that. Declan said to me it was incredibly erotic.' Siobhan laughed. 'Didn't look erotic to me. It just looked mind-numbingly cold.'

Julian laughed. 'I think that's a divide between the sexes, right there.' He placed the pan down on the hob and looked around for a couple of plates.

'That cupboard over there,' said Siobhan. Julian took two plates out, placed them beside Siobhan, and tipped out the scrambled egg. He turned to the toaster, saw Siobhan's two slices of cold toast and reset the plunger. Julian allowed the toast to warm up for nearly a minute before taking it out and throwing a slice of each on the plates before Siobhan. He took a chair and sat down beside her, not across the table.

'Are you okay?' he asked, tucking into the eggs. 'We can take this over, if you want. What you're digging up at the moment, well, it's worth investigating.'

'I don't actually have anything though, do I?'

'No, and yet you're extremely close to things. How close have you got?'

'It's all been a watching brief,' said Siobhan. 'I have infiltrated nowhere. I haven't gone inside any buildings. Done research through the library. I've tailed and followed someone because Kylie got followed.'

'Kylie got followed?' said Julian suddenly.

'Not by anyone professional. By the redhead we were tailing. That's how I knew where she lived. Kylie called me up and said this redhead was following her. She'd also had a weird experience at the library where the librarian, at least one of them, was very awkward about Kylie doing the research on the witches.

'The woman I tailed is Lorraine Campbell. I've checked her bank details and other stuff and she's living in a house and driving a car she can't afford. She doesn't seem to have any men in there and yet she's dealing with some of the nastier sort that live on some of the Belfast estates and she's slapping them about. I thought, at first, she was some sort of high-class hooker, but she's not. She's anything but. She's in charge, not them.

'After days of looking around and following her, we get this. Suddenly everyone's wearing a witch's gown, dancing naked, and I've got a missing person from their coven, or rather their group. I'm trying not to call it a coven. Every time I call it a coven, I get a voice in my head of how things could be supernatural, how they're influencing stuff, where their power comes from to do that.'

'That's how we'll keep it,' said Julian. 'Everything that makes sense, everything rational. Don't believe that there's nothing in the witches' idea. The very idea carries a weight. Things don't need to be supernatural for people to believe, to be influenced by them. As long as people think that's what it is.

'We're talking about the power of belief. Won't go down well in a land like this, talking about it that way. Many people here believe a lot of things, trust in a lot of things because of it.'

'God—the Church—is one thing,' said Julian. 'I'm not saying that there's nothing out there. I'm not decrying people's beliefs. All I'm saying is that your belief, right or wrong, can drive people to do lots of things. Don't dismiss the idea of a publicly visible coven or one that's visible to the right people to make them do things.'

After eating their scrambled eggs, the pair went to Siobhan's office and spent the next three hours watching the videotape of the witches' dance. Halfway through it, there was a knock on her office door, and Kylie popped her head in.

'Why's Declan sleeping in the front room?'

'We were out last night, as you know, but we found something. Look at this,' said Siobhan. She stepped aside to let Kylie come closer in to look at a screen that Julian was in front of.

'Bloody hell,' said Kylie. 'Last night? It was minus figures last night. Minus figures, I'm telling you. Who in their right minds would do that?' Then she stopped suddenly. 'That's that redhead. That's Lorraine Campbell. My goodness, look at her! I mean, they don't even care, do they? Was anybody watching?'

'Just me and Declan,' said Siobhan.

'Declan was watching this?' said Kylie suddenly.

'Declan was filming it.'

'Were you there?'

'Kylie, I was lying on my front on the cold ground. Declan was lying beside me. I was watching them; Declan was filming them. It was investigative work. It was . . .'

'It was a load of naked women dancing about,' said Kylie. 'It's no wonder he can't wake up now. He must be exhausted looking at that.'

Julian nearly burst out laughing and shot a glance towards Siobhan.

'Julian comes from the Service,' Siobhan said to Kylie. 'In the Service, we have a bit more decorum. We don't get overexcited about who's done what or whatever. Declan was doing his job.'

'You're telling me that Declan just sat there the whole time, filming it, and felt nothing and didn't enjoy it at all?'

'Whether or not Declan enjoyed the view—' started Siobhan.

Kylie laughed. 'Yes, I knew it.'

There came a knock at the door and Declan stuck his head in, looking bleary-eyed.

'Oh. It's you, Siobhan's friend.'

'Julian,' said Julian, standing up. 'Good morning, Declan. I hear you had an interesting night.'

Declan's face became a grin. 'Yes, it was quite something.' Then he caught the look on Kylie's face.

'You dirty perv,' she said to him.

'I was following Mrs D's instructions. She told me to film it. Not my fault the load of women got naked.'

'Do you mind,' said Siobhan. 'If you two are going to have some sort of lover's tiff, can you get out?'

'Excuse me,' said Kylie suddenly, 'lover's tiff?'

'You seem quite bothered by what he saw. Is there some sort of jealousy going on?'

Just for a moment, Kylie blushed, and Siobhan thought she was on to something. When they first got together, when Siobhan took up the house, and Kylie had been introduced to Declan, there had been a glance. But she'd kept him at a distance. Declan was slightly younger than she, and Kylie had a rough time, previously.

Declan clearly had always liked Kylie, but making a place in her life had not been easy. The investigations were drawing them closer together. Now jealousy on Kylie's part had been highlighted. More than that, Declan, for although he wasn't the wisest of people, could see it. He was now grinning like a Cheshire cat.

'What are you smiling at?' asked Kylie.

'Out,' said Siobhan. 'Julian and I have work to do.'

'I can help,' said Declan.

'I'm afraid it requires a level of expertise,' said Julian. 'I suggest you follow your employer's instructions. Nice to meet both of you. Wouldn't mind a cup of coffee if there was any going, though.'

'She's not big on the coffee,' said Kylie. 'Although she apparently seems to like dancing in the middle of the night.'

Kylie stormed out of the room. Declan followed, now looking less pleased with himself. He closed the door behind him, and Julian laughed.

'Something going on between those two?'

'I think so, but not that they know it,' said Siobhan. Siobhan moved behind Julian as he watched the screen. Almost absentmindedly, she reached down and rubbed his shoulders.

'They don't do that in the Service.'

'Yes, they do. Sometimes.'

'The thing about the Service, though,' said Julian, 'is you can't carry through any of this, can you?'

'I'm not in the Service anymore,' said Siobhan. She didn't know why. Maybe she was tired, but at this moment in time, there were thoughts about Julian running through her head that needed to be pushed aside. She was delighted to have him here, delighted to work with him, just to have him close.

'We've got some facial recognition being run,' he said. 'It'll take a moment.'

Siobhan kept rubbing his shoulders. 'I'm not going anywhere,' she said. She leaned forward, allowing her chin to sit on top of his head. Her arms slipped off his shoulders and wrapped around his neck. She pulled herself close into him, cradling the top half of him in her arms. 'Thank you,' she said. 'I know you're not here just for the Service.'

'It helps justify the time I spend here. It's good that you're able to find something of interest. Otherwise, I'd have to come here out of my own volition.'

'You're welcome anytime,' said Siobhan.

'I know,' said Julian. 'The thing is, if we go down that line, I'll have to walk away from the Service. I'll have all this stuff I can't tell you.'

'You can't tell me it now,' said Siobhan.

'No. There's a reason I've never really got close to anyone in the Service, or close to anybody outside. I think the sort of relationship, the one that I really want, demands closeness, demands no secrets.'

Siobhan pulled him closer. 'Well, I'm not in the Service,' she said. 'That's really your call, but don't leave it too long.'

Before he could answer, the facial recognition software gave a bleep, and Julian scanned it.

'This is showing two IDs. I'm surprised how we've even got that. It was so dark. The match rates aren't that high.' Siobhan watched Julian skimming back through the video, and she stood back upright seeing that the moment had gone.

'Eileen Quigley, Beyonce Smith. Beyonce Smith's a minor thing. Photographed once because of demonstration, public order demonstration. Eileen Quigley is interesting. That's not come from the police; that's come from the Service. Rumours, words, involvement with the paramilitaries and with others.

'Find anything concrete?'

'No, nothing concrete.'

'Well, we've got two, haven't we?' said Siobhan. 'We've got two contacts now that we can go to. I wonder.'

'Whatever you're going to do,' said Julian suddenly turning around, 'be very careful. Eileen Quigley's tagged with high risk. They have proved nothing, but she appears merciless.'

'That's about right,' said Siobhan. 'I mean, we are looking at witches.' She smiled, but Julian wasn't smiling back.

Chapter 14

That afternoon, Siobhan sat down and tried to work out a plan of how best to exploit their knowledge of Eileen Quigley and Beyonce Smith. Eileen Quigley was clearly a big player, one that the Service had been interested in, though Julian hadn't fully explained why. She had simply been tagged, but tagged in such a way that people understood she was dangerous.

Maybe there was no evidence behind it. Such reports in the Service were not uncommon. Sometimes this was to protect informants, with the actual information only revealed to those who were close to the issue. Other times it was because there was no evidence to be had, just suspicion, suspicion that was probably true.

Beyonce Smith, on the other hand, was a low-level offender, pulled up for a protest, and finding her was really a shot in the dark. Julian happily furnished the last known address for the woman, which was on a rough estate in Belfast. As far as he knew, she was a woman on her own in her twenties, but there was little other information.

Siobhan wondered if the woman could be played, if anyone could get close to her, but she needed to know more about the woman first before she would play that card. She had in her head that Kylie had been asking all the questions, and Lorraine Campbell knew this. Maybe Kylie could get into the group. Maybe Kylie could say she was looking for a way in, say that she noticed what was going on. She would look clever. Maybe that was how they could fill up that thirteenth witch role. Siobhan had decided that getting inside was the only way to know the truth about what had happened to Deborah. After all, that was what she was being paid for.

Siobhan took a hire car and drove out to the estate that evening. It had just gone dark, and Siobhan deliberately dressed suspiciously, wrapped up in her black coat and hat. She wanted to give the air of a player. She tucked her hair up inside the hat and had a scarf that covered most of her face.

There was a risk to this. She wasn't sure who Beyonce was, and if she was someone important, maybe there would be violence. Maybe people would come to sort her out. Maybe people would try to get rid of the nosy, interfering woman. Siobhan trusted she could read this and at least get herself out of the situation, if not take charge of it.

The evening was cool, frost beginning to fall on the ground. Car windscreens were misting over as Siobhan walked the streets up to Beyonce's house. The house was dark. No lights on inside, and she wondered if the woman was in. Carefully, she made her way up to the windows, and saw the place looked truly deserted.

It was a semi-detached house, and Siobhan decided to try the neighbours. She stood before a green door and rapped on it, spotting that there was no doorbell or knocker to use. The door opened to a woman holding a small child. She was dressed in fluffy slippers and had a dressing gown around her.

'Evening,' said Siobhan, the scarf lingering just under her nose, so most of her face was covered. 'I was looking to speak to Mrs Smith next door.'

'Miss Smith,' said the woman. 'Beyonce's not in. I saw her go out earlier.'

'I was just wondering what she was like as a neighbour, wondering if she had anything special about her.'

The woman's face looked slightly scared, but she quickly turned and, flicking her head over her shoulder, she shouted for a man in the rear. He came forward in jeans and a T-shirt. He was square with a paunch belly, badly shaved, and his hair looked a bit of a mess.

'You asking about Beyonce?' he said.

'I am,' said Siobhan.

'Well, don't,' he said. 'Just bugger off. There's nothing here for you. She has friends. You don't want to annoy them.'

Siobhan nodded and walked away to hear the door close hard behind her. She went to see the neighbours on the other side. This time, the door was opened by an elderly man. He had downy grey hair, glasses, and looked doddery on his feet.

'I'm looking for Beyonce Smith. She's not in at the moment. Do you have any idea where she's gone? I was wondering if she'd be into receiving a visit from a prospective employer.'

The man started to close the door. 'Don't involve me. Nothing to do with me. Don't involve me.' He closed it in Siobhan's face.

She thought about knocking again. The man was clearly scared. She retreated to the first neighbour she had tried, rapping the door again. This time, the man with the rotund belly opened the door.

'I thought I told you to bugger off,' he said.

'I can't bugger off until I've met Miss Smith. When's she going to be in?'

I don't know, and I don't care. Bugger off.'

He slammed the door in her face. Siobhan stood for a moment, thinking about her options. She could break into Beyonce's house, but that wouldn't be a good start. She wanted to find out about the woman, not give her cause to worry. Siobhan rapped on the door of the neighbour's house again.

'I thought I told you to bugger off,' said the man, opening the door. 'I've said it once and I'll say it again—just get the hell out of here. You don't care what she's involved in, what she's doing. She's not involved in it with me. Clear off.'

Most people wouldn't have answered the door, thought Siobhan. *He's not here protecting his family. He's a watch on the house, unlike the old man. The old man's just a neighbour who's obviously seen things and doesn't want to get involved. This one isn't. This one's part of them.*

Siobhan heard someone coming up behind her. She glanced over her shoulder and saw a man with a shotgun. It wasn't a common thing in these estates, but there were certainly people here who would have weapons and wouldn't be that shy about using them. Gunning somebody down on the doorstep wouldn't work well. The police would come. If they were just trying to keep people away from Beyonce or just acting as a doorkeeper for her, it really wouldn't do to shoot them.

'A friend of mine says he's told you to bugger off and you won't. You're not from here. This estate doesn't want you. I don't care what you think you've got to offer. You're not offering it here. Now get the hell out of here, woman, before I blast you.'

'You can catch yourself on for a start, sunshine,' spat

Siobhan.

'What did you say?' asked the man. 'Are you wanting to be filled with lead?'

'Are you wise?' Siobhan said, turning round. 'Look fella, you shoot me here, police will be all over this place. I doubt Beyonce's going to want that, not with the stuff she's into, stuff that I might want to get involved in. Just need to know a bit of information about her.'

'You're going to start walking,' said the man, 'or else I'm going to take you inside of this house. There I will shoot you but not with this but with something else and they won't know anything about you and there won't be no police. I will bury you in some unmarked grave somewhere. She doesn't like visitors. She really doesn't like visitors.'

'You don't say. Least she could do is come and tell them herself though,' said Siobhan. 'I'm afraid you'll have to take me inside.'

The man reached past Siobhan and knocked on the door. The green door opened, and the fat man looked at the man behind him with a shotgun.

'In here, Jack? Why the hell in here?'

'Is the kid up? Get the kid upstairs with the missus. It's all right. We'll keep it clean, then I'll get her out of here. I don't want to walk it anywhere else. Too many people have seen her walk in. We'll sort it out. This bitch isn't going anywhere.'

Siobhan felt the shotgun being pushed into her back, and she stepped inside the house. The woman with the child walked past her, glaring at her, and took the child upstairs while Siobhan was pushed in towards a back room. There'd be one more threat, one more chance to let Siobhan walk away. They didn't want to do this. Siobhan was a hassle to them, a real hassle.

'Go get the gun,' said the man with the shotgun. 'The quiet one. You, get down on your knees,' he said to Siobhan.

'Get down on your knees yourself,' Siobhan said. 'I'm not taking that crap from you.'

The man reached forward, pushing her to spin her around. The other guy had left the room. The man with the shotgun had fallen into Siobhan's trap. As she spun around, she whipped her hand down and across, pushing the shotgun to one side. She continued to spin and drove an elbow into his face. The man lurched backwards, his hand releasing on the shotgun. Siobhan took it and pointed it straight at him.

'One word and I'll blast your balls off,' she said. 'This is how this is going to work. You're going to get on your knees right now. If you don't, there'll be trouble.'

The man didn't flinch. Siobhan knew she couldn't carry through her act. She wanted him to think she was involved in all of this. If Beyonce was involved in something this deep, maybe this was somebody coming to talk to her, somebody big, somebody who could handle themselves. Siobhan drove the butt of the shotgun into the man's face. He yelled.

'Shut up,' said Siobhan, and pointed the shotgun directly at the man's head. His colleague came bursting into the room and took one look at the man on his knees.

'Your weapon,' said Siobhan. The man looked at her, panicked, and then handed over his weapon.

'On your knees too.' Siobhan then pulled a kitchen chair across the room, sat down on it, and pointed the two guns at both men.

'One of two things is going to happen,' she said. 'You're going to talk to me and then I'm going to leave, or the other option is that the good lady upstairs is going to have a hell of a lot of cleaning to do in this room. I think I'll put you on that wall,' said Siobhan, 'you on the other one.'

The men were shaking now. Whatever act Siobhan was doing, she was doing it well. She'd roughed up people before, but to kill someone, you didn't do that in the Service often. Well, not with what she had done. As an operative, sometimes it became necessary, but it hadn't been necessary in such a long time. There had been two that she remembered, but they'd asked for it. If she hadn't had done it, she wouldn't be here. Still, there was a shiver inside her at the thought of having to have done it.

'Please,' said the man, 'take it up with her. She doesn't allow us to talk. She doesn't allow us to say anything.'

She's that high up, thought Siobhan, *that they're actually contemplating not saying anything with their life on the line.*

'What's she got on you?' asked Siobhan. 'Tell me. What's she got on you?'

'They've got it on us. They've got it on everyone. If you're trying to muscle in, woman, just you get out. I'm telling you now; get out of this.'

The man was kneeling, and she could see him urinate. It was a miserable sight, but the man beside him didn't flinch away. He was terrified, too. Siobhan could see him shake. These men were going to let her kill them.

'What's she got on you? What is it you can't say? How did she get a hold that you're about to die for her?' asked Siobhan.

'Everything. What we can do; where we can go. They can do things to your family, things to you that you wouldn't dream of.'

Witchcraft raced through Siobhan's head. She stopped

herself. She didn't want to put words in the mouth of the men. If they said it, if they came through with stuff like that, it was one thing. She wouldn't say it for them.

'Look,' said Siobhan, 'I need to know. I need to get in. You don't have to kill yourselves for her.'

Faces looked at her. They were white, their eyes bulging. *They'll do this*, she thought. 'Damn it.'

Siobhan stood up, swinging the shotgun round and planted the butt into the face of first its owner, and then the tubbier man. They both fell backwards, rolling around on the floor. Siobhan cracked open the shotgun, emptied the shots, and then took the other gun, dropping the rounds out of it as well.

She walked out into the hall, throwing the guns on the floor, closing the door behind her. She marched straight to her car and drove it away. As she dropped it back to the hire company, glad she'd used one of her other identities, she wondered just what she was getting involved in.

She expected that Eileen Quigley might be something, but Beyonce Smith? The woman was twenty-one. How could she have such a rap that it would do this to men? Then it came to her. It's the group, not just Beyonce Smith. It's not individuals. They are who they are as a group. She needed to get in on that group.

Maybe, we could do it. They are a witch short, aren't they? Could she get in close, or better still, could Kylie get in?

Kylie had shown that she was interested in the witchcraft. She'd asked all the questions. The librarian would back that up. She wondered if it might look like somebody strange coming. Siobhan would have to ask Kylie. She'd work it out, see if she could get her in, but she'd need to monitor Beyonce first. Eileen Quigley was too big a shot to go at. Kylie would be a better fit with Beyonce. Beyonce Smith might just be the key to getting inside the coven.

Chapter 15

Siobhan decided to tail Beyonce now that she knew where she lived. After disguising herself, changing her hair colour, and donning a more low-key outfit, Siobhan returned to the estate. She had picked up a second-hand car, a battered Ford Fiesta, and was dressed in joggers and training top, finished by a baseball cap. Her hair was now red, and she was lucky enough to catch Beyonce on the move.

She'd spotted the woman walking from one house on the estate back towards her car. She'd briefly popped inside before taking the car and driving to a local gym. It was posh, and Siobhan entered the gym with her, working out at a large group of weights, after paying at the front desk. Beyonce didn't seem to work too hard, instead talking mostly to several men in the gym. They were young as well, and Siobhan was sure that messages were being passed out.

For the next three days, Siobhan was able to follow her, and Beyonce came back to this gym a lot. Siobhan entered the gym three times, each time with a different hair colour, and trying to look a different age, disguising herself up each morning. Having decided that this might be a place for Beyonce to meet someone, Siobhan thought hard about whether Kylie was the right person. Siobhan was older than Beyonce. It would look like she was trying to make a move in, as there wasn't anything in common between them. Kylie was Beyonce's age. Maybe she could get close. Kylie had that quality about her that she could get close to people. Siobhan sat her down in the living room to discuss it.

'I want you to get alongside Beyonce Smith,' said Siobhan. 'She works out of a gym. I think she passes instructions to others about what's going on or conveys any messages that need to be sent. The same group of men are usually around there. She's also a twenty-one-year-old woman. I think you could get close. Don't go in trying to find out anything about her, just get close. Comment about her workout, comment about your workout. Talk about the latest things, I don't know, music, whatever you people do,' said Siobhan. 'Just get close. Mention nothing about the investigation. Say nothing about witches, unless she brings it up, and see what you can do.'

The next morning, Kylie caught the bus to Belfast, and then took another out towards the gym. She entered under Siobhan's watchful gaze from a distance. Siobhan would stay there as backup, just in case Kylie was taken away. Thankfully Kylie exited after a few hours, catching the bus back down to the city centre where Siobhan picked her up.

'How did it go?' she asked.

'I said hi. That was it,' said Kylie. 'I worked out close to her, and I said hi. She said hi back.'

'Good,' said Siobhan. 'You're back again tomorrow.'

'How do I explain being there, though?'

'Trying out a new gym.'

'Where do I live though?' she asked.

Siobhan wrote an address down. 'If you have to, you can

give her this, but don't volunteer an address, say this area. It's a reasonably decent area. She won't be expecting any trouble from it. It'll make out that you really are just a gym goer.'

'Okay,' said Kylie, pleased with herself. The next day was similar. Kylie had gone in and she'd looked like she'd done a workout by the time she came out.

'I think she enjoys watching people doing the boxing.'

'That's right, there was a punch bag or two on the side, wasn't there?' said Siobhan.

'I'm going to do some boxing tomorrow.'

'Do you know how to box?'

'No,' said Kylie, 'but I thought she might jump in and help me. You never know.'

'You're thinking smart now,' said Siobhan.

As they drove back that night to Siobhan's house, she thought about how these things take time. The investigation would be long-lasting. She couldn't rush this. If Kylie went in too quickly, Kylie could get into trouble. If Beyonce Smith was lined up with somebody like Eileen Quigley, if there really was such power and coercion going on, it would be nothing to them to get rid of Kylie. Kylie may be naïve enough not to see it coming.

Siobhan dropped Kylie off at the bus station again and watched from outside as Kylie entered, wearing her third gym outfit. This time, when Kylie exited, she had a smile on her face. She got on the bus, but by the time Siobhan picked her up, Kylie still looked like she'd just finished a workout.

'Are you okay?' asked Siobhan.

'It's good. I engaged with her today. I actually spoke several times. She was asking me if I wanted to learn to fight because I was doing the boxing. I was telling her it was for fitness. She told me quite a bit about her fitness.'

'Does she like you, do you think?'

'Not like that,' said Kylie.

'I wasn't suggesting like that. Friendship-wise, just some-body else that she could talk to.'

'I hope so, we'll see. I said I'd be back tomorrow. She said she would too.'

'After tomorrow, you don't go. It's just going to get ridiculous if you keep turning up day after day. She's there for a reason. You have no reason to be there day after day. Everybody has to take a day off working out. Everybody has the day they can't make it. We need to filter that in. You need to be real.'

'Okay,' said Kylie. 'I'm enjoying this, though. I think I'm quite good at it.'

'Don't get cocky. Keep it simple, keep it plain. She's the one who invites you in. She's the one who puts the offer before you. Don't force it and make it happen. If you do this right, she won't suspect anything.'

'Okay,' said Kylie. 'You do go on, don't you?'

Siobhan pulled the car over, stopping in a lay-by. She turned in her seat to Kylie.

'Understand what you're doing. You're undercover. You're trying to go in with someone who's potentially dangerous. When I talked to Julian, he said Eileen Quigley had been noted by the Service. Noted by the Service and yet there was no evidence, nothing. We don't do that lightly. That is someone who is a serious problem. She may be a killer.

'You're talking to the potential friend, colleague, workmate, whatever, of a killer. You do not let yourself relax for a moment. Everything you do is looking to protect you. You keep it simple. Everything you say could be said by a friend, by just a nobody. You don't look for the information; you wait for it to come, because if you look for it and they make you, you'll be dead.'

'Okay, if it's that bad, why are you letting me do it?'

'Because you want to and you're the right person. I can't get in with Beyonce. I would have to get in with Eileen Quigley, and that is much more dangerous. Just watch your back,' said Siobhan.

As she drove the car onto towards Bangor, she could feel the tension in the car rise. Siobhan was having to tread a fine line. Kylie needed to be relaxed. She couldn't be looking over her shoulder all the time. But she also had to know that she couldn't drop anything and hint who she was and what she was doing.

Two days following, Kylie emerged looking happy. As she stepped into the car, she plonked herself in the seat beside Siobhan, putting her sports clothing at her feet.

'I did it,' she said. 'We're going for a drink tomorrow night.'

'Where?' asked Siobhan instantly.

'Centre of Belfast. I said I'd meet her in the centre.'

'Good, plenty of people about. Don't go back to her place whatever you do. Make your excuses. You have to be back; you have to be away.'

'Okay, okay.'

'How did she invite you out?'

'More boxing, more talking about it, more about what we were doing with our training, and then she started asking me if I enjoy clubbing. I think she likes me at the core of it. That's what's behind it all. She simply likes me and wants us to get on.'

'I hope so. At any point during this, have you overheard or been close enough to overhear her talking to any of the men about anything dodgy?'

'She's never spoken to them within earshot of me.'

'Good,' said Siobhan. She stared hard at Kylie. 'Take it easy. Don't come on strong. Have a few drinks, don't get pissed because then you won't know what you're saying. If she tries to make you drink too much, play the Catholic card.'

'What do you mean, the Catholic card?'

'It's an old one we used to have in the Service, works in a lot of the Latin American countries as well. You're a good girl, you go to the chapel, you're not someone that does the alcohol. Make sure if you take any, you act like you're pissed or at least reasonably so.'

'This life you had before, you really were deep in it, weren't you?'

'You have no idea,' Siobhan said to Kylie. 'I hope you never have to come across and do some things I've done.'

Siobhan decided the next night when Kylie was going out for drinks that she would be about. Rather than follow Kylie into bars or whatever clubs they were going to, she decided that instead, she would hang about outside, telling Kylie that if she needed to run, she had someone to run to.

It would be an unusual location to take someone if you'd suspected them of anything. You didn't take them into the city centre. You'd have taken them to the pub in the estate, ask them to go to somewhere without people. Siobhan was fairly confident that Kylie would be okay. She just had to keep in the manner that she'd done so far.

Siobhan walked down the street that night between four or five different pubs. She only stepped inside two of them, and each time she did, she saw Kylie sitting, chatting to Beyonce. Kylie was dressed nice but looked like she was clubbing. Her skirt was short, the top was tight. Siobhan had noticed that Declan had hung around quite a lot at the house that day when Kylie was asking Siobhan if she looked the part. More than that, Kylie hadn't complained when Declan was hanging about, either.

Siobhan had kept Declan completely out of the loop on what was going on. He couldn't be around Kylie in that way because he would overreact. Siobhan was necessary. Siobhan was there to step in if things went south. She knew what to do. Declan was liable to step in and make things worse.

At around two in the morning, Siobhan was hanging on the edge of a bar looking down at a rather drunk Kylie. She was worried that the end of the evening could go somewhere else. Beyonce ended up walking Kylie over to the taxi rank, putting Kylie in, and paying the taxi driver to drop Kylie off.

Kylie was good. She got out of the taxi, and told him she was fine, though he stayed to make sure. She turned to walk up the drive of a house on the estate where she said she had lived. Siobhan was watching closely from her car. The taxi driver, now satisfied, was out of sight before Kylie got close to the front door of the house. There was no one else about, no one else watching. Kylie walked out and along the street before Siobhan picked her up.

'I thought I told you not to get drunk.'

'I am not drunk,' she said. 'I'm holding it together.' She burped loudly and then she farted. 'But maybe I'm a bit drunk.'

'How did it go?'

'Weren't you watching?' said Kylie rather loudly. Siobhan was glad they were in the car.

'Of course, I was watching. Seemed to go well, but I didn't come inside for the whole evening. Did she say anything to you of note?'

'We talked about witches.'

'Really?' said Siobhan.

'She brought it up.' She said that there were witches about; she enjoyed watching witches on the TV. Named a lot of the shows, the films and that.'

'What else did she say?'

'She thought witches were cool. Said she heard a lot of stuff about witches.'

'And what did you say?' asked Siobhan.

'I said that I liked witches. Never really saw any.'

'Good,' said Siobhan. 'How did she react to that?'

'She's invited me to a party.'

'Excuse me?'

'She's invited me to a party. I'm going to a party with Beyonce. She said it's quite different, something exclusive, but there were people there who would know about witches, so I said I would come. I think I've done rather well,' said Kylie.

She was lifting herself up in her seat looking all haughty and Siobhan was wondering if this was a good thing. Of course, it was for the investigation, the talk of witches, but had it been too quick, too soon? They'd taken their time, hadn't they? Although it'd been what? Less than a week.

Kylie fell asleep in the car as Siobhan drove her home, but Siobhan wasn't for sleeping. She was worried this was too quick, worried about what was going on. There wasn't a second drink out on the town; there weren't a few weeks of getting to know each other. There was talk of witches and then suddenly an invite to a party. Siobhan went to bed that night a little uneasy.

Chapter 16

Kylie was excited. She came to show Siobhan her outfit for the party Beyonce had invited her to. It was going to be on the estate close to Beyonce's house, something which Siobhan was not entirely happy about. But she couldn't find any reason that Kylie had her cover blown.

Everything Kylie had said was true. She had an interest in witches. If anyone had got back to Beyonce about Kylie's efforts at the library, that would still hold. Siobhan just didn't like the idea of Kylie being off on her own, especially on an estate like that. It was harder for Siobhan to gain access. She'd try to watch from outside, try to peer in through windows, but it was going to be up to Kylie to gather what information she could.

'But do I look all right?' said Kylie.

Siobhan thought she looked like she was out clubbing again. She had a small pair of boots on, a skirt that Siobhan felt would have been cold in summer. There was a top that she felt didn't just highlight Kylie's figure, but made sure every detail was shown. Maybe it was just the young ones. Maybe she was like that back in the day.

These days it was more subtle. Siobhan didn't have the same

figure to show anymore. It was more mature. It was more refined, less vulgar when she used it in an alluring fashion. She certainly wouldn't have pitched up in front of Julian in an outfit like this. Then Julian had more class.

Siobhan stopped herself. Was she just being unkind? Was she just annoyed that Kylie was at the forefront now? Declan was certainly annoyed that Kylie was at the forefront. At least until she came down in her outfit. Then Declan was all encouragement. Then got annoyed again when Kylie said there was no point in Declan coming with them.

The whole point of the ruse was she was making friends. She didn't need to turn up with a pretend boyfriend. Kylie could listen, finding things out without Declan being there. Siobhan at least agreed on that point.

On the night of the party, Kylie was dropped by Siobhan at the bus station. Arriving on the edge of the estate by bus, she walked and was met by two men. They seemed quite rough, but in fairness, their approach to Kylie was all courtesy and they escorted her round to Beyonce's house. Siobhan noted that more men came to the edge of the estate and that, clearly, it wouldn't be a matter of simply walking along the street to peer in the windows. Siobhan was going to have to do this the old-fashioned way, by staying out of sight, and peering in from a distance.

She wasn't happy to let Kylie just go. It was okay while Kylie was playing the part, but the other thing that Siobhan had been trained in was how to get out of somewhere fast. That involved using your wits and thinking very straight under pressure. You had many skills to disarm and work your way past people, but also an ability to kill if necessary. Kylie didn't begin to have any of these. If her cover was blown and she was in trouble, Siobhan would have to get her out of there.

At least she looked more convincing in this disguise than she had when they tried to dupe the Russians. Kylie was dressed up as one of the male heavies, or not so heavy. Siobhan almost laughed out loud at that one, but she contained herself and moved her car away from the edge of the estate. Changing inside the car, Siobhan emerged completely in black. Even her hair was wrapped up inside the black balaclava.

She always enjoyed the black, always enjoyed being able to disappear into the night. As an operative, it wasn't used that often. You were more used to being out in the open, daily exposed, right in their faces, ready to run at an instant in case your cover was blown.

Siobhan had to her knowledge at least twenty successful nighttime missions, working on her own as recon. In each of them she'd be dressed up in the black. But that was also some time ago and there was no call for the black as an analyst. In truth, she wasn't worried. You didn't have the same sort of protection around here. They thought they were good and tough, but they didn't spot things. They didn't spot people working from a distance, either.

She threw a small rucksack over her shoulder and disappeared around the edge of the estate, nipping down a few back alleys and then amongst some trees. Siobhan calculated exactly where Beyonce's house was. She shimmied up one tree, hiding within the branches, looking for the view she wanted.

She adjusted herself several times before finding a comfortable perch with a sight line into the living room of Beyonce's house. It was through a window and part of the room was cut off from sight, but she could get a good idea of what was going on. Inside were many men and women, most of whom looked like they were from the estate. Some men were clearly there to make sure that nobody untoward came in. There were also several women hanging about. They seemed to range in age, and Siobhan wasn't certain of who any of them were.

She saw Kylie come in. The woman was as calm as anything. *Good girl*, thought Siobhan as she watched her talking to Beyonce. Beyonce seemed quite animated with Kylie. Siobhan found it hard to see any deception in what the woman was saying. If anything, Beyonce seemed quite fixated on Kylie. Kylie had said nothing in terms of anything sexual being between them. No looks, no comments, discussions, and Siobhan had dismissed any idea that part of this was beyond friendship and was to do with any physical need.

Looking through the window, she wondered now. Of course, she knew nothing about Beyonce's orientation, but it was something she'd ruled out that was now coming back into play. She didn't like that thought, though. That meant Beyonce could play beyond her limits, which could take Kylie into trouble as well. A good spy, a good operative or the leader of any organisation knew to distance their feelings from their decisions. *Sometimes easier said than done*, thought Siobhan.

Siobhan stopped watching as she heard a sound on the ground below. Looking down, she saw a man walk past the tree she was hiding in. He said nothing but just kept walking. He was looking around. Clearly, he was the scout put out on the estate. He never looked up, telling Siobhan what an amateur he was.

If someone was watching, they will not stand here, thought Siobhan. *You're going to be up out of the way. You want a perch you will not be disturbed from.* Once she made sure the man had disappeared around a corner, she turned her eyes back towards Beyonce's house, and then Siobhan's eyes widened.

There was a man with a tight haircut, almost bald, and he was dressed in a tight jumper that showed his rippling muscles, but he wasn't what was turning Siobhan's head. It was the woman he was talking to, or rather, the woman he was agreeing with and almost backing away from. Eileen Quigley was at the party.

She was dressed in a snappy grey suit with a blouse, and clearly was someone that many people didn't really want to talk to. They came to chat to her almost as if they had to, as if it was expected. Siobhan likened it to the Godfather, the man in charge of a mafia family. At weddings and other family occasions, people would come up to him, maybe giving a gift or saying some pandering words. Of course, if they didn't, somebody would grab them and bring them to say those words and give them a reminder that next time they wouldn't get a second chance.

Eileen Quigley gave off that air, and yet she had no powerful men with her. There were those hanging around, but they seemed to take orders from Beyonce, not from Eileen. Maybe Eileen just didn't need to give any, for everyone seemed to have a good idea who she was, in the sense that they were avoiding her if they could.

The party wound up around about one in the morning, but Siobhan noticed Kylie didn't leave the house. Even the security people, those tough guys Beyonce had brought in, had disappeared by then. Some of them stood outside, still protecting the estate, but Siobhan wondered who was left inside.

She glanced at Kylie walking past the window, Beyonce with

her. Then a light went on upstairs, possibly in the bedroom. Siobhan took her binoculars out and watched closely through them, trying to see if there were any shadows through the curtains. There wasn't. She became uneasy, wondering what was going on.

Quickly, she climbed down the tree. She tore through back gardens, leapt over a fence, and then climbed a spout up towards the bedroom. Siobhan didn't like this. She was out in the open. Although there weren't that many lights, she couldn't hang up near the window for long. She needed to grab a snatch of conversation, hear what was happening. As she hung there, she leaned in close to the window.

Kylie laughed. 'I've seen none like that,' she said. 'How many of these have you got?'

'Several. I've read them all through. I understand them all. You should read them at some point. Come over. Learn about them. The black arts are something that can benefit a woman, especially a woman like yourself.'

There was silence then. Siobhan heard a dog bark. She turned. In an alleyway not far away, she saw one guard walking around the estate. Siobhan slid down the drainpipe as quick as she could, disappearing out of sight behind the fence at the rear of the house. She crept up close to it, listening for the man to go past before leaping out and retaking her position in the tree.

It was another hour before Kylie left. As she exited the house, and Siobhan looked at the time, she realised there'd be no buses. A taxi pulled up, and Kylie was whisked into the night. Siobhan legged it back to her own car as quick as she could. Once inside, she drove straight to where Kylie would ask the taxi to take her, but Siobhan was too late.

When she got there, Kylie was already getting out of the taxi, and this taxi wasn't for moving. Kylie walked up the short driveway up to the front door that she hadn't knocked on previously when she was dropped off. She turned to look at the taxi, but it hadn't driven away. Kylie turned and knocked on the door of the house. Siobhan watched, wondering if Kylie would remember what she was told.

The door was opened by a middle-aged man who suddenly smiled at seeing Kylie. He took her inside, and Siobhan watched the taxi drive away. Quickly, Siobhan made her way up to the house, rapped on the door, and it was opened again by the same middle-aged man.

'Two peppers with a parakeet,' said Siobhan, and stepped over the threshold of the door inside. The door was closed behind her. She looked back at the man holding a gun towards her.

'Two people in the space of five minutes, or less,' said the man, 'both quoting the code word. I've had nobody come here for the last seven months. Who are you? She's not service,' he said. 'Who are you?'

'Sorry to barge in like that. I was given the code by one of your colleagues. Said I could use it if we were desperate.'

'Who?' asked the man.

'The gentleman,' said Siobhan, quoting Julian's codename. 'You know him how?'

'Ex-service. Worked with him. I worked abroad though. Never worked here in the province. I'm no longer in the Service. My name is Siobhan Duffy.'

The man nodded. 'Welcome, Mrs Duffy. A good job with the Russian mobsters up at the causeway,' said the man, 'but it doesn't explain who just came in before you.' The man was still holding the gun and pointing it at Siobhan.

'That's Kylie, who works for me. I'm now a private detective, and she was running cover. Part of that cover needed an address. The gentleman said we could use this one. That taxi driver wasn't waiting for fun. He's gone away quite happy, so I thank you.'

'Inside,' said the man with the gun. Siobhan walked inside, still dressed all in black, and saw Kylie sitting on a couch with her hands cuffed behind her. She looked quite solemn.

'Don't panic,' said Siobhan. 'They're using protocol. It's what they're meant to do. The password gets you into the building. It doesn't mean they trust you. The man at the front is going to make a call to the gentleman, one of my friends. He'll square everything up, and that will be that and we'll be on our way.'

Siobhan looked over at a woman sitting in a seat in the far corner. She had a gun trained on Siobhan. 'Until that happens though,' said Siobhan, 'they won't trust us, so I'm going to sit beside you.' Siobhan turned to the woman across the room. 'If that's all right, you don't mind me sitting beside Kylie?'

The woman nodded, but the gun stayed trained on Siobhan. Five minutes later, Siobhan was escorting Kylie back out of the house and off to her car. Once there, they drove back to Siobhan's house, but Siobhan wasn't waiting till there for a debrief.

'What happened when you went upstairs?'

'You will not believe this,' said Kylie. 'She has esoteric volumes.'

'Esoteric? Where did you learn that word?'

'Tonight. It means creepy or spooky.'

'No, it doesn't. It means it's intended or likely to only be understood by a few people with specialised knowledge or interest,' said Siobhan. 'The word "esoteric" doesn't mean there's anything strange about it. It just means that only some people are going to get it. What was the esoteric volume?' she asked.

'All this stuff about witches. Loads and loads of stuff about witches, their lore, their history. Beyonce's got loads of it.'

'And it's what?'

'It's local, a lot. That's what I couldn't get. I was looking at pictures. Some things they used to do,' said Kylie, 'were quite shocking.'

'And she was showing you this—why?'

'Because we were talking about witches and what we collected.'

'And you told her you collected what?'

'Just stories and the odd bit of clothing, stuff that I could back up by producing if I have to one day.'

'And she told you about this, did she?' asked Siobhan.

'Yes. She showed me these volumes. I don't know if she was meant to or not. She said that she could probably get me to see more witches, real witches.'

'And you said what?'

'I said bring it on,' said Kylie.

'Did you see who else was in that room tonight?' asked Siobhan.

'No. Why, who was there?'

'Eileen Quigley, the one the Service was worried about.'

'Oh,' said Kylie, but she was sitting back with a satisfied look on her face.

Siobhan's heart sank. *Kylie doesn't get it*, she thought, *really doesn't understand. This woman was trouble. All Kylie is seeing was Beyonce being nice to her.*

Siobhan was worried. Something inside of her smelled a rat. She couldn't put her finger on what, but call it instinct. Instinct from years in the field. She'd have to play this carefully but if something really big came up, Siobhan was going to pull the plug on this one.

Chapter 17

Kylie was back in the gym two days later, and Siobhan was once again watching from outside. Everything seemed cool, and when Kylie emerged after an hour and a half, Siobhan thought things must have gone well. Kylie was beaming, absolutely beaming, but Siobhan didn't know why and waited for Kylie to take her bus trip back into the centre of Belfast. Once there, Siobhan drove her back down to her home on the coast. Kylie was looking smug all the way back, but she said nothing, not until they got back to the house.

'Get Declan,' she said. 'Get Declan in here.'

Siobhan wondered what Kylie was doing, but she called Declan from the garden. The young man came through and Kylie was now standing in the kitchen, having taken off her tracksuit top, hanging it over the back of a chair. She was standing in her Lycra leggings and Lycra top, smiling over at Declan.

'You're not going to believe this,' she said, clearly talking at Declan and not at Siobhan, 'but I've only gone and done it.'

'Done what?' asked Declan.

'Yes,' said Siobhan. 'Done what? What exactly have you

done?'

'I've been invited.'

'You've been invited. Great,' said Declan. 'Where?'

'To the dance.'

'I'm sorry,' said Siobhan. 'What dance? What hall is it taking place in?'

'No, the dance. The one you and Declan saw.'

'You've been invited to the naked dance?' said Declan. 'You're going to need backup.'

Kylie looked at him. 'Is that the first thing that came into your head? Do you realise what I've just achieved? What I've gone and done all on my own?'

'Where and when?' asked Siobhan, her eyes narrowing.

'Oh, it's great. It's great what you've done,' said Declan, 'but you're going to have to get your kit off to do it. You'll probably need some backup; people hanging around. Just in case . . .'

'Seriously, Declan. I tell about my achievement, I tell you how well I've done over this last week or so, and all you can think about is how I'm going to look.'

'Well, yes,' said Declan.

Kylie shook her head. 'There's no way you're coming for backup.'

'Excuse me,' said Siobhan. 'This is the boss speaking. Declan, stow it. Start thinking with your brain. Kylie, where and when?'

'Two night's time. I've got to go to the dressmaker. She's going to fit me up with my robes.'

'Awful lot of effort just for you to take them off again,' said Declan.

'Declan, shut it,' said Siobhan, 'the grown-up needs to talk.' Siobhan rounded on Kylie. 'You didn't tell me that as soon as you came out. You've hung on to this. Why? To stand there and gloat and to say, look at me, how well I've done?'

'You didn't think I could do it. You wanted to watch over me the whole time. What did you do? Nothing. You didn't have to interfere at all. I was magnificent.'

'Excuse me, but you weren't,' said Siobhan. 'You missed plenty. If I hadn't set you up with that safe house and a code word to get in, you'd have been taken back by that taxi and you wouldn't have come away from that estate.'

'What about all the things I did? At the gym every day, getting on, talking with . . .'

'And you got on well. Are you sure she was telling the truth? Are you sure she's not playing you?'

'Of course, she isn't. I was magnificent,' said Kylie, 'and I'm a really personable type of person. People like me; people gravitate to me. You might not find that, Siobhan. You might find that people don't . . .'

'I like Mrs D,' said Declan.

'Well, that's appreciated, Declan. Shut up,' said Siobhan. 'We're not here talking about me; we're talking about you, Kylie. We're talking about what you actually know and what you've agreed to.'

'Well, they're taking me to the dressmaker.'

'Who is?'

'Beyonce is. She's organising that. Then, when we get my robes and come back from that, the following night, we're on. She's teaching me about what the dance means.'

'And what does it mean?' asked Siobhan.

'It's about us all becoming one. One sisterhood. It's about having dominion over people. Power, control, but we do it on the quiet, in the shadows, so they don't know what we're doing.'

'Why do they do it naked?' asked Declan.

'That's not really a key point at the moment, Declan,' said Siobhan. Then she stopped. 'Well, yes, actually,' said Siobhan, 'why do they bother with that side of it?'

'Well, that's easy. It's so we're open towards each other. There are no secrets kept within the coven.'

'Believe that when I see it,' said Siobhan.

'Anyway,' said Kylie, 'I've got to go tomorrow to get my outfit. Beyonce's going to pick me up. I said I'd meet her in town. I thought that was easier than trying to get her to pick us up from that safe house again. We don't want any of those people holding guns at us.'

'Who's holding guns at who?' blurted Declan.

'Declan, for the last time, shoosh. I need to have a word with Kylie here.' Siobhan turned, rounding on Kylie. 'When we used to work in the Service, when we committed to something like this, we would sit down. We would go through every moment of the conversations that we had with the person whose group we were trying to infiltrate. Pull out every reaction and we would sit with others and go through them all. I need you to sit down and detail everything out from scratch.'

'I can't remember,' said Kylie. Siobhan rolled her eyes. 'But I'll tell you this,' said Kylie. 'It feels good. I think she's into me. Do you know what? I think she might be into me in a more-than-friend's way.'

Siobhan put her hand up towards Declan. 'Don't even start. Okay?' *The poor boy*, thought Siobhan. 'Look Kylie,' she said, 'we're going to go and we're going to get this dress outfit made for you and you're going to tell me everything that happens.

When you come back from that, we're going to sit and you're going to detail everything. Based on that, I'm going to make an assessment whether you should or shouldn't go.'

'Shouldn't that be my assessment, too? Shouldn't I be getting a say on that? In fact, I should probably get a veto,' said Kylie.

The annoying thing about this was that Kylie was right. She was the one going in. She was the one who should turn around at the end of the day and say, "I do" or "I do not want to go in". You couldn't make somebody do something like this. Kylie wouldn't be the one who would get to say if the operation was a go or not, but yes, she could veto it.

Siobhan felt uncomfortable, but there'd also been a lot of work put into this and now they were close. 'Okay. Go get your cloak tomorrow and your witch's outfit. But tomorrow night, we sit down and we talk and you detail everything about the conversation you have.'

'Okay,' said Kylie. She left the room in less spirits than when she arrived, and Siobhan hoped that she'd knocked some sense into her. The last thing she needed was Kylie being giddy going to this fitting. As Siobhan thought through the worries on her mind, she realised Declan was still in the room.

'What's up Dec?'

'Mrs D, I'm sure you're going to agree with me that if she goes to this dance thing, you're going to need backup. You're going to need me. There's lots of them, not a lot of you, and I mean, you took me last time for surveillance. I could record everything, we could get more faces, we could . . .'

'Declan, if we cover this and I need you there, please understand the one thing; I will not tell Kylie that's what's happening. Can you imagine Kylie dancing like that, knowing you're watching?'

Siobhan saw the man's face and put her hand up again. 'Declan, it wasn't meant to be a chance for you to think about that, to imagine it. I'll decide if I need you, but if we do, it's business and you have to keep all thoughts out of your head and do what needs done.'

'That's understood, Mrs D, it's just that . . . it's just that . . .'

'And be very careful how you approach this. Kylie was busting to tell you how she'd done such a good job, how she'd been a brilliant operative, for want of a better word, working undercover. All you could see was a chance to see her with nothing on. I'm not sure that went down well.'

'Mrs D, I don't think you understand how modern love works.'

Siobhan had thinking to do, and the last thing she needed was to get into some sort of debate with Declan about how relationships work these days. It was hard enough talking to the man about gardening sometimes. He sometimes talked about the flowers and the bees, and it seemed a lot more animated than what Siobhan remembered.

'Go home, go to bed, Declan,' said Siobhan.

The following morning, Kylie was back in a good mood, and Siobhan dropped her into town. She didn't tail her this time, worried about who else could have been there, and was relieved to pick her up round about four o'clock.

Kylie was carrying a large bag, and when she brought it back to Siobhan's house, she pulled a large cloak with an undergarment from it. Siobhan hadn't realised that the undergarment was so thin. The cloak was the item keeping the women warm when they were out there before their dance.

Standing in the living room, Kylie closed the curtains, making sure Declan wasn't there, as she showed Siobhan how the outfit worked. As she let the cape and the inner outfit fall away, leaving her just in her underwear, Siobhan looked at the outfit. It had the same wonderful design, but this was unique. This was very much a one-off.

'It was Lorraine Campbell that made it,' said Kylie suddenly.

'They took you to that shop?'

'Yes. She asked me what I was doing last time. I said I was just interested, really interested in everything. That's why I was going around trying to see if I could get an outfit made, trying to see if there was any detail on witches and covens. That's why I'd gone to the library. I'd learnt about it from one of the senior librarians there. She seemed pretty cool about my responses, and I think Beyonce certainly trusted her.'

It's definitely a chance, thought Siobhan. *This is a big, big play. If Kylie gets in amongst them and becomes one of them, she could expose the complete operation. Highlight whatever is happening. So far, we're still none the wiser.*

'Tell me, Kylie,' said Siobhan, as she watched Kylie dressing back up, 'what's your gut feeling about this? Are you scared at all?'

'Of course, I am. It's going to be freezing as well, but this is a way in, isn't it?'

'I guess it is. I guess if they weren't happy with you, they might have just stopped it there and then. Why go through the whole charade? Why not just take you out somewhere else?'

'So, I'm going to do it then,' said Kylie.

'Yes, you are,' said Siobhan. 'You're going to dress up, you're going to go with them, and you're going to dance like they dance. You're going to show that you're into it, carried away with it, and hopefully after that, they're going to tell you a lot more about them.'

'I honestly can't think of anything,' said Kylie. 'I can't think of anything that blew my cover or showed them I wasn't who I said I was.'

'Okay,' said Siobhan, 'we'll do this then. We'll do this, but I'll be watching. I'll be nearby. There's no way I'm letting you go in on your own.'

'I'll be all right,' said Kylie. 'You better make sure they don't see you.'

'I get that bit,' said Siobhan. 'I'm the expert here. You make sure you remember that.'

'Will Declan be there too?'

'I don't know. If we were doing surveillance, I would say yes, but we're not. We're trying to get you through this rite, or whatever it is, and then you're in the organisation. The reason for me being there is the same reason I've been here for the last couple of weeks—to pull you out if things go wrong. I don't think Declan will be of use for that. Better if I only have to look after one of you if things go wrong. You've no idea what it takes to get yourself out, never mind getting somebody else out as well.'

'That's a pity,' said Kylie.

'A pity?' queried Siobhan. 'I mean, I can phone him up and bring him round now if you really feel that you need to put yourself on display,' said Siobhan, eyes wide, looking at Kylie incredulously.

'It's funny, I know I had all the issues before with, well, the pregnancy and my child and losing it, but before that all I ever wanted was for guys to look at me, to want me. I'm now at a point where I think I want that again.'

'Trust me,' said Siobhan, 'the one thing you won't have to

do is run around naked in a field with a lot of other women to get Declan to want you. I think the guy's bought and sold on you the day he saw you.'

'Do you really think so?'

'Why is it,' asked Siobhan, 'that every time I say something, everyone questions me, wondering if I'm a talented investigator or not? I can read people.'

Kylie stepped forward and kissed Siobhan on the cheek. 'Thank you. Thank you for that and thank you for trusting me. This is one of the most exciting things I've ever done.'

'Why do you think I stayed away from home for so long?' said Siobhan. 'There's nothing like it, not when you get to the thick of it. Let's see how you go tomorrow.'

Chapter 18

Siobhan let Declan drive Kylie up to Belfast, where she would be picked up by Beyonce. Kylie was clearly excited. Thankfully, a little trepidation was also showing. Siobhan had found through her years of experience it was best not just to be excited. You needed to have something to ground you, a fear. She wasn't sure that Kylie had it.

Siobhan remembered how the fear was less until the first time that she failed. The first time she had failed in the field as a spy, someone had died. After that, every job she did made her think, made her plan, and there was a core fear that was healthy. A fear that meant that she checked everything through. She saw the vulnerability—was desperately looking for it.

Siobhan had bought another car. Beaten up, but with enough power in it because the car had come from a boy racer. Someone who had taken up a beaten old wreck and made it into something. It wasn't something she'd be seen dead driving around in normally, but it had speed, speed to get her away if needed. Declan was to follow Beyonce at a distance, a proper distance, and just make sure she was heading in the general direction with Kylie, once she'd picked her up.

Already in position and dressed in her camouflage jacket, Siobhan was wrapped up against the winter chill. Once Declan had texted that Beyonce had entered Greenisland, he was to turn back and disappear. Siobhan had parked the car up and was now hunkered down in a field, waiting to see cars arrive. Hopefully, they would park up in the same place as last time using the hollow field.

Siobhan wasn't sure at what time this would happen. Kylie had gone up late and eleven o'clock was scheduled for the pickup. Siobhan had been in place since ten-thirty.

Sitting in the cold, she received a text from Declan. Beyonce's car had gone to the estate. Siobhan thought as much. If they were going to do their dance or whatever in the middle of the night, they wouldn't hang around out here for a couple of hours, not like her, getting cold. She cracked some of the heat pads from her small backpack, stuffing some up the inside of her arms, and dropping one inside her chest. It was Baltic out here.

At one o'clock, Declan said that Beyonce's car was on the move again and having followed it out to Greenisland, he texted to say that he was moving on. Siobhan watched as her car arrived, parked up and then waited. Other cars arrived. She counted them coming in until there were twelve there in total. Only then did the cloak-clad witches move towards the field with the hollow.

Two of them were carrying between them a brazier. With her infrared glasses, Siobhan could see Kylie marching with quite a jig towards the middle of the field. She was then taken towards the rear, where she seemed to kneel with two of the witches. Siobhan sat and watched as the fire was lit and the women moved back to their positions.

Kylie was brought forward and placed in that thirteenth position, as the women all stood around in a circle. It was only then that Siobhan noticed a difference. It was hard to tell through the infrared glasses, as you didn't truly get an image of a person. You got the outline, the features, but each of the witches was wearing a mask. Siobhan couldn't tell if they were ornate or not, but they covered at least half the face. Everyone was wearing a mask except for one person, Kylie. An unease grew in Siobhan. This wasn't normal. This was not what had happened before.

It reached the point where Siobhan was expecting the women to disrobe and begin their dance around the fire. Instead, somebody said something in a language that Siobhan didn't understand. Then the two witches on either side of Kylie turned and grabbed her wrists, dragging her forward towards the fire. Siobhan struggled as the light distorted the view through the infrared glasses. She tore them off and then saw by the light from the fire a large knife being brandished.

Siobhan was quite a distance away. Far enough that there was no way she could reach in time, not if they intended to kill Kylie, but she'd planned for this.

Quickly but calmly, she reached inside the backpack that she carried, pulled out a gun, and fired into the air. The witches scattered, but they ran away from the flame into the dark. Siobhan quickly tried to identify where Kylie was, still holding the gun in her hand. She put back on the infrared goggles, then noticed somebody being dragged by two of the other witches. They were heading towards the cars. Siobhan didn't believe she could reach it before they departed, so instead, she turned and ran for her own car. It was sitting out on the main road.

As the cars departed from the field, Siobhan tore over towards them. She wore a balaclava over her head, keen not to be seen, and drove up quickly beside the first car. There was only one person inside. She braked, letting the car disappear ahead of her. As the next car shot up beside her, again she pulled over close, crashing into the side of it briefly. She looked over, but again, there was only a single person inside.

Siobhan felt her own car being shunted from behind. Her seatbelt saved her, and she looked up into the rearview mirror. She could only see one person in that car as well. Where was Kylie? The one thing she wouldn't be doing was driving. There were only twelve cars, so somebody had her. Would it be the car that had arrived with her? She couldn't tell. It was so dark on arrival that Siobhan didn't have a clue about which car belonged to who.

As she got closer to them, she tried to scan into each car until she realised that the eighth car had Kylie in it. She was bouncing about in the back, and a masked witch drove at the front. Siobhan pulled the handbrake to turn the car around to follow her, but as she did so, two other cars rammed into her side. Siobhan was buffeted back and forward, but the car's engine was still going.

She put her foot down and drove off, hearing the scrape of metal. Up ahead, cars were peeling this way and that, and she fought through the mind fog of the accident to see which car was the one containing Kylie. Three cars spun off to the right down a road that headed back into Greenisland. Siobhan tore after them, convinced that the middle car was the one containing Kylie. She drove fast, not hesitating, and went smack into the rear of the car in front, smashing her own headlights. She now only had side lights operating, but the car she had smashed into had gone off at a side angle, and she was now directly behind Kylie's car. Glancing in the rearview mirror, however, she had seen that several other cars were now tailing after her.

Siobhan drove hard around the country lanes, coming close to the rear of the car in front of her, until she went for it, at a tight bend. The car in front slowed, knowing it would have to take the bend, but Siobhan kept the accelerator down. She drove hard into the side of the car, smacking it into the hedge up ahead.

The action had the required result, as the rear of the car in front went up on the verge. The back wheels were lifted off the ground. Its engine had conked out as well, and by the time anyone had recovered, Siobhan was already out of her own car. She pulled open the rear door, pulling Kylie out. Someone got out of the front of the car, staggering towards her, but she fired her gun off into the air.

Kylie was staggering and clearly had a cut or something to her head, because blood was evident. Siobhan ignored it, opened the rear door, and threw Kylie into the back of the now beat-up Fiesta. The engine was still running as she stepped inside.

She tried to reverse, but found a car hit her from behind this time. She was thankful she had grabbed the seatbelt, clicking it just in time. Kylie, however, hit the back seats. Siobhan saw that the Fiesta had been bent slightly, but by putting her foot down on the accelerator, she squeezed out from between the car melee. Metal scraped along metal. There were cries and shouts, and Siobhan hoped no one had a weapon of any sort because they were so close to the witches' cars.

Having pulled out of the melee, Siobhan turned the car back in the opposite direction from which she had come. Several cars were now bearing down upon her, heading towards her with force. Siobhan didn't hesitate, spun the wheel and drove clean through a hedge on one side, into a grassy field beyond. The wheels slipped on the icy ground, but at least it was firm.

Able to keep going, she found the gate to the field, and then drove through the hedge back out onto the road. She flicked her head round to look behind her. Kylie groaned, moaning away, but she saw several cars had reversed and were coming towards her. Siobhan picked up her phone, dialling Declan's number.

Declan answered. 'Something up?'

'Where the hell are you?' asked Siobhan.

'I'm heading back down the road like you told me.'

'Turn around, turn around, head towards, head towards…' Siobhan thought hard. *Where should they go? Where was the obvious place?* 'Down to the docks, M2—M2, three junctions along. Sit up the top of the flyover. Yes? You know what I'm talking about? Up the top on the motorway.'

'Okay,' said Declan. 'What's up? What's the matter?'

'It's all gone to pot. They're after us. I'll be dropping my car off, getting in yours, and we'll be getting out of there.'

'Right,' said Declan.

'They're going to be behind me. I need you to have petrol with you. A canister of petrol.'

'Where the hell do I get that now?'

'Petrol station, 24-7. Go get it. You should easily be there, well before me.'

'Okay,' said Declan, but he sounded nervous.

Siobhan closed down the phone call. He'd better be there, because if he wasn't, they would be screwed.

Once clear of Greenisland, the roads were wider, but still so quiet. It was the middle of the night, and Siobhan wasn't too sure that the witches would want to keep up with them for too long. Her hope that they would soon fall back and cut their losses. Hope floundered, as she saw at least three cars continuing to follow her. Maybe there would be more up ahead. She cut off the main road, racing up and then down through Monkstown, before rejoining at the M5.

She saw police cars leaving the station at the bottom of Monkstown, but heading the other direction. Gunshots had obviously been reported. She took great delight, as she was heading the opposite direction from there. As she reached the motorway, she realised that she probably had about thirty seconds lead on the cars that was chasing her.

As she neared the turnoff for the flyover, where hopefully Declan was waiting, she looked up to see him in his own car. Hopefully, he'd have the wit to do what she'd always told him to do if ever they were really in trouble. She peeled off to the left, up to the top of the flyover, and parked up about ten yards behind Declan's car. Jumping out, she pulled open the rear door, hauling Kylie out, still dressed in her witch's robes. Declan was out of the car in a flash, carrying a canister of petrol and some matches in the other hand.

'Take her. Get her in the car.'

Siobhan passed Kylie over, taking the canister off Declan. She opened the top of it and started pouring it over her Ford Fiesta. Reaching inside and grabbing the last of her gear, she flung the bag over her shoulder and stood, desperately trying to ignite matches. She had three wrapped together in her hand, watched the orange flame ignite and then dropped them into the petrol.

An almighty whoosh forced Siobhan back off her feet. She scrambled round, heading towards Declan's car. As she came up to the rear, she noticed he had taped out his registration number. *Good lad*!

As she raced round to the passenger side, jumping in, she cried for him to go and placed the now empty canister and matches at her feet.

Declan pulled away, and looking behind her, Siobhan could see cars pulling up to the now flaming inferno that was the Ford Fiesta. Declan had just disappeared off the roundabout and no doubt there would be police cars arriving soon with such a flaming wreckage at the top of the flyover. Siobhan told Declan to drive back into Belfast. They made a circuitous route encompassing over fifty miles of travel before arriving back at the house that night.

After making sure they weren't being followed, Declan had removed the tape, allowing his number plate to be seen again. They arrived back at the house where Kylie was taken inside and Siobhan told Declan to go home, and park his car up in his usual spot. Siobhan turned out all the house lights and took Kylie into the front room to a large sofa. She laid her down before quickly taking off her witch's clothing and then wrapping her up in blankets. The clothing was taken and put underneath the floor in Siobhan's study.

Siobhan then strode back into her front room and sat in the dark, the gun taken out of her backpack held in her lap. She didn't think anybody would find them; didn't think anyone was coming, but she needed to be sure. She was always safer in this house. Her defences were here, and if they wanted to come, they could come.

As she sat in the dark silence, Siobhan thought about what went wrong. *At which point had they made Kylie? At which point did they know she wasn't one of them? How late on? Or had she simply been voted out?*

One thing was for sure, Kylie would no longer be part of this investigation. They'd found her and they knew. It was time to either close the investigation or for Siobhan to take the lead. Either that or hand it over to Julian.

Chapter 19

Y ou're out. Understand me? You're out of it completely.' Siobhan stared hard at Kylie, not believing that the girl was still contemplating coming back into what they were doing. How could she? She'd been made. They were going to kill her. Still, Kylie wanted to work on the investigation.

'I can still be useful, though. I can still find out information, can still tail people.'

'You got tailed yourself. They know who you are, Kylie. I need to take you out of this.'

'I don't understand why. You've had trouble before. You've had to continue with the investigation. I mean, you've still had people talk to you.'

'I was a full-blown operative,' said Siobhan. 'Even I got pulled out of my own way at times. It's about the operation. It's about what we're trying to do here. We're needing to prove that Deborah died at the hands of these people. So, we need to play our hand secretly. They obviously realised that you were trying to break their ranks, get in amongst them. If I'm to do that again, you have to be out of the picture. They have to believe that we've pulled back completely.'

'That won't work, though, will it?' said Kylie.

The pair were standing in Siobhan's kitchen, Siobhan looking out the window at the sea, while Kylie argued, sitting at the table. This had been going on for the last hour as they awaited Declan.

Siobhan hadn't realised until now that she liked Declan about. He was quite happy to pitch in against Kylie, but he would do it in a quieter way, a more soothing way. Siobhan spoke harshly, like she was running an operation. She was still trying to understand how this worked, with the two novices alongside her.

In the Service, you spoke candidly. Nobody took offence. Well, nobody took easy offence. Not that difficult to offend anyone at the end of the day. With Declan and Kylie, she had to be more coercive. She had to be less straight-talking. They didn't react well to being told they couldn't, or they were unable, that they were lacking in certain things. It was a fault.

Maybe it's society. We constantly get told we can be anything, we can do anything. Siobhan was all for maximising your potential. But do anything? Siobhan would win no marathons. She realised that. She might run one, or at least have run one, but she would never win one. This old girl wasn't quick. She wasn't built like that. As a spy, she was good. As an analyst, she was even better. She felt she'd maximised her potential in those worlds, but she would never be a marathon winner.

Unfortunately, that didn't play well these days. The younger ones seemed to think they could do anything, and half the time, without the work. She stopped herself. Yes, she was thinking like a fuddy-duddy. Thinking like a really old person. But she was right, wasn't she?

The world had changed in the last lot of years. The world

had changed between something that you worked hard and got your rewards in, to a place that had to look after you. Well, who cares? We'll just sit and do nothing, and we'll be looked after.

There was no society anymore. We weren't together. We didn't work for the better of everyone. Take what you can for yourself. Oh, we'll talk about it, and we'll say nice things. *The truth was, though,* thought Siobhan, *that the harshness of saying the truth was a kindness in itself if it stopped you from doing stupid things and getting yourself into a place you couldn't get out of.* She turned around and looked at Kylie.

'I have said no. Absolutely no.'

'Why? Give me one good reason,' said Kylie.

'Because, and this one is the best reason, and unlike the several dozen I've given you so far, it might even strike into that thick head of yours: you will get yourself killed.'

'But . . .'

'There are no buts when you're dead. That's it. It's done. It's dusted. Having done what I've done, if I was in your position, I wouldn't be volunteering. I would get myself out of the way. One thing you have to learn in this game is when to haul your backside out of there. Now catch yourself on.'

The doorbell rang.

'Oh, thank God,' said Siobhan. 'Maybe Declan can talk some sense into you.'

'Declan will be on my side.'

Not if I get to him first, thought Siobhan. She left the kitchen, walked to the front door, checked the peephole, and saw Declan outside. Opening the door, she smiled at his beaming face.

'Morning, Mrs D. Looks like we got away with it.'

'It looks like we did, Declan.'

She hadn't told him about sitting throughout the night, watching over Kylie. Neither had she told him about the gun she had held in her lap. She didn't tell him about how she was prepared to kill if anyone had come through that door. Siobhan liked Declan. But as she'd just thought to herself earlier, she needed to work on a slightly different plane with him.

'It's on the news about the car being burnt out, but I don't think the police know who it is. There's also reports about gunshots being fired. They're mentioning it being terrorism or by paramilitaries, though they don't know which side it is. The police are in a right flummox about it.'

'They are, are they?' said Siobhan. 'Go into the kitchen. Oh, and when you do, Declan,' Siobhan held him by the shoulder, 'if Kylie tells you about getting back into this investigation, about being at the centre, tell her no. Tell her she'll get herself killed.'

'Will she?' said Declan.

'Undoubtedly.'

Siobhan gripped Declan's shoulder and put on her most serious of faces. It was overkill, but she wanted to make sure the point was taken by Declan. He cared for Kylie—that was clear. Hopefully, he cared enough to tell her sense rather than just go along with whatever she would want to believe.

Siobhan waited out in the hall so that she wouldn't seem to back Declan up, or vice versa. She wanted to give the two of them a moment. There was something brewing, a closeness coming. While the situation demanded that she take Kylie out of the picture, she didn't want to impede that. Genuine feelings in life, true and passionate ones, were short on demand. You didn't know when they were coming. Maybe, you might see the inkling of them. You might have to explore them. Half the time some other idiot got in the way.

Siobhan had her own regrets. The Service had impeded Eamon. The Service at the moment was getting in the way of Julian. In this whole idea of settling down, she wanted someone to settle down with. Not these two youngsters. They were great to have about the place. They kept you feeling alive, kept you feeling fresh, but she wanted that special someone. Siobhan listened for a moment and heard Declan raising his voice.

'No. You shouldn't do it. You'll get yourself killed.'

'That's what she says. You're just saying what she says.'

'She's the expert,' said Declan loudly. 'She's the expert. Kylie, listen to yourself.'

'You just don't think I'm good enough at this. You just want to take the limelight.'

'Kylie, that's not it. I just don't want to see you get killed. I don't want to lose you.'

There was silence in the kitchen. *That was a big statement,* thought Siobhan. *A big statement. It wasn't a case of, I don't want to see you get killed. It was, I don't want to lose you.* He was probably making quite an assumption to believe that he had her in the first place, Siobhan mused, but he's not far off. She took a moment to smile, to enjoy the tenderness Declan was showing. It had been rough, the last twelve hours particularly.

The doorbell broke her thoughts and Siobhan spun round to look out of the peephole. An immaculately dressed man in a suit with a tie smiled at the small viewing port. Siobhan opened the door to Julian.

'Well, haven't you been busy? I take it somebody's cover got blown.'

'Yes,' said Siobhan. 'Somebody is sitting in the kitchen at the moment, telling me she should still be involved in this investigation. I want to bury her. I want to put her far away from it as possible.'

'You've told her that, haven't you?'

'Of course, I've told her,' said Siobhan. She took Julian's jacket and hung it up.

'Well, then, that'll be that,' he said.

'I'm afraid running a detective agency isn't quite the same as running the Service. I'm believing that the Service is a lot easier.'

Julian grinned and walked into the kitchen. Siobhan followed behind. Declan was currently over at the window, looking frustrated. Kylie still had eyes of defiance. Julian simply sauntered in, sat down in the chair on the opposite side of the table from Kylie.

'When our cover is blown, when we have been identified, and when we have been followed, we remove ourselves from the situation. This is a team task, and the head of the team determines who goes in next. You're not head of the team. The head of the team is Siobhan. You will withdraw yourself.'

'How am I meant to get experience if I withdraw myself?'

'You gain experience by being alive and getting yourself involved in the next investigation that comes along,' said Julian. 'I have a vested interest in seeing that we come to a successful conclusion of this investigation. In truth, it seems to be growing arms and legs beyond what I thought was there. That being so, I believe that Mrs Duffy is currently in the correct position to continue those investigations. If, however, certain elements of her operation go rogue and cause that to be a problem, I would be forced to remove Mrs Duffy from the investigation. That may be by polite, or rather more robust efforts. Kylie, stand down and stay stood down.'

Kylie stared at Julian's immovable face. *He'd done it politely, incredibly politely, but that was the Service,* thought Siobhan. *The hard things said straight and direct. There was always a promise that behind it all, things would move fast; things would move violently if necessary, but usually there was a polite statement at the beginning.*

Kylie looked up at Siobhan. 'You're the boss.'

'Thank you,' said Siobhan. 'I don't want this to sound condescending, but Julian could do with a cup of tea.' Kylie stood up and moved over to put the kettle on. 'We need a better way in,' said Siobhan openly to the room. 'Kylie needs to fade into the background, but we need to get in close again. Beyonce was an excellent target, but that target is gone.'

'That target will be gone,' said Julian, looking at Siobhan. Siobhan understood what he meant. Beyonce would be dead. Maybe not yet, but soon.

'Why is she gone?' asked Kylie.

'She brought you in.'

'But she brought me in to their instructions, surely? I wouldn't have got that far without everybody else knowing.'

'When you're in a secret society,' said Julian, 'or a group of people, if you bring somebody in who turns out to be not what they say they are, you haven't done your job. You haven't vetted them correctly. Can't keep doing that. You can't do that, and the society survives. If you make a mistake; you pay for it.'

'I think Beyonce wanted more than just to bring you in as a witch. I think Beyonce saw you as a friend, and from some things you've said, possibly as much more than a friend,' said Siobhan.

Kylie swallowed hard. 'But she tried to kill me. They all did.'

'That, they did. Thank God, I got you out. Thank God for Declan, who did his part remarkably well. I sat and briefed you after everything, and I probably should have called it. You need more experience. This was a difficult situation, and these are brutal people. Maybe not Beyonce, but the surrounding people. Certainly, the person at the top.'

'That aside,' said Julian, 'you're going to need to pick a new target.'

'We only have two,' said Siobhan. 'Eileen Quigley and Lorraine Campbell. Lorraine Campbell was there in the shop. Kylie spoke to her. They don't know we know about Eileen Quigley.'

'She was at the party,' said Kylie. 'When I was at Beyonce's, she was there. They know I've seen her there.'

'When they went to kill you, they all went masked. Why? Because they didn't want you to know who they were. When they were at the dance before, there were no masks. They all know who each other is. But you didn't know. You knew Beyonce. You knew Lorraine Campbell. But you didn't know Eileen Quigley. We also need to approach this differently. You went alongside Beyonce as a friend.'

'You thinking of going in as something else?' asked Julian.

'You're going to get to play the part of a mobster again, Mrs D.'

Siobhan looked round at Declan. 'Not quite, Declan. I was thinking, Julian, that maybe you should put out that one of your agents has gone rogue, looking to make a bit of money.'

'Well, the way they pay us these days, that wouldn't be out

of the question,' said Julian. 'I can manage that.'

'Good. I target Eileen Quigley. She's down two, or she will be down two witches.'

'You're serious about Beyonce? They won't just throw her out.'

Julian and Siobhan looked at Kylie together, but Declan got in before they could speak. 'That's the way these things work, Kylie. You've got to be on your game or you're out the door.' Siobhan turned and looked at Declan. When did he become such a professional?

'I don't know if he's picked it up from YouTube, but Declan's right.' Siobhan watched as Kylie picked up the kettle just as it clicked. She poured the water into a cup holding a tea bag, but her hand was shaking, some of the water spilling slightly on the side.

'Whoops,' she said. Siobhan raced round the table, put her arms underneath Kylie as she fell. She held her close as the girl flung her arms around Siobhan, her head laid on her breast. She cried.

'Yes,' said Siobhan. 'It's okay. It was that close, but we got you. I got you. That's why I'm here.'

Julian appeared beside Siobhan, took her tea out of the way and mopped down the counter. He returned to sit at the table while Siobhan hung on to Kylie.

'Good,' said Siobhan, as Kylie finally broke her embrace. 'It's got through to you. Let these things sink in. They're not pleasant, but it will keep you alive in the future. Trust me. We've all been there.'

'Well, except for Declan,' said Julian suddenly.

'After last time,' said Siobhan quietly, 'even Declan's been there.'

'Thanks, Mrs D,' said Declan. 'I'm not just a man made by YouTube.'

* * *

Lindsay McLaughlin walked along the streets of Carrickfergus, watching her breath in front of her in the frosty morning air. They'd given her a few days off after she'd found the body of Deborah Lynch hanging on the Witches' Pillory. She was grateful for it, but she still felt shaken by what she'd found. On her first day back, she looked in every corner, every side street, thinking that someone might jump out, or that someone might be slumped against a wall.

Now, coming towards the end of her shift, she would clean the street down to the pillory. She would be ready to understand that these things didn't happen all the time. This was a one-off. She'd been incredibly unlucky, as her supervisor had said. It wasn't unknown that those cleaning the refuse of a town came across bodies. After all, those in the building trade sometimes dug up skeletons. Bad things happened, and sometimes good people ended up finding the bad things.

It was okay; she would get over it. Things would go back to normal. These first days would be like that, would be somewhat nervous. It was to be expected that she would see things, that she would be anxious.

Lindsay had refused to have someone come out with her, mainly because they were going to put John with her. John, frankly, liked Lindsay, but Lindsay didn't like him. She didn't need that sort of thing when she was struggling with just doing her job.

The Witches' Pillory was at the end of the street, but she was keeping her head down as she pushed the cart forward. She stopped, took out her brush, swept in some rubbish she saw on the ground, and put it into her bin. She put the brush back on her cart and pushed forward again. Looking down, she saw the mazy pattern of the frost. She looked left and saw the grit lying in the middle of the road; the lorries had been out much earlier.

As she got closer to the pillory, Lindsay found herself not able to look up. Instead, she pushed the cart, looking at her feet. Then she looked to the left and saw the shop fronts. She would be opposite the pillory now. On her right would be the pillory. In her mind was what she saw last time. The woman had been hanging there, heart cut out, the blood, the white dress. The eyes had been missing.

She was shaking now too, and she put both hands on the cart, steadying herself. 'It's all right, Lindsay,' she said. 'It's all right. We just turn, we take a quick look. There'll be nothing there. It'll be just the pillory. We'll get our brush, and we'll sweep.' Slowly Lindsay turned her head and looked.

The figure there wasn't the same. A more petite woman had the same things done to her. The hair was different, the overall body size was different, but it had happened again. Someone had killed a witch and left her in the pillory. Lindsay put her eyes straight back down to her feet for a moment. Was she seeing things? Was she? She glanced back up. No, the shape was different. This was a different woman, but she was just as dead.

Lindsay turned and ran as hard as she could back up the street, screaming all the way.

Chapter 20

It took Siobhan a few days to set herself up in a small flat near to her own house. It was anything but salubrious, yet she could operate out of it and the rumour that she had disappeared from her own house would be true. Siobhan had discussed with Julian about keeping Kylie safe and though she was going to live at Siobhan's house, Julian would monitor the place. Until this was over, Siobhan was worried that Kylie could still be a target. After all, she had evidence.

Siobhan was now going off to become a rogue agent, or at least pretend to be one. She had gathered much of the tools of her trade and moved them into the new flat. She would wait a few days, bide her time, and then she would make a move on Eileen Quigley. Siobhan needed to appear as a player, an actual player. Not someone with a lot of collateral behind her, but someone with the ability to take charge, the ability to be part of the coven. She had seen how Lorraine Campbell had operated. That was the type of person who was required and that was what Siobhan needed to do: make herself appear to be one of those people.

Julian, meanwhile, had been spreading the story about Siobhan going rogue. He'd even included some of the previous details about the Russian mobsters and Siobhan's involvement, though never confirmed, in making that deal happen. The deal that went sour.

It was a complete fabrication, and in fact, Siobhan had tidied up the previous incident, allowing many to be brought to justice. But Julian could tell a good story. He had, after all, covered up most of what had happened last time. Siobhan was also glad of him being involved, for she felt like she had backup. This had developed from being a simple murder, in as much as any murders were ever simple, and developed into a much more expansive operation. At some point, she might have to hand it over to Julian, but he could see for now that she was best placed to be a part of this.

With the coven being involved with many of the players in the paramilitaries, Julian didn't like the idea of his operatives, or those that worked with him, being the ones to make contact. It was too easy to get known, to be spotted. Siobhan was different.

Julian had found out Eileen Quigley's address, which was a rather large house on the Holywood Road. Quigley was a socialite, generously giving to charities, with a fortune made in unknown fashion. She wasn't ridiculously wealthy, but she had more than enough money, apparently.

The previous day, Siobhan and Julian had scanned the house quickly, noting that it had a few security guards around it. There were at least two, but there could have been more who didn't come out of the house. If she was being careful, whilst being protected, she didn't want to give the idea that she had so much money that she could afford massive security. She wouldn't be able to justify where it came from. Quigley had a long list of husbands who had died over the years, which

Julian found highly suspicious.

Siobhan decided the best way to get her attention, though, was to make a statement entrance. She wouldn't sneak up to her on the sly. She would be there, right in the woman's face, announcing her attention to be part of whatever action Eileen Quigley was involved in. The Service knew Quigley was involved in something. Quigley would know they knew that, so an operative going rogue and trying to come in and take part in that action wouldn't look suspicious. At least, not too suspicious.

Declan turned up just after midnight, picking up Siobhan from outside the flat. Siobhan wore a large coat that covered up the black outfit that she wore underneath. She had a balaclava in her pocket, and a small rucksack that contained a gun with drugged darts. She had several lock picks, ways to incapacitate systems and run the odd bypass, but she doubted that the major system would be activated.

There was a difficulty when you had security guards patrolling. There would be cameras, however, and she would be sure to take them out. To do so, she'd have to hurry, in case there was somebody sat watching them the whole time.

Declan was in a buoyant mood as he drove up the Bangor Road towards Belfast. The house was located just outside Holywood and had a front facing onto the main road. They would route in behind, and Siobhan would approach through the gardens of at least three other houses.

'You ready for this, Mrs D?' asked Declan.

Was he going to give her a pep talk or something? 'Completely prepared, Declan.'

'Good,' he said, 'because you're the professional here.'

This was his new watchword, the professional. He'd also

described himself as rising above the level of a YouTube addict. Declan was hilarious, but he learned. He wasn't as headstrong as Kylie, and he listened, but he always had the banter to act as if he knew more than he did.

Taking the back roads, Declan dropped Siobhan off under a couple of trees by the roadside. She'd picked the spot the previous night. Leaving her coat in the car, she stepped out completely in black, with her balaclava on. In an instant, she'd disappeared over a fence, and into the gardens of a house. As Declan drove off, she sat for a moment, running through what she was about to do.

The night was frosty, extremely cold, but she wore gloves that were tight to her fingers. Despite that, the chill was getting through. She couldn't wrap up too warm, because she needed to move quickly. With the small rucksack around her back, she stole through the foliage on what was also a calm night. She could hear the occasional crunch of her feet moving over the frosted ground, and stepped out and ran across the grass instead.

She scanned the building for any security lights, keeping well away from them. The joy about these houses was that they had such extensive gardens. There was plenty of room to linger in. Siobhan stole across the three gardens that led through to the house of Eileen Quigley. Once at the fence that surrounded Eileen Quigley's, she stopped, took out the backpack, and removed the small gun that fired the drug darts. She'd need to be reasonably close, and the darts would act pretty fast. She needed to be watchful in case she missed or if they didn't take effect quickly enough. You could always knock them out and let the drug do its work.

As she crouched in the foliage at the corner of the next-door neighbour's garden, Siobhan thought back to those days in Russia. She had leapt through a few embassies. Now they were fun. Less gizmos in those days, less automatic lights, more people operating them manually. Reconnaissance was all about not being seen.

Siobhan climbed the fence surrounding Eileen Quigley's. It wasn't electric, nor did it have any security on it, other than being reasonably high. Quigley was in a dilemma. You couldn't make your house look like Fort Knox. It would give away how you had either incredible amounts of money or something important inside. It was like when she went to the estates; they were people at the bottom end of the rung. The fact they had money from their various activities was hidden from day-to-day view. But when you approached, people in other houses knew you were coming. They had their own network of security; they knew you would be there. Quigley, however, was living in a classy part of the province, and even though she had security guards, they were rarely in view.

Siobhan landed in the grass on the other side, stole around behind a small sculpture, watching, looking for the security lights on the house. One came on, as a man walked out. Siobhan could see that there was a weapon concealed at his hip, and she saw the camera on the house looking down. The man was in full view of it. There was no way she would take him out at this time.

She stole further round, keeping her distance from the house as a whole. Her access would be through the rear door. That was the one they came in and out of. She could see the camera pointed at it. The door wouldn't be open. Rather, she'd have to have an electrical fault occur with the camera, and then someone would be sent. That was when she would make her move.

While the guard was outside, she carefully stole over and took a pair of pliers out from her bag. The camera was just over Siobhan's full height. She ran up towards it, jumped, pushed one foot on the wall, throwing herself up higher than her full height. Reaching up, she cut the wire running into the back of the camera with one go. As she dropped back to the ground, she ran away from the house, behind the bush sitting in the middle of the lawn.

She peered out from it, and watched as the man, who'd been outside the house, came round. He had only taken twenty seconds to respond to the outage, so someone was watching the cameras. As he walked up towards the camera, and before he could reach in and make a report on the radio clipped to his collar, Siobhan fired a dart into the side of his neck. He reached up, and then he collapsed.

Siobhan stole forward, putting herself up against the wall, so no one could see. She heard the automatic lock on the rear door activate and knew someone would come soon. She took a dart out of the gun, placing it into her own hand. Ten seconds later, a guard stepped out, and before he could even see his colleague, a dart was driven into his neck by Siobhan.

The man fell to the ground, and Siobhan put her foot in the door, stopping it from closing. She slipped through quickly and heard the lock reactivating. This would be important, but she wouldn't have long before she would need to move. Whoever was on the cameras, watching outside, would only have a finite amount of time before they would panic that something was truly up. Siobhan would quickly need to find where they were and incapacitate them.

She took another dart out of her backpack and hurried

through the kitchen. There was a large corridor, and she saw a door leading off to the left. Given the geometry of the house, it seemed a strange place for a room. There would be no outside window, no windows on any side. Siobhan bent down to see a lock beneath the door handle. The door could be locked.

She peered inside, and saw coloured lights. This would be it. She stood up, composed herself for a moment, turned the door handle, and, opening the door, stepped in quickly. A man was watching screens, and had just started talking into a radio, asking for a report. He never finished his sentence, turning his head as a dart was placed into his neck. By the time he saw Siobhan, he'd crumpled in the chair.

Siobhan closed the door of the room and listened intently. Three men. She wouldn't have any more. Not many more, anyway. Too risky. Too much, as well. She had to be subtle with her protection. Not too subtle, though, she noted, realising that the man, now slumped in the chair, was armed.

Siobhan tore through the rather large house, finding stairs that led upwards. Quigley would be in her bedroom. After all, it was now two in the morning. As Siobhan stole along the upper floor, she could hear sounds. Someone was enjoying themselves. More accurately, two people were enjoying themselves. This would be interesting.

Siobhan loaded up a dart into the gun, listening intently and following the sounds of vigorous exercise. The moments of pleasure. In all her years, she'd always realised that these were the times people were truly off guard. It was difficult to not lose yourself in a moment like that. Whoever you were, it was when people were at their most defenceless, as they indulged themselves in somebody else.

As Siobhan arrived at the door that the activity was taking place behind, she prepped the gun. Slowly, she opened the door and saw that the room had a light on. It was casting a dim glow across the bed. A young man was upright, covered from the hips down by the bedclothes, but his bare back rippled. His arms were placed in front of him, clearly in the act of lovemaking. There was a woman there too, but Siobhan couldn't see her from the current angle.

She aimed the gun and fired, the dart hitting the man in the back of the neck. He continued vigorously for a moment, then swayed before falling forward. Siobhan was impressed by how the woman extricated herself out from underneath him quickly, and rolled over in the bed, taking a gun off a bedside cabinet.

Siobhan strolled in, hands in the air, with a wide grin.

'Eileen Quigley. You might have heard of me. My name's Siobhan Duffy. I've come home and I'm not getting the due reward that I was promised. It's about time I got myself a little cash. I was hoping you could help me. I hear you're quite the entrepreneur.'

The woman in front of her was at least as old as Siobhan, and her auburn hair, for all that it rolled down onto her shoulders, was looking thin. With the gun pointing at Siobhan, Eileen Quigley was not ashamed of her nakedness, and calmly stepped out of the bed, coming closer.

'I could shoot you dead,' said Eileen. 'You could have just sent a note. You could have just asked to go out for coffee.'

'But you've not met me,' said Siobhan, 'and I haven't met you. I could help you with your security arrangements.'

'And I could just put a bullet in you and hand you back to the Service, but why wouldn't I do that?'

'Because you've heard rumours they're on to you. You've heard rumours they know things. Somebody has been speaking. I understand how the Service works. I know how they play the game. You could do with someone like me. I could do with the money. Five, ten years. Then I will happily sod off somewhere hot with someone like him,' said Siobhan, pointing to the man in the bed, 'and spend the rest of my life enjoying myself. Gave too much for this country and they shafted me. Time for me to return the compliment.'

'Tomorrow, eleven o'clock,' said Quigley. 'I'll pick you up in front of the city hall. We'll talk more then.' Quigley put the gun down, placing it behind her on the small bedroom cabinet. Close enough to use if necessary, but showing trust to Siobhan.

'And I shall leave your establishment. Sorry to barge into your home, but I do like to make an entrance.'

As Siobhan turned to walk away, Quigley shouted after her. 'The drug in the dart, how long does it last for?'

'Two, three hours,' said Siobhan. She heard Quigley swear as Siobhan stepped back out onto the landing of the house. At least she wouldn't forget Siobhan's entrance.

Chapter 21

Siobhan stood in front of the City Hall in Belfast, watching the traffic racing past. It was always busy along this road and the building behind her was iconic. From having flags flown that were debated to the bitter end, to the winter market that lit the place up and showed a better side of Belfast, the building formed a central feature of the city. She remembered being on one of those large Ferris-type wheels at the far end of the City Hall, and she had seen Belfast Lough, and even towards Lough Neagh.

There was something about standing here waiting that reminded her of Belfast in a worse time. She remembered people going shopping and having to go through checkpoints at the end of the street, walking into shops with their bags being scanned. Not anymore. Belfast was open. Belfast was, she wanted to say, free, but the word free had such connotations in this wee country where you learnt to choose your words carefully.

All these things had sent her away. Oh yes, her husband had remained at home. He'd made his fortune by replacing the glass in the buildings that had been bombed. In some ways, she had the troubles to thank for the fortune that she had in the bank. That was a fortune she would have gladly given up.

When she'd gone off to work as an agent, to be an operative for the Service in foreign countries, she'd had to learn about the politics there. It meant she could throw away the politics here. People always talked about which side of the divide you sat on in Northern Ireland. Were you Protestant? Were you Catholic? Loyalist? Republican?

There always was another group of people, she had long thought—those who wished they'd all just take those politics and throw them away. If they had problems with each other, take it to an enormous field and shoot it out. Then, when you were done, come back in and see if you could actually get this place to work with the rest of us.

She'd been driven out, she thought, driven out by this land claim, this so-called history. Like anywhere in the world, history governed a lot of what happened in Northern Ireland. It was interwoven with criminal activity, one-upmanship, and the everyday struggle to just get on in the world. In her heart, she loved the place and yet she also wept for it.

When you saw somewhere that you loved struggle and tear itself apart, you naturally built up all the good bits. In Northern Ireland, there were plenty of good bits. Not just the scenery, not just the areas, but the people, too. They could be so warm, and yet the country had seen some of the most horrific acts committed by humanity on itself. The world was a crazy place. Sometimes she wondered if back home here was as crazy as any of the rest of it. Maybe every country just had its own flavour of craziness.

Siobhan was feeling good though, regarding this investigation. She stood in a long black leather coat that went down to her knees. She had boots underneath, a skirt that was business-like, and she wore her favourite jumper on top. Most importantly, she would have to act like someone who knew what she was doing. She thought for a moment. *Act. I know what I'm doing.* She'd seen enough over her years to be a player, to understand how a player should look. She'd have to not antagonise Quigley, but let Quigley know who she was.

Siobhan was also carrying a gun. She kept her weapons particularly secret. The darts that drugged were no big deal, for they weren't intended to kill. The small handgun concealed inside her coat was deadly. While she didn't intend to use it, having it there for effect in case she needed to show it was all important.

A black BMW had pulled up at the curb in front of Siobhan, with blackened windows. One was rolled down to reveal Eileen Quigley's rather serious-looking face.

'Won't you get in, Mrs Duffy? I think it's time we had a proper chat.'

Siobhan opened the door and climbed into the rear seat. Beside her, Eileen Quigley was dressed in a smart business suit over an immaculate blouse. She had a very impressive figure and sat with her hands together on her lap, staring at Siobhan. There was a glass screen through to the driver and front passenger seats where two men sat. The one driving didn't look round, but the other did and then got a nod from Quigley. He faced the front.

'They can't hear us. I have this soundproofed. They're good boys, but you have to take precautions, and they don't need to know all the things I know. Welcome, Mrs Duffy, or shall I call you Siobhan?'

'I apologise for barging in on your activity last night. He was quite cute though, wasn't he?'

'I wondered when you would come,' said Eileen. 'He'd been there for the last three nights. You put the word out, which was good. I'd hate to have shot you before our relationship began.'

'Well, we know how to do things in the Service. We get taught well. However, they are after you.'

'I had heard rumours. Are you aware of my operations?'

'I know that you've got fingers in many pies.'

'One of the things about Northern Ireland,' said Quigley. 'Of course, I'm talking to a local. Our wee country here, I've always thought it had tremendous potential, but it was divided. The political process tried to bring them together. Of course, what it did was instead of having the Brits now make all the decisions or even the Irish involved too, we now have to work with each other. That's not going so good, is it?'

Siobhan gave a grin. Quigley was really stating the obvious.

'There's always been coercion and money being made,' said Quigley, 'and I thought maybe I should make it. I belong to a rather forward-looking group of ladies. You see, you can't leave the men to it. They are good at certain things, but to really see what could be done, you need a woman. Somebody once told me that a woman could be much more ruthless than a man can ever be. If you threaten a man's children, he'll ward you off. He may even inflict violence on you to keep you away. Unless you actually go to kill them, he's unlikely to kill you. There are the odd exceptions, of course, but they're delusional, unstable.

'A perfectly stable woman, if you threaten her kids, will react with savagery. She will stop you, put you in the ground, and then she'll turn and act normally to her children. She'll carry on acting normally. It's like a switch where we know what needs to be done. We can trigger the worst part, they say, of us—or possibly the best part, I've come to believe. You seem to trigger it too, from the stories I've heard.'

'We can't let the men have all the fun,' said Siobhan. Quigley tapped the partition between the driver and herself, and the car headed out into the various residential areas around Belfast. Some of those they drove through would be called ghettos to a degree, the police not venturing deep into them. Others looked like normal estates. As she looked around her, Siobhan saw everybody going about their daily business.

'I control all of this,' said Quigley. 'There's a group of us who operate together. Well, I'm at the head. You see, I've found that I don't need to be there for everything. You'd probably say I have my generals. I call them sisters. Are you aware of the witch trials that used to happen?'

'I've read some stories. I'm not that well-informed.'

'People get very suspicious about the past. Some think that it controls us. Rather, we let it control us. You can see that with the Protestant and Catholic heritages. Fantastic what people will do in the name of a land that they can never truly own.'

'People have died for that belief here,' said Siobhan.

'Sad really, isn't it?' said Quigley. 'Above all, most people want to have something and to exist. I've put a sort of cohesion on everything. If people work with me, and for me, they get a lot of what they want. People's aspirations are different. Some men that control these estates want money, want to feel they have power. That's fine. I can let them feel that, as long as they know who's in charge. They get their posh cars; they let everybody know that they're one step higher up the rank.

'Some people below couldn't care less because their kids are getting an education. They do things for me, they talk to me about stuff, and I'm able to make the money off the top, able to run the place. Even some people in the government will help me with that. Of course, nobody knows who's helping who. Nobody knows who's with me and who isn't. It's always good to keep people on their toes, but there is the rumour of the witchcraft,' said Eileen, smiling.

The car headed out towards Greenisland, eventually pulling over at the coast, giving Siobhan a glorious view of the water that she could see from her home. This was from a slightly different angle.

'Around here, witchcraft took place back in the day. I don't know what you know about witchcraft. I think it's more to do with the mind than any deals with the devil. The devil's not real to me, but it's real to a lot of other people. It's all to do with the ceremony, the show, the parade. People must get in their head that things occur, and some of my sisters believe deeply in it. You're not a woman who would, which is why I'm telling you this, but you understand the power of control that could come from it.

'The thing about you, Mrs Duffy,' said Quigley, 'I understand what you want, to make some money, then to clear off. Maybe from here, set yourself up. You want to come back out of it. You've no desire to control. Don't have that hunger for power. That's good. I want to be in control, so you not having that works well between the two of us. You want the money. Excellent. I can give you the money. And I want someone I can trust to oversee what's going on from a distance, not out in the field. I see you have that experience, and if necessary, you may have to reach out, but I think you'd be better at controlling the sisters.

'You could oversee the operation, understand what's going on, tell me when the Service is leaking in. You know how they operate; know how they break groups up. It's important I have somebody from that side of things. I have no experience with you, your team, the way you operate. I understand you tried to deal with the Russian mobsters last time, and they wouldn't let you. You hung them out to dry. Excellent. I was impressed by that. Now I understand fully what went on. I have watched you, and it will be a slow build for our partnership. Be assured, I am in charge, and I'll tell you what I want from you . . . tell you how my operations work. I take a far-off view, let people get on with it.

'Look after things, make me profitable, and make the business work well, and I'll happily keep feeding you the money. Don't cause me to come after you. There'll be certain things you'll have to do, certain ways in. That's to be expected.

'At the moment, let's say we're not sisters. We're more enterprising business partners, looking to learn more about each other. One thing you'll have to do is to get on board with the idea of the witches in our coven. You'll have to become part of the show. That's all right. I've got someone in mind, and I still got space for you afterward. I've had some recent losses.'

'I heard about the deaths at the pillory in Carrickfergus,' said Siobhan. 'Certainly, showing people who did it, even if they didn't understand why.'

'Very bloody, but it buys into the whole witchcraft thing. People go along with it. You'll have to become familiar with it. You'll have to become familiar with what they fear. Learn to use it. But I think, given your expertise, I'd like you on board. You've also got a gun on you, haven't you?' Siobhan smiled. 'Of course, you have. You know who you're dealing with, don't you?'

'I think I'm well aware,' said Siobhan. 'I'm here for the money, here to make things go with as minimal fuss as possible, get done what you need me to do, and then I will get out. Unlike yourself, I won't be sitting in a house with some young lad on top of me entertaining me. I'll go to a beach somewhere nice and hot and have him entertain me for the rest of my days.'

'Good,' said Eileen, and tapped the partition between the driver and herself. A little window opened up in it.

'I think I'll go for some lunch. Private though. Mrs Duffy will join me.'

'Thank you kindly,' said Siobhan.

'It'll be a working lunch. I'll take you through some things, get you started. You probably don't realise how much there will be to learn, how much there will be to engage in, but you'll get there. Like I said, this is the start of us learning about each other in this business. Welcome on board.' Eileen Quigley held out her hand. Siobhan took it and shook.

'Here's to a beautiful partnership,' said Siobhan.

'Indeed,' said Eileen. 'A slow-burning one that will hopefully turn into a large flame.'

Siobhan stared into Quigley's eyes. Everything had been smooth, but everything had been smooth with Kylie as well. Siobhan believed Quigley was far from trusting her and the time to earn her respect was only just beginning.

Chapter 22

Siobhan felt like she hadn't seen Declan and Kylie for the last two weeks. Every day she'd been in Belfast taking instruction, often from Eileen Quigley directly, about her organisation. Declan was busying himself with the garden and generally looking after the house. Siobhan checked in regularly, usually via Julian, who would pop by every day to make sure Kylie was okay. Siobhan knew he was doing more than that and a watch was being kept on the house for her, but she didn't let her employees know.

Living in her nearby flat, Siobhan would walk past the house every evening, something that Julian noted to her in one of their daily phone calls. Siobhan would sit down every evening, typing out exactly what had happened that day. Quigley had an extensive network. Siobhan was far from sure of the full extent, and she was convinced that she didn't have all the information, but things were certainly progressing well.

At the end of the second week, Siobhan was being shown around by other people, Lorraine Campbell being one of them. She followed her out to meet with some paramilitary leaders, although they weren't introduced as such. They were more people who owned certain estates or business gentlemen.

Siobhan saw them as hoodlums, people extorting money and using racketeering. All names changed, even though activities didn't.

It was at the end of the second week that Siobhan was told she needed to drive out towards Greenisland in the early hours of the morning. That evening, she called Julian.

'They're going to induct me,' said Siobhan. 'I got measured for a suit the other day, but the measurements they were taking weren't right. There were other measurements involved. I think Quigley's playing things close to her chest. She's not sure how I'm going to react to all the witch shenanigans. I think she's just being cautious in case I react against it.'

'You know what happened last time Kylie went up for that? They tried to kill her. Do you want cover?'

'Totally,' said Siobhan. 'But nobody within the Service.'

'Why?' asked Julian.

'Because she knows the Service is looking into her. Somebody in the Service is talking to her. I don't know how or why.'

'I've thought as much,' said Julian. 'That's why you're off the radar.' Siobhan laughed down the phone. 'I guessed that. Why are you using me? Why are you working with me when you could have just taken this entire investigation over? I thought for a moment it was because you liked me, but . . .'

'You know the Service comes first and I'm sorting that out. In case you hadn't noticed, I'm quite into you as well,' said Julian, and then he laughed. 'Into you enough to come and watch you do some rather fun dancing tonight.'

It suddenly hit Siobhan what she was looking forward to. She'd have to do this dance and Julian would be watching. Siobhan wasn't a prude, but neither was she a show-off. The idea she'd have to do this dancing bothered her a bit, but it was for the job and it needed done. While she was dancing around with a load of other women in the altogether, it didn't seem that bad. Knowing that Julian was watching, however, changed things. It could have been worse, though. Could have been Declan watching.

'I hope you're going to maintain a professional attitude while I'm doing this,' said Siobhan.

'I'm thoroughly professional. Do you want me to record it?'

'I don't think that's necessary. We don't need to clock faces anymore.'

'I just thought it was maybe key evidence that could be brought up later,' mused Julian.

'I thought you'd prefer a more private dance at some point.'

There was a sudden silence on the other end of the phone, and then Julian laughed a little. 'Stop teasing me with this!'

'Who's teasing?' said Siobhan.

She didn't know what was coming over her, or maybe she did. She'd been talking to Eileen Quigley about her dream of being on a beach and having young guys look after her. Quigley, it seemed, had a reasonable sexual appetite, and seemed to like well-honed younger men, but that wasn't Siobhan. She said it to Quigley to have a point of commonality, but in truth, she wanted more than just a body to be with.

Siobhan wanted a guy who stimulated her mind as much as her body. Julian did that. Julian could talk all day to her. She could sit with him and not be bothered about what they talked about. He seemed to enjoy her company, too. Always had. He was erudite, clever, but he could challenge her.

That was the thing about Julian. Declan and Kylie, Siobhan could ride over if she wanted to. She could knock them out of the way. Not Julian. Julian knew how Siobhan worked, or at least he seemed to. Turning fifty, she didn't have time to mess around. She knew that. She'd pondered over the last week about Julian. What was the point hanging back? Did she wait until he was sixty-five, and out of the Service? Had his pension and no longer had complications?

She could be dead by sixty-five. After all, nobody knew. She was getting to the point of life where you felt different. As a young person, you never thought about death. You never thought about time running out. She was fifty. There were plenty of years ahead, but there probably were fewer years than there were behind. Not so much to terrify her. Not so much to give her relief that this body wouldn't have to go on much longer, either.

Siobhan intended to have fun over the next twenty or thirty years. Absolutely. But that was the point. She wanted to have fun with someone who really got her. Someone she really wanted.

'Two in the morning,' she said suddenly. 'I expect you to be there watching. It'll probably help me dance better.'

Siobhan put the phone down, feeling rather cheeky when she thought about how Julian would react on the other end. She hoped he was putting on that little grin he had.

That evening, Siobhan drove up to Belfast and ate out late. It was about ten o'clock by the time she left the restaurant she was eating in. She drove off to a bar, waiting. It was good sometimes to get out somewhere with a lot of noise so you could think, everything else happening around you. It was one o'clock by the time she left the bar, having not touched a single drop of alcohol. She had impressed herself. Instead, she'd gone for the alcohol-free varieties, going to the toilet before she left. After all, it would be cold. Embarrassing to have to interrupt a ritual like this just because she needed to disappear behind a bush.

Siobhan arrived at the ritual site, the hidden field with the large hollow, around about a quarter to two. There was no one else there. Ten to two, another car arrived, pulling up beside her, and she recognised Lorraine Campbell.

She came over to Siobhan's car, opening the door and said to her, 'I need you to put something on and I need you to understand what we're going to do.'

Lorraine stepped inside Siobhan's car, sitting beside her, and detailed the ceremony that Siobhan had already witnessed. Siobhan tried to show an element of shock when she was told she would have to dance naked, but in truth she'd been prepping herself for most of the day. Lorraine Campbell left her and Siobhan changed within the car into the witch's outfit. She noticed how easily it slipped off, but was glad of the surrounding cloak, keeping her warm within the car. It would be even colder when she stepped out.

There was a tap on the window of her door, and Eileen Quigley looked in. Siobhan opened the door and stepped out.

'Yourself and twelve of us,' said Eileen. 'This is you becoming part of the coven. Many of the sisters here take this very seriously. Do what they ask. Perform it well. Be part of us. As I said before, the show matters. Some here actually believe that the devil gives his blessing. I don't judge them for it, but I use them,' said Quigley, without a smile. 'Now come on, let's get this business done and we can get you home and warmed up again. I'm sure you'll be happy to get into your bed tonight. I know I will.'

'You got someone waiting?' asked Siobhan.

Quigley smiled. 'Always. What's the point of all this power and wealth if you can't enjoy it?'

Quigley led Siobhan out into the field, and she was shown where to go. Quigley told her to dance like the others. There was no formalisation to it, but you had to give yourself an abandon.

A brazier was placed in the middle of the field and set fire to, and soon Siobhan found herself dropping her clothing and dancing along with the rest. She imagined Julian watching and tried to throw herself into an abandon as if she was merely in her bedroom with him. The cold air made it feel somewhat different.

Five minutes later when she was putting the cloak back on, Siobhan was grateful, wrapping her arms around herself as every extremity felt frozen. *These people must be insane*, she thought, '*if they actually think that this does something. Surely nothing could be so evil to demand dancing on a night like this.*

As she returned to the car, Quigley called over to her, asking her to step inside her own car. It was unusual to see her in the front seat of a car, and Siobhan stepped into the passenger seat. The car was rather sporty. Quigley said it was an indulgence, but one that she felt she deserved.

'Now listen,' said Quigley. 'You're just beginning on this journey. You've seen the lie of the land, but you haven't seen the detail of what happens underneath. You've seen some of the extent of what I'm into. Tomorrow, I will take you to a place that is key to our operations. It's known only to the sisters here. No one else knows about it. No one else ever will. Giving away information about what is inside of it, or indeed where it is, means instant death. There'll be no questions. There'll be no investigations. The slightest suspicion will end up in your death.'

'It's your secret files, your storage cabinet. It's that bit in the office that the employees are not allowed to look into,' said Siobhan. 'I get it.'

'Good,' said Eileen. 'I was impressed tonight. You didn't hang back. You danced with them. Freezing it is. Absolutely freezing. I'm going back for a hot soak and then to enjoy myself before getting back to work in the morning. We don't do these things that often, although we've had to do it more often recently. You're part of the coven now. Never speak ill of it.

'If you talk about it to anyone else, talk about it with a sense of fear to them. That even their knowledge of it is something that they should be worried about. Never talk about any of our sisters as being weak. Whenever I speak through one of you, it's as if I speak. It's as if the coven speaks. Many people don't fear me. They fear what I'm involved in. This story of the witches—this story of the darkness, of the control, supernatural control—is important. You may laugh at it in private. I do,' said Eileen suddenly, breaking away from the rather mysterious conversation she was having.

'I laugh out loud sometimes, but I do it to myself and no one else. It's surprising how worried those paramilitary leaders and hoodlums are about the potential consequences I could bring, even from a distance. They actually think that the little doll and the pins might be something. Although that's probably because one of them suffered serious pains after he crossed me once.'

'A fortunate coincidence?' asked Siobhan, raising her eyebrows.

'No, nothing like it. I doctored his drink, and he suffered.

He suffered badly, but he thought he suffered badly because I was sticking needles into him. One of our sisters is a doctor, and understands so much about the body that we can do this type of thing. She's like you; looks at the mystical side of our organisation and laughs at it, but she plays it. She is the one who enables some of the mystery to happen.

'You will be too. I may call on you to visit places. Your powers of reconnaissance and stealth, according to the Service, are quite good. Very good, in fact, even if it has been a while. When you got to me, that showed that you knew what you were about, and I think there's more to come for you. Anyway, tomorrow you'll be taken to where you need to know about.'

Siobhan took a bath that night as well, warming herself up before she got to sleep around about five o'clock. By nine o'clock the next morning, she was in Belfast, dressed up in her long black coat and being picked up by Eileen Quigley's car. Quigley wasn't inside it though, Lorraine Campbell was, and Siobhan sat back as they drove the long distance out to the foot of the Mourne mountains.

They were like the Scottish Highlands squashed in all together down by the sea. A place you could enter in no time at all to see the majesty of mountain life. A wondrous place, but like all of Northern Ireland, condensed. Close to it was Tollymore Forest Park, a place where, as a kid, she'd gone for barbecues, to camp out, to take forest walks.

In the shadow of the Mourne mountains, Siobhan saw an old house. It was large, very large, and while it wasn't dilapidated, it didn't have the look of a modern building. Inside, she thought it would be cold. When the sun came across it in late afternoon, the house cast such a shadow and gave an eerie look. It wasn't worn down in any way; it was just imposing, and Siobhan understood why it was chosen as a place of mystery, the place of the witches, the place of the coven.

Anyone coming near it wouldn't want to enter it. It looked foreboding. She'd arrived there around lunchtime. She was shown the outside of it briefly before Lorraine Campbell had taken her off for a meal. This was an opportunity to run through some of what Lorraine was doing regarding the illicit businesses. By four o'clock, as the sun was setting and the shadows were cast, Siobhan was brought back to the building.

It sat among the browns and the bare trees of winter, with some patches of frost still lingering from the morning in the shadows. As they pulled up in the car, Siobhan could see Eileen Quigley dressed in her robes, the same ones she'd been wearing the night before. Glancing around, Siobhan could see no one, and she walked towards Eileen.

'This is it,' she said to Siobhan, 'the safe at the back of the office. You will have appointed times when you can come here, for not everybody comes at the same time. If you are here outside of those times, you'll die. Only I have access all the time. Do you understand that?'

'I do,' said Siobhan.

'Good. Given where you live, I thought it best if your hours were later in the evening. You may come any time between four and ten. Outside of that, you should not be here.'

'Thank you,' said Siobhan. She took Eileen Quigley's hand as she held it up for her, and together, the two women walked towards the heavy wooden doors that marked the entrance to the house.

Chapter 23

Over the next few days, Siobhan grew into her role. She visited the house near the Mourne Mountains on two different occasions, but each time someone else was always there. The first time, it was Eileen Quigley, and she kept a close eye on Siobhan. Siobhan had access to several things, but everywhere there were locked drawers. They were all old-fashioned, not a digital lock in sight, but you had to have keys to get into them, and Siobhan didn't. With someone always watching her, the one thing she couldn't do was use her lock picks to break into them.

The second time she went, Lorraine Campbell was there. She wasn't sure if it was Lorraine Campbell's time to be there or if Eileen Quigley had just sent her over to keep an eye. Certainly, the element of trust Siobhan wanted to foster wasn't fully there, and Siobhan wondered if she was being monitored. The one thing that was difficult to decide was if someone was there all the time. Was somebody looking out for her?

She dropped by a few times, but there were no cars, and the lights were out. A few other times, she dropped by, and she could see either Eileen Quigley's car or someone else's. To all intents and purposes, the house at the foot of the Mourne's was being used as it should be, the members of the coven entering during their allotted times. This was where the secrets were, though, and Siobhan was determined to get them.

In order to do this, she decided she would have to break in outside of her allotted time for two reasons. One, if she had to escape, but leave things open, she couldn't be accused of opening them herself unless they caught her. Two, if she tried to tamper with the locked drawers during her allocated times, it made her a pretty obvious candidate.

Siobhan wondered why there wasn't more covert surveillance of the house, but she remembered what Eileen Quigley had said. The whole idea of the coven, the whole idea of mentioning witchcraft, was to make people wonder, and think, and believe. If, as she said, several of the coven believed in witchcraft, you couldn't very well mount all these security cameras to protect what was their fortress.

Having been inside, Siobhan had seen various symbols and hexes, not knowing what any of them meant. Eileen Quigley was putting up a terrific masquerade, and it was working too. Combined with her ruthlessness and business-like attitude, she did indeed seem to have control of many of the more nefarious elements, certainly within the Belfast area.

On Siobhan's third visit, she looked around because she was on her own. She stopped herself from opening any of the other drawers. Instead, she focused on the information she'd been advised to read; she sat there dutifully, just in case she had an unseen observer. Her eyes scanned the rooms, looking for secret compartments, places where people could hide. There was certainly no evidence of any covert electronics.

As she left that night, Siobhan put into action a plan that

had been a day in the making. Arriving at her car, she drove off to turn into Tollymore Forest Park, and at the facilities there, she changed, donning her full black outfit. She would reconnoitre the building. She would go in, open everything, and set it back the way it was. The secrets were here, and with her small camera, she would reveal them all.

Siobhan approached the eerie-looking house by the single road that led to it, realising that no one was there. She reversed the car and parked it about a mile away, hidden beneath some trees in a small car park. From her boot, she removed some false number plates, attaching them to the front and rear of the car. She loaded up her small rucksack on her back and headed off across the fields towards the house.

A final check told her that there was still no one else in the house and no cars outside until she crept towards the front door. She had a key to get in, but rather than use it, she took out her lock picks, opening up the three locks of the door. It took her less than a minute because they weren't that advanced. She then stole inside, locking the door behind her again. If anyone was going to intrude on her, she wanted to hear them opening the door. Siobhan crept into the entrance hall, ignoring it, and the various pictures of former coven members that hung along the wall. Instead, she made for what had been described as Eileen Quigley's private office. Surely, some of the greatest secrets would be in there. Secrets that were less operational, more discreet, information and actions that you wouldn't want anyone to find out about.

The office, set to the eastern side of the house, had a frosted glass pane on its door. There was a single lock, and Siobhan checked around the entire doorframe in case there was an electrical trip. There was none, and she quickly opened the door with her lock picks. It was wooden, and as she swung it back, it made a creaking sound, freezing her to the spot. She could hear nothing else, though.

She closed the door and re-locked it. If anyone else came in, they wouldn't come in here unless they were Eileen Quigley. She turned around and took a torch out of her rucksack, and began shining it around the room. Siobhan hadn't been in here yet. She'd only been told what it was. There was a large desk with an impressive leather chair behind it. Various esoteric symbols were located around the room. The whole place spoke of witchcraft, and yet, there were some obvious and modern filing cabinets. Siobhan went up to the first one, saw a lock at the top of it, and picked it. Just as she'd opened it, she heard a sound.

She switched off her torch and dropped to the floor. She listened closely and could hear footsteps. Slowly, she crept towards the door and tried to peer through the frosted glass. She nearly tumbled backwards as an apparition, a ghostly white figure, seemed to cruise the hallway outside. Siobhan froze. What was that?

Eileen Quigley had always said there was nothing of the supernatural about the coven or the place. Siobhan was banking on it because, at the moment, her eyes had her doubting. After repicking the lock, she reached for the handle of the door, turning it slowly, and then pulled the door back.

Outside, she saw what looked like skeletal white hands, a floating gown. As she looked up, she saw some hair. It was white and attached to…, a skull? Siobhan looked more closely.

There was indeed an apparition outside, but it wasn't a supernatural one. It was being projected from somewhere. Siobhan must have triggered something. Maybe this was there for the more superstitious of the coven. To have got this far inside you would have had to have broken in like she had. If you were worried about those sorts of people, you'd have put more dangerous traps to overcome, but this door wasn't meant to be opened. Siobhan had set off the trap somehow, but she reckoned it must have been from inside, not outside.

She turned, looking past the filing cabinet, and saw a wire running out of the back of it. So, it was the filing cabinet that did it. She turned back to the lock at the top of it, quickly used her picks and closed it. The apparition vanished.

Simple but effective, she thought. *Any of the witches that believe would be scared witless by that.* Siobhan undid the lock again, and the apparition reappeared outside. She pulled back on the cabinet files and pulled one out. It had the name of A McGinley and below detailed in code. Siobhan thought they must have been operations concerning the man. She could break the code. It would take time, but better if she handed the code over to Julian and his cohorts.

Siobhan went to take her small camera out, but then she heard another sound. There was a clip, footsteps from the outer hall, the one you came into just as you entered through the front door. Siobhan stood up, put the file back, closed the cabinet, quickly worked her lock picks and switched off the apparition. She then hunkered down behind the desk.

Someone was walking around and she wondered who. Siobhan caught her breath as the clipping of the feet came closer to her. A voice spoke, and she recognised it as the sharp tones of Eileen Quigley.

'Do your walk around and meet me back here. Remember, if she turns up, don't give the game away.'

Siobhan's heart thumped. This was a test. This was her

being examined. They told her to go nowhere else, not to be in the building, and yet there she was. If they saw her now, it would be over and she wouldn't have any of the concrete evidence. What would she have to tell people? The Service might believe her, but even they needed some sort of information to go on. They would have to justify why they would bring Eileen Quigley down.

As long as she doesn't come in here, thought Siobhan, *I can wait it out. I can hide all night if I have to. It's not a problem. No one's going to miss me until morning.*

As Siobhan hunkered close to the door, she heard a key turning. Without hesitation, she sprinted round to the back of the desk and worked her way underneath it, pulling her feet in close. She was trapped. Trapped because somebody was coming through the door and it had to be Eileen Quigley, it couldn't be anyone else. Surely only she had a key for her own office.

A light went on in the room, causing Siobhan to blink, but she didn't flinch, staying completely quiet. She heard Eileen's footsteps walking round the desk. Siobhan wondered if Eileen could see her hidden deep within the well of the desk. She moved as close as she could to be, as far away from the chair at the entrance to the well. The chair moved back and then the feet stopped. She was going to sit down.

Siobhan saw Eileen Quigley's feet move in front of the chair and then the woman sat on it. Siobhan had to spread herself up against the inside of the well of the table and as Eileen's feet came through, she found herself in the most awkward of positions.

Just hold it, she said, *just hold it. Maybe she'll move again soon.'* Siobhan kept telling herself this. Eileen would move soon; Eileen would move soon, but by the time she'd got to the twentieth minute of saying this, she was feeling sore. Her concentration lapsing twice, she nearly dropped an arm and touched Eileen.

The woman was writing something on the desk and eventually slid back out from under it. She walked over to the filing cabinet Siobhan had been at earlier and Siobhan saw her reach behind. She must have flicked a switch or something because when Eileen undid the lock and opened it, no apparition appeared outside. Carefully, Siobhan crept forward, peering out from behind the well. Eileen had her back to her.

Siobhan looked along the floor. The door was open; it was ajar. Slowly Siobhan crept out from under the well as quietly as she could, stepping ever so lightly. She got over to the open door and snuck through, heading along the hallway towards the front door of the building. As she did so, she heard footsteps around the corner in that hall and flung herself into a small alcove. Seconds later, she saw the hair of Lorraine Campbell walk past her, but the woman hadn't spotted her.

Siobhan rolled out of the alcove, looked in the hallway, saw no one and made for the front door. She opened it carefully, glanced outside, saw no one, and closed the door behind her. Without hesitation she ran, hurtling over a fence and then dropped, spinning around to watch the house again. She took out her binoculars, the infrared ones, and watched. Eileen Quigley, Lorraine Campbell, and another of the witches left approximately twenty minutes later. They locked up in what seemed a normal fashion and then all drove away.

Should Siobhan go back? Was now a time to look inside again? She decided against it. Clearly, they were testing her. They were there to do a search, to see if anyone was outside of their hours. Just didn't seem normal. You would trust most of the witches in the coven. Siobhan was new, and they knew when she was meant to be there. Were they just checking her outside of hours? Eileen talked about whether someone was there. It must have been Siobhan that she was mentioning.

Siobhan went home that night and trembled in the shower. It had been close, too close, but now she understood she was still in a period of being assessed. It was three days later when Eileen Quigley said to her that the house was open full-time for her in the Mourne Mountains. She could come and go as she pleased. Evidently, she'd passed that trial. Siobhan smiled happily at Eileen as she said it, giving the impression that she'd done nothing wrong. Deep inside of her, she felt an unease at how close she'd come to getting caught. She didn't think she'd have done that back in the day.

Chapter 24

The following week, Siobhan was called to the main house in the Mourne Mountains. She wasn't happy about the way the news was delivered, as Lorraine Campbell approached her when she was on a call in Belfast. Eileen Quigley had asked her to speak to a certain leader on an estate, but when she arrived, Lorraine Campbell was sitting in the house instead. She told Siobhan that Quigley expected her in four hours' time at the Mourne Mountains headquarters. There was nothing else said, and Siobhan felt uneasy. She made the trip over, making sure to carry her firearm with her; on the way, she called Julian.

'Unexpected though, isn't it?' said Julian. 'Why suddenly? Why now? Unless she's got something afoot. You don't think she could be planning something, getting you to organise it?'

'But why not just call me? Why go through this charade?'

'Has to do with the house though, isn't it? Maybe she doesn't want anybody else in the coven to know. She seems to use Lorraine Campbell quite a lot as a go-between. Maybe she trusts her. Maybe Campbell's the number two.'

'She certainly used Campbell to tail Kylie,' said Siobhan. 'I'm not comfortable with it though.'

'Are you going to go anyway, though?'

'Of course. We've got to follow this through. Too much spade work done now. If things look dodgy, I'll come out. Maybe this could be something else. Maybe it could be a chance to really get in close. I won't know unless I go.'

'No, you won't,' said Julian. 'Absolutely not. Do you want me to be close by?'

'If it's that big, they'll be looking. No, I've got a good feeling about this,' said Siobhan. 'We'll see how it goes. I can handle myself.'

'Are you sure?' asked Julian.

'Yes, she said. Trust me. Besides, I think you owe me.'

'What do you mean?' asked Julian.

'You got to see me dance. I want to take you back to that field and watch you dance someday.'

Julian laughed, but then his voice went serious. 'Make sure you do,' he said. 'All caution on this one. They really are nasty people, really.'

'I am aware,' said Siobhan. 'But I will do.'

Siobhan drove up to the house, this time not in any covert fashion, but parking her car in front of it. It looked foreboding even at this time of day. Using her keys, she unlocked the front door, and stepped into the hallway. She could hear no one, and the whole place had an eerie quiet about it. However, it was clean, always clean. Somebody came in and cleaned this. Nobody ever said 'Hi'. Maybe one of the coven was tasked with this every week. There were ranks within the coven. Certainly, people who were above others. Siobhan was going to be quite high up. At least, that's what she was told. Siobhan trusted nothing that Eileen Quigley said.

She would hold it all in her head and wait to see if it was

true. She heard footsteps coming from beyond the hall and then a head popped around the doors of the hallway. 'Siobhan, you got my message then.'

'I did. You could have just called me.'

'No, I couldn't. I wanted to make sure you were coming, and I wanted to make sure that nobody saw me messaging you about this one. Come in.'

Siobhan walked along, her boots clipping on the hallway's wooden floor. Eileen Quigley, who was once again dressed in her black cloak, marched along to the large room at the end. She opened the door that Siobhan hadn't been allowed to open before. It led upstairs with small wooden stairs that were tight. When she reached the top, a large room was presented. It had oak panelling, several leather chairs, and many desks. They had library lamps, and on the desks, were plans.

'You might think it quite crazy of us to leave this sort of stuff lying around. After all, there's no formal protection here, is there? No one gets access up here except for a few of us. We don't speak of what we have in here, only to me. You don't know who else knows this stuff. It's the plans, it's our schemes, it's who knows what in what we do.

'You will oversee it. You will make sure that there are no cross purposes in what we do, that we aren't exposing ourselves from one side of the operation to the other. If you find an issue, you'll be talking to me about it. It's all written down. That's how I do things. Easy to torch this place. There's a system already here which I can activate. The insurance policy I call it, as I can't go to an insurer's and get a proper one. So, if all comes to nought, I can flick the switch, so to speak, and all the plans, all the evidence goes up in smoke.'

Siobhan was impressed.

'This is it, all in here. You realise that this is me trusting you. You're in fully. Not just doing that silly dance. No, this is you working properly for me now. The rewards will come as well. You'll find tonight there's a significant amount of money in your bank account. Ties you to me, or to one of my offshore holding companies. You work for me, and I will honour you to ten years. After that you can enjoy whatever young sprite you want in the sunshine. I'll leave you alone for a while. Come down and see me when you've gone over the recent material. It'll take quite a while to come up to speed with all of this.'

Eileen Quigley disappeared down the wooden stairs and Siobhan walked around the room looking at all the various information in front of her. It was what she was expected to do. She couldn't possibly memorise all of this, but she could bring a camera in with her and photograph it. She now had everything in front of her, or so Quigley said. This was the point where Siobhan could go to the police.

She could tell them all about it. She could tell them all about the activities that were happening. If they were clever, they could just monitor, make sure the information was correct.

Siobhan didn't feel Quigley was lying to her. They'd set up their trap, and Siobhan had sprung it and then escaped, but nobody had been the wiser she'd been there.

Siobhan wandered between the different tables. Quigley's operations truly covered the province. There were connections into the south as well, some across to the UK mainland. As she read through, Siobhan realised that most of them would be difficult to tie Quigley to. She was so high above it. This whole place would need to be infiltrated. It would need to have all of its information taken, and even then, you'd have to work hard. To go back through all the loops and the code names to find Quigley's orders at the top would be difficult.

This was the only place that anything was written, for she'd seen nothing communicated by paper outside. Quigley was good. She didn't use computers either. There was no tracing Quigley except from her own personal matters and those were not criminal.

Siobhan swept her hair back with her hand. She'd done it. She'd infiltrated, and now she was ready, but something was bugging her. Was it too easy? No, it hadn't been that easy. She'd done well, but Quigley wasn't showing any sign of suspicion. Maybe she was just an excellent card player. Maybe she kept everything close to her chest. Siobhan didn't know. That was the problem—she didn't know.

Kylie had thought everything had been all right with Beyonce. Yes, Kylie didn't have Siobhan's experience. Neither did Beyonce have Quigley's. Siobhan was up against a master, the person who'd orchestrated all of this. She wouldn't trust someone lightly. There'd be something coming.

Siobhan continued her work before traipsing down the stairs and making her way round to Quigley's office. Quigley came out from behind it and locked the door.

'You've seen most of it. Where do you think the weakness is at the moment?'

'You want to watch what we're doing out in Fermanagh. Tyrone too. That seems rather stretched. I've only had a brief run through. The other thing is you haven't given me a key to get up there.'

'No, I haven't. I was wondering to see if you would leave it open.'

'Why?' asked Siobhan.

'You know why I'm checking. I don't take people on board lightly. You need to remember that. So far, everything you've done has checked out well. But I tell you, you cross me, if you take anything from in here, or tell anyone about any of it, especially the upstairs, you die.'

'You've communicated that clearly and frequently,' said Siobhan. 'You need to remember that I come from the Service. We try not to make mistakes. When we do, we're not usually back for a second go. I'm used to operating with this level of intensity. You can trust me with it, or rather you can pay me and I'll come through with you. However you want to do it. The level of trust that you give out is up to yourself. I'm here for the pay packet,' said Siobhan. 'Nothing more, nothing less. I won't be happy until I'm on that beach enjoying the attentions of some young-looking stud.'

'Speaking of young-looking stud, I have one awaiting me soon, so I'm going to go.'

'Key first, please,' said Siobhan.

Quigley reached inside one of her pockets within her cloak and handed Siobhan a key. Siobhan made a point of going over to the wooden stairs, switching the lights off up above and then locking the door. She put the key away in her pocket and accompanied Quigley out to the front door.

'Very good,' said Quigley. 'I hope that fills you with confidence, all that I've shared with you. Work well, and you shall be rewarded.'

Siobhan nodded and made her way to her car. Driving away, she realised Quigley was laying down the law. She was determined to make sure that Siobhan knew who was in charge. Siobhan was never in doubt, though. As she drove off, she placed a call to Julian.

'I just thought I'd let you know I'm okay.'

There was a sigh on the other end of the phone. Relief? How very un-service like.

'Did you find out any more?'

'She's opened it up, Pandora's box. All the secrets are there for me.'

'That's rather simple,' said Julian.

'I know. I'll try to photograph it in the coming weeks, but slowly. Just got a feeling that something's coming. She hasn't tied me to the ground yet. I don't feel she's truly tested me. They may have been making sure I didn't come into that house out of sight, and out of the hours I was allotted. But to hand over the keys to the kingdom, just like that? There's a kicker coming. She'll be checking if I'm passing information on first, so I'm telling you nothing.'

'Quite wise,' said Julian. 'I wouldn't want to accept anything at this time. It's still compromised information until we confirm that you're good within the organisation.'

'Exactly,' said Siobhan. 'What's troubling me is I'm not sure what she's going to have on me, unless somebody's going to come back with something from the Service. My service record is excellent. There's nothing in there, no catch. There's nothing in my service record where I sit and think that I really wished I hadn't had done any of that. Even the two that I killed; they were necessary, incredibly necessary.'

'I know,' said Julian. 'I've checked it throughout. Just sit tight then. Sit tight. I'm pleased to tell you that the blossoming relationship between Declan and Kylie seems to go strong.'

'Why? What's happened?'

'He appears to be staying over.'

'Is he not aware that you're looking after her?'

'What can I say? It seems the Service doesn't let itself be caught that easily.'

Siobhan laughed. 'It's probably good for them to distract themselves at the moment. Otherwise, they'd get heavily involved in this. I'll sit tight, but I'm warning you, the sooner I'm out of this, the better because I'm still waiting for that dance from you.'

'That's why I'm hoping this investigation lasts until the middle of summer. I'm not sure I could be so brave in the cold.'

Siobhan laughed as she closed down the call. Julian made her laugh. He worried about her. He understood so much of her. She couldn't wait for this investigation to be over, either.

Chapter 25

Two days later, Siobhan was summoned to meet Eileen Quigley, but this time it was in a restaurant in Belfast. Siobhan had dressed up neatly with black trousers and a smart leather jacket. Her dirty blonde hair was pulled tight into a ponytail at the rear. She looked businesslike, which was what she wanted to convey. After all, now she was helping to look after a lot of the operation.

She had learnt over the last couple of days so much about how Quigley was operating, how ingenious many of her methods were. She really was the floating hand high above. Various people were working hard for her, some of them committing high levels of extortion and forcing people with the use of guns, knives, or the threat of harm. But there were also issues within banking and other sectors. Her reach was incredible.

So far, Siobhan hadn't been privy to anyone within the political sector, but she was sure they must have been involved as well. It would only be a matter of time before she found out. But as she had discussed with Julian, Siobhan had photographed none of the information. She had been sent off to give the occasional order and to be introduced to various parties, but not as many as she thought. Maybe she was still under surveillance. Maybe she was still not trusted.

The restaurant was not long open, highly modern, and was busy. As Siobhan entered, she found this an unusual place to meet to talk. But she was escorted through to the back, up a small set of stairs and into a private room where Eileen Quigley sat, sipping on a glass of wine in front of a set table.

'I took the liberty of ordering for us. You're not vegetarian, are you?' Siobhan shook her head. Like Quigley didn't know. 'Good, because the beef here's rather good. Sit down, please.'

'I haven't come prepared with anything. Is there anything particular you wanted me for?' asked Siobhan. 'You didn't say.'

'No, I didn't because, well, this will be between you and me. What are you drinking?'

'Just a glass of water,' said Siobhan.

'No, she'll have some of the wine. You might need it after this one.'

A waiter approached and poured Siobhan some wine. Then Eileen gave a nod. Lunch was served before Eileen told everyone to leave the room as Siobhan tucked into her beef, which was indeed excellent. She saw Eileen show a moment's hesitation, but then she spoke up.

'This is really where we come down to see just how much of a partnership we are,' said Eileen. 'To become part of our circle, at some point, and especially up into the ranks that I want you to be in, you have to kill someone.'

Siobhan tried not to show any shock on her face. She wasn't working for nice people. In other parts of the world, loyalty to gangs by causing the death of another was not uncommon. Just because there seemed to be a refinement about this so-called coven didn't make it immune to any of the normal ways and means of operating.

'Who would you like me to kill?' asked Siobhan, trying to hold her voice steady.

Eileen took out a small brown envelope and handed it to Siobhan. Siobhan ran her nail across it, opened up the envelope and then tried not to look horrified. She saw photographs of Declan, Kylie, and herself, all in Siobhan's garden.

'I think you'll find I'm cleverer than you give me credit for.'

'I didn't think I was not giving you credit,' said Siobhan, stoically.

'I wondered who had come for Kylie. Beyonce introduced her. Beyonce said that she'd met her, and Beyonce had fallen for her, wanting her to be part of us. Well, amongst witches, that sort of thing isn't a problem, and we are in a modern age after all. But I was slightly suspicious. Anyway, it turned out that Kylie seemed to have friends.

'I wasn't actually going to kill her if nobody turned up, but then somebody did, firing a gun. I realised then she was working for you. This was your way of getting in. You needed information. You wanted to know who you were joining. That's all quite laudable. I haven't got a problem with that, but I want to know I can trust you, so I need her dead. Firstly because, well, she's seen Lorraine. She's seen Beyonce, and we had to remove Beyonce because of her lack of judgment. I'm sure you can appreciate that.'

'Absolutely,' said Siobhan. 'Kylie shouldn't have got herself into that situation.'

'Lorraine said that somebody must have helped her because she was tailing her easily, and then suddenly she wasn't. But there was no sign of anyone. Put that together with a Service operator suddenly talking to me. Someone who came in and also rescued her.

'That, by the way, was quite audacious. You couldn't have known how that would have gone. You've got other people working for you as well. Declan there. He's incredible. You think he's a gardener. Everybody that's seen him thinks he's an idiot. Oh, and by the way, the two of them have got quite close lately, so it will not hit Declan well if you kill her off. You might want to move him on. I'm not telling you how to deal with your own people. That's up to you.'

'I'll take it under advisement,' said Siobhan. Inside, her heart was pumping. They wanted Kylie dead. If Siobhan was going to keep this going, if Siobhan was going to get to the bottom of it, Kylie would have to die. How did she make Kylie die? How was this going to be a good ending? More to the point, she couldn't bring a complete halt to it. Kylie and Siobhan would be marked targets, as would Declan.

It wasn't like the Service when you were working elsewhere. They didn't just grab you and move you somewhere else. She was out on a limb here. Somebody in the Service must be working with Quigley. To what extent, she wasn't sure. Julian was possibly at risk as well.

'Why do you still trust me?' asked Siobhan. 'Why not just put a bullet in my head? Call it quits. I mean, this seems quite an underhand approach. You might be worried I want to take over.'

'No. I have my contacts in the Service. That's not you. You've never wanted to be on top. You do your work, you're very thorough. Apparently, you haven't got as much money as you thought coming from your husband. He worked in the glass trade. In fact, I think I had several windows repaired by him once. He was good. Was it a sham marriage?'

'Not so much a sham,' said Siobhan, 'more like we realised we weren't really compatible, but hey, we made it work as an arrangement. He was happy with it and I was happy with it.'

'And you still got to play around with that Eamon guy? Any others?'

'No,' said Siobhan.

'I like that. You're under pressure and you tell me the truth. You don't deny any of it.'

'I want the money.'

'That's your roadblock,' said Quigley. 'That young girl's a pity. She's quite pretty, isn't she? I'm sure he'll be devastated. Are you close to her? I've heard that you're close to her.'

'Not so close that she can't be removed from the operation,' said Siobhan.

'Oh, you're closer than that. But I like how you hold yourself. You give nothing away, do you? I said to a certain contact, what was Siobhan Duffy like? How did it go with these Russians? They were very complimentary. Extremely so.'

'I need time to plan it. I can't just make her disappear.'

'You have till the end of the week,' said Quigley. 'Otherwise, we part company. And as we're still within our ten-year tenure, unfortunately, that means a more permanent goodbye for all of you.'

Siobhan wanted to stand up and smack the woman clean in the face. She acted all civilised, yet she was a complete and utter bitch. More than that, she was happy to murder, have others murder. Wanted people to kill friends. She was cold and callous.

Siobhan had seen plenty of people like that come from the

province, but Quigley was one of the best. There were some darn good people where she lived, but there were a lot of others who were as evil as they came.

'You haven't touched your wine,' said Eileen. 'You really should. Guess your appetite may have gone. No, don't waste that beef. It is rather good.'

Siobhan handed back the photographs to Quigley, picked up her knife and fork, and sat for the next twenty minutes, eating her meal and drinking her wine. She even made small talk with Quigley. At the end, she stood up and went to leave the room, but Quigley called her back.

'You won't have been expecting this. I know it's harsh. I didn't want to do it, but this is business and, well, there you go. Make sure it's a quick clean kill. She deserves that. But I love the way you stayed. I love the way you never got angry. If you need a new house cleaner—that's what she masquerades as, isn't it? Well, if you do, just drop me a line and I'll make sure I get you someone sorted. Might even get one of the coven to come round. Because once you've done this, you'll get to know us a lot better.'

I need a new plan, thought Siobhan as she turned away. *A plan that involves the death of Kylie. I need to stage it. I need to be trusted so I get some way of exposing what this cult is doing.*

Siobhan didn't know how, but she knew she was going to. She hadn't been simply threatened. Not simply been told that she could be killed or any of her friends could. This woman had actually told Siobhan to kill a close colleague, a friend, and she'd given her less than a week to do it.

She'd need Julian's help. It would have to be done between the four of them. Declan would have to be angry. Declan would have to be throwing the book at Siobhan. They were going to need to act and act in a big way. The most important thing was Julian. He had to buy into it. She couldn't do this on her own.

The last thing she needed was for Julian to bottle it, to come screaming in and take over. She'd need to tell him he wouldn't find his mole. He wouldn't find the guy, whoever it was in the Service, passing details about Siobhan. If Julian stuck with what Siobhan was going to do with her new plan, he'd find the mole, too.

Julian will do it for me. He'd do it because it's the right thing to do and he'll do it for love. Then I am getting myself out of this and he is going to leave that damn service. She got into her car outside the restaurant and drove off. Siobhan called Declan.

Hello Mrs D. What's the biz?

'Declan, I need you to call Julian.'

'Why?'

'Shut up. I don't need to tell you why at the moment. You don't need to know. You need to call Julian. Explain to him you really like kippers for tea and also drop into the conversation that Carrowdore has always seemed like a suitable spot for a holiday for you.'

'What?'

'Do it and make it seamless, okay?'

She looked at her watch. She had approximately two hours until Julian would meet her. It would be in a forest just above Hollywood in the Craigantlet Hills. There she would have to plan the death of Kylie, her later resurrection, and a way out of this whole mess. If she didn't, they could all end up in a box in the ground, or at best, having to live the rest of their life somewhere in South America.

Chapter 26

'I'm presuming we don't actually want to have her killed,' said Julian, sitting on a tree stump. Siobhan looked up and saw him smile at her.

'It's not time for jokes, Julian,' she said, but she appreciated him trying to break the seriousness of the situation. He knew as well as Siobhan did that this was a major problem. It wouldn't be easy to fake Kylie's death, not at Siobhan's hands. How much influence did Siobhan really have? How many links did she have in the medical community? Because someone would have to sign off the death as accidental. It would have to have been done quickly as well. What would the mode of death be? How would it be executed?

All these thoughts ran through Siobhan's head and then Kylie marched into clearing. 'Declan said you wanted to see me. Are we on a nature hunt?'

'Don't joke. Is Declan there as well?'

'Yes, he is. Dec, come on. Where are you?'

Declan strode in, nodded a look at Julian, and then turned to Siobhan. 'Mrs D, looks like we're all here then. What's up?'

'I've obviously been working away from the two of you for quite a while. I told you the reasons and I've kept you out of it pretty much because things got a lot more serious. Julian's watched the house rather closely.'

'Really?' said Kylie. 'I haven't seen him.'

'Exactly,' said Julian.

'Didn't watch it that closely then,' said Declan.

'I don't like to break confidences,' said Julian, 'but I believe Kylie has the sort of hair that really gets you going.' Julian smiled at Declan, who blushed. Siobhan folded her arms and looked at her pair of employees.

'How did you know that?' asked Kylie.

'I was watching and don't worry, I won't reveal anything else. I'm not spying on you. I'm protecting you.'

'Sounds like spying to me,' said Kylie. Declan said nothing.

'Julian has done a good job,' said Siobhan, 'and he's going to have to help me do an even better one. Unfortunately, I have been invited into the witches' coven, and I now have a last test to prove that I'm truly loyal to them.'

'That doesn't sound unfortunate to me, Mrs D,' said Declan. 'Seems to me you've done well.'

'They want me to kill Kylie.'

'What? You can't do that. That's not on. Mrs D, you can't do that,' blurted Declan.

'Obviously, I can't do that, Declan,' said Siobhan. 'I haven't asked her out here to finish her off. Wise up. We're here to discuss how we make it look like I'm killing her off.'

'I will not help you,' said Declan.

'Declan,' said Julian, 'what Siobhan's trying to say is we're going to have to stage Kylie's death. As someone who is evidently close to her and has been watched, so that they will know that you're close to her, you'll have to portray the correct amount of grief.'

'Right,' said Declan.

'I was thinking something undramatic,' said Siobhan.

'Am I not worth a dramatic death,' said Kylie. 'By the way, what happens after I die? And for how long will I be dead?'

'Yes, for how long?' said Declan.

'Long as it takes,' said Siobhan. 'Look, I haven't been completely forthright. We've got a problem. They know you live with me, Kylie, and they think you work for me, that you were out there getting information.'

'That's true, isn't it?' said Declan. 'Mrs D, she does work for you. So do I.'

'Yes, but not in the way they think. They're not seeing us as a group of small private investigators. They're seeing me as an annoyed spy coming out, turning on her masters. That I've decided I haven't got enough money. Obviously, this detective lark isn't any good, so I sent someone in because I had notions about the coven. All your groundwork was done to discover all about them and give feedback to me. Which is actually true, just not quite in the way that they believe. We're going along with that because if they think we're detectives or we're private investigators, we're dead. We're just dead. If we're not dead, we're in South America.'

'Are you sure that's what they think, Mrs D?' asked Declan.

'Julian spun a heck of a story about a disgruntled spy. She's bought it completely. They tested me in other ways which I passed. But now we're sitting in the situation of needing to kill Kylie.'

'I think the easiest is that she slips away in her sleep,' said Julian, 'back in the house. We'll obviously have to have the coffin in the house. I suspect they'll want to see the body at some point. Certainly, have it signed off. I'll arrange for that.

We may need to have an open coffin, though, at some point. Let them come and see.'

'How does that work?' said Kylie. 'You expect me to lie there pretending I'm dead? All these people come and look at me.'

'We can immobilise you, make it look like you're dead. We can slow the heart rate down. Furnish the coffin in such a way that they can't see you breathing. Things can be done.'

'Let me do it,' said Siobhan, 'and quick. I've got to the end of the week. Three days' time.'

'I haven't agreed to this yet,' said Kylie.

'You're dying one way or another,' said Siobhan. 'I hope you get that.'

'Kylie, I'm the last person who would want you dead,' said Declan, and Siobhan swore there was a tear in his eye, 'but if this keeps you safe, you're going to have to die.'

'There really are better ways to phrase all of that,' said Julian. 'I'll go away, get the plan, put things in place. Expect to be dead in about two days' time,' Julian said to Kylie and then motioned Siobhan to come out of the clearing with him.

'I'm not sure how long we can keep this under wraps,' he said to Siobhan on the path to the car park. 'I can put her in a safe house, but how long does it go on? People know when safe houses are being used. It can't be a year. After a couple of weeks, we'd have to get her out of the country.'

'Don't hit her with that yet. If it goes on more than about a month or two, you might have to get all of us out of the country.'

Julian stopped and looked around. He smiled at Siobhan. 'I hope not. I quite like your pad down on the gold coast. Looks like the right retirement plan.'

'Offer's still open,' said Siobhan. 'You could join me.'

'I could, but I don't want to be thinking about that at the moment. I need to concentrate on everything. We need to get you through this,' he said to Siobhan. 'I put you into it. I used somebody outside the Service because I thought we had a small leak, which apparently, we do, and now you're in trouble because of it. Trust me, I will get you through this and then consider options. I'm too emotional at the moment to consider them properly.'

Siobhan took a step back, surprised. 'You really are serious, aren't you?' she said. Julian stepped forward, put one hand on her shoulder and, leaning in, kissed her. He went to withdraw after such a delicate kiss, but Siobhan grabbed him, pulling him close, kissing him harder. Her hands roamed his back briefly as she held him, pulling him tight towards her. After a few moments, he stepped back.

'Quite emotional,' he said. He turned, smoothing his jacket and fixing his tie. 'Time to go to work,' he said. He went to say more and then he stopped.

'What?' said Siobhan. She could see him thinking. Julian was always the thinker. Then he just shook his head.

'Sorry,' he said. 'Lost for words. Really lost for words, but superbly so. Bye.' He turned and walked out to where his car was parked. Siobhan watched him walk all the way. *Why now in the middle of all this? Why?*

She wanted to run after him; wanted to pull him back; wanted to say, 'Stay with me.' She wanted to kick Kylie and Declan back to their car and have those first few tender moments when a relationship begins. They were precious, weren't they? Always precious.

'You all right, Mrs D?' said Declan.

'Fine, Declan. Why do you ask?'

'Never seen you kiss anyone like that.' Siobhan froze. He'd been watching. She'd missed him watching.

'Hi.' She turned around quickly. 'Don't need to read any . . .'

'Now you catch yourself on,' Declan said to Siobhan. 'He's a bit posh, but he's nice. Certainly likes you. And he's going to help Kylie out, so he's all right in my book.'

Siobhan nodded. Well, if she had Declan's seal of approval, how could things go wrong?

In the dead of night, two days later, Kylie was visited by a member of the Service, unknown to Siobhan. They didn't tell Siobhan how. But the next morning when Kylie didn't come to the house, Siobhan tried to call her. She sent a text, sent emails. Siobhan banged on Kylie's door before she opened it with her key, went in and found Kylie dead in her bed. She called for the ambulance, tears streaming down her face as it arrived.

Declan arrived for work, and fair play to him, completely broke down. He wept as they took Kylie out of the house, sobbing bitterly, but not like he was on the stage, just like he was experiencing it for the first time. Siobhan was proud of him.

Two days later, in a casket in the living room, Kylie lay silently. Siobhan didn't quite understand everything they'd done to her, but her face was motionless. If you put your hand up really close to her nose, you could feel the breathing. Because there was only the small area at the top of the casket open, her chest couldn't be seen rising and falling. As it happened, there was no need for this part of the facade.

No one came who they didn't know. Kylie had little extended family, and those that did were so far removed, they were there more as a courtesy. There was no church service, just a small token of remembrance in the front living room. Siobhan didn't tell or make known to anyone outside her small circle. She believed anyone else would soon have to come to her after hearing rumours of Kylie's death. Much easier to go back on those than to have informed everybody of her death.

Quietly, she was taken away and slipped out of the casket before it was buried in a churchyard. Julian watched the churchyard to see if anyone would come to check the grave, but for two days, no one did. Siobhan didn't make contact with the coven during this time. After all, she would mourn a colleague, and as tight-faced as she'd been, she wanted them to believe it had truly affected her.

It was the third day after her funeral that Siobhan first saw a contact from the coven. Lorraine Campbell was watching as Siobhan visited the grave. She didn't come close, but she watched Siobhan like a hawk from a distance. Declan arrived, and Siobhan walked off. He stared at Siobhan, putting on angry eyes.

The boy's a player, Siobhan thought. *A true player*. Leaving Declan by the graveside, Siobhan disappeared in her car, off to a nearby cafe, where she sat down and picked up her phone. She dialled a number that nobody else knew to a mobile that had not long been bought.

'How are you feeling?' asked Siobhan. She gave no names, didn't mention her own, and didn't expect the person on the other end to give her name, either. The reply meant she knew exactly who it was.

'Like death warmed up,' said Kylie. 'A little bored. Not much to do here, but I have to be careful. I can't fire through the internet either. Can't go looking at my things, but it's okay.

Still feeling funny from what they pumped into me. Our friend said he wouldn't be dropping by that often, and I'm to spend most of the time on my own here.'

'He'll be watching,' said Siobhan.

'I hope it isn't a long time before I get out of here.'

'I hope not, either. We'll do our best. At least you're still alive. We all are. We might get to the end of this, but if not, we might have to run somewhere. I'll make sure it's somewhere sunny.'

Kylie laughed. 'How is our, or rather, my close friend doing?'

'The greatest actor I ever watched. He misses you.'

'Tell him I miss him, too. I never thought I'd ever say that.'

'No, but none of us pick who we fall for. Take care,' said Siobhan.

'I will do.'

The call was closed. Siobhan knew she wouldn't be speaking to Kylie for a while.

Chapter 27

As part of the charade, Siobhan had a headstone made for Kylie. Now, five days after her supposed funeral, it was ready. They'd placed it on the ground in the graveyard, and Siobhan went to visit it. As she arrived, dressed in her black jacket and with a red scarf around her, she approached the grave to see Declan there.

The team had made it a thing that they would continue to visit, Declan keeping up an angry front towards Siobhan. Siobhan could see Lorraine Campbell watching from the car park again. She didn't look at her, but took some flowers out of the boot of her car before walking along the path towards Kylie's grave. Declan shouted at her.

'Just go away. You don't deserve to be here. Don't deserve to be anywhere near her. You betrayed her.'

'I'd watch your tongue,' said Siobhan. 'You need to be quiet. You don't speak like that in public.'

Declan was doing a magnificent job. Tears were streaming from his eyes, and as Siobhan came close, he turned, took three steps towards her, and threw an almighty punch. Siobhan stepped to one side, Declan swinging past her. He tripped up, stumbling to the ground. It wasn't an act.

She had told him previously, throw punches, do whatever, and he'd put heart and soul into it. The surprise of Siobhan simply stepping out of the way so easily had caught him unawares. He'd overbalanced and gone down to the ground.

Siobhan calmly walked past him and placed flowers on Kylie's grave. Declan stood up, walked over, and picked up the flowers. He started throwing them around.

'I'll kill you for this,' he shouted, pointing at her. 'I'll kill you.'

Siobhan stepped forward quickly and, with a pacey move, stepped around his back, her arm going around his throat. A knife emerged from within her coat in her other hand. She pressed it to his neck. Holding it carefully, she caused a small nick. It shocked Declan, surprise written all over his face.

It was perfect, exactly what was needed. She pretended to whisper something in his ear but said, 'Top stuff, but that's enough. You need to get out of here before I have to overplay this. If I didn't deal with you now, it would look wrong. Walk away.'

She let Declan go and he stumbled forward. He turned, pointing and swearing at her, and then half ran towards his car. He tore out of the car park, and Siobhan calmly began walking around, picking up the flowers he had tossed about. It took a couple of minutes of looking extremely undignified, but slowly she placed them all back on the grave. She knelt down in front and let tears fall from her eyes. As she did so, she heard the crunch of footsteps on the gravel path.

Siobhan turned and saw Eileen Quigley walking towards her. She was dressed in black as well. Calmly, methodically, she approached the grave to stand behind Siobhan. She said nothing, showing her respect for Siobhan as she continued to cry over the grave. Then Siobhan wiped her eyes, producing a handkerchief from her coat. After a few heavy sniffs, she stood up, stepped back from the grave, and felt Eileen Quigley's hand go to her shoulder.

'Hard times,' said Eileen. 'Hard times and sacrifices we all have to make. We've all done it. We've all had to show our loyalty. One of my newest recruits had to despatch Beyonce. Pity as she'd grown very close to her. That was why I chose her. You have to lay down a sacrifice. Between you and me, that was for business reasons to know you were genuine, that I could trust you. It was trust with a friend from the coven as well, only she believed she was doing it for our master.'

Eileen pointed up to the church at the far end of the graveyard. 'Isn't it fantastic, belief?' she said. 'We all put them in the ground, hoping for them to rise again. My friend in the coven believed in the opposite of this. Well, the enemy rather, doing it for the devil, for the devil would give them power. Even the good guys say that's a lie. How she could fall for that one, I don't know, but people are vulnerable. They're silly. You can prey upon them in that way. Look at me. I run an empire, and I don't get my hands dirty. Stand at the top and get others to do things, but I have known it. I have known the pain.'

'Didn't take you for someone who would hesitate. Thought you would just despatch those who were no longer required,' said Siobhan.

'I have my loves as much as anyone. I have friends, those I hold dear. When I joined the coven, they asked me to kill my first love. We were still in love. You are fortunate. I didn't want you to be seen as implicated in Kylie's death, so I let it be decided by you how she went. You did it quietly. It shows me you can do that with others.

'Your skills are quite excellent. You obviously have real training. We could have taught you how to do these things, or come and done them for you. Matter's not. The point is, you get the job done. When I had to kill off my lover, they wanted it to be in the throes of passion. I killed him when we were at our closest, when we were abandoning ourselves to each other. That's because the woman that ran the coven then, she believed in this power.

'She was deluded. It didn't save her. She ran the coven for about a year before I took it over, a year from being the lowest of the sisters to being the top dog. I killed her as well. I killed her for making me kill him, but she did me a favour. He was a weakness,' said Eileen, 'a true weakness.'

Siobhan stared at the woman and saw tears coming from her eyes.

'I am better for it. Doesn't change the fact that he was my lover. He was mine, a part of me. He would have followed me all the way into taking over this little part of the world. We were meant to enjoy it together, but we all pay the price, and I've paid the price for that. Lorraine there had to do a similar act.'

Siobhan handed over her handkerchief to Eileen Quigley. She wiped her eyes. She handed it back, and Siobhan pocketed it before the two women embraced.

'Thank you for that,' said Quigley. 'Some people would have walked away. I think you and I are going to have a superb relationship. I think it's going to benefit what I do, and I think it's going to give you what you want in the future. When you come next time, don't look at this as something you've lost. Instead, thank Kylie for what she's giving you.

'Her sacrifice is going to make all the difference. Take another day or two, and then I will show you what we're really about. I will show you where the money's coming from and the money that you're going to take from it. You'll get a ten percent cut of everything we make.' Siobhan's eyes widened.

'Oh, yes,' said Eileen, 'it'll be a lot, an awful lot, but you won't get most of it until ten years' time. That's what we're agreeing? I'll obviously give you funds in the meantime, but you can't be seen to be living beyond your means.'

'I'm not.'

'It'll all be in a bank account somewhere else. But every time you look at the numbers in that account, you can tell yourself about the beach you'll be on. A young man keeping you happy, telling you how beautiful you are. Even if he's lying to himself about your ability to dispose of him for another one if you ever get bored with him.

'Too many people buried here,' said Quigley, pointing to the graveyard, 'go into that ground dreaming of a better life the next time round. You get a better life now. That's the secret of the coven, the secret of what we do. That's the genuine joy of it. As I said to you, give thanks to Kylie. She's the one that got you there.'

Eileen Quigley took Siobhan's head in her hands and, making Siobhan bend forward slightly, she kissed her forehead, much like a mother would kiss a child. The tenderness was incredible, and Siobhan swore she could not have been acting. Siobhan played her part so well and yet struggled to keep the facade on her face.

This woman was talking about Kylie. She was talking about killing off someone, close people to you. For Quigley, it was the closest. And then thanking them for money, for power. There was no love in this. She was deluded. She was pathological in her hunger for the future.

Siobhan let the tears flow, watching Quigley walk away. She felt the genuine horror within about this woman. The rest were pawns, and Quigley was the queen bee. Siobhan knew that if everything went wrong, like a queen, she would fly away and start up again. She had the money on one side. What was she doing this for now? How much money could you require if all she wanted was her happiness? No. This was a woman who wanted everything. She had to be stopped.

Siobhan waited until Quigley had disappeared in the car, along with Lorraine Campbell. She took a few more moments, then walked back to her own car before driving off to a cafe. Spotting the man who was watching her, probably one of Quigley's, Siobhan sat on her own with a coffee until he had disappeared, probably to make his report. She picked up her phone and called Julian.

'Safely installed?' asked Julian.

'I'm truly in. She's bought it, hook, line, and sinker. I don't know how much longer for,' said Siobhan, realising she was still feeling teary. 'She embraced me, Julian. She killed her own lover, killed him to get into the coven. Quigley killed him as they made love, at their closest. From the sounds of it, she made sure the coven wasn't far away to see. She wants everything. Already has money put away—she said as much— and yet she's still going. She needs to be brought down.'

'I can't move in. There is somebody within the Service, somebody who knows. I've cut all links. Nobody knows what I'm doing for you. The safe house Kylie is in, I have told no one about. I'm keeping her safe by making sure no one knows. She is dead to the Service world, as well as our own. Only my doctor who made her sleep in the coffin knows she's alive.'

'Then we need to move soon. This needs to end soon.'

'Do you want me to come round?' asked Julian. 'You sound like you might unravel.'

Siobhan half laughed on the phone. 'Do I want you to come around? With everything inside of me, I do, but you can't. I'll go back to the coven within the next day or two. She's got something to show me, something to tell me. She's going to lay out the full extent of her business. Once I know that, we'll work out how we bring it down.

'We can't keep this going for too long. She's got inside of me, Julian. You're not meant to hit your mark. Not meant to feel anything about them. You're just meant to do the job. Right now, I feel as if she had me kill Kylie. I feel like it's almost real. This needs to end soon.'

'It will,' said Julian. 'It will. Hold on. You're strong enough. You can do this.'

'You sound like a man from the Service now.'

'Except that I know you,' said Julian. 'I know you more than a report on a file. Know you more than just working on the side. You can do this because I know you want that retired life, and you want it with me. You can do this.'

Chapter 28

Two days later, Siobhan, having composed herself, spent several hours disciplining herself on how to act around Eileen. To purge the anger she felt towards the woman, Siobhan returned to the coven headquarters at the base of the Mourne Mountains. As she drove up, over an hour away from her home, she once again realised the beauty of the area she was in. How the Mournes swept down to the sea, just as the song said, but inside she felt an anger.

This darkness, this nastiness, was right here. She'd always felt this about Northern Ireland, about the wee country, the province, whatever you wanted to call it. This part of the world should be so beautiful, and yet why was it infested with a horror? When you sat back rationally, it did not differ from anywhere else in the world. There was great beauty, always, but it was tinged with sadness, always sullied with corruption, hatred and evil. But why?

Maybe it was because she was outside of the Service. They had very strict lines not to cross. You were doing things for a reason, because other people had ordered it. It was simple. Execute what you are told to do. Follow it through. Now she needed to execute what needed to be done.

Angela Lynch had called Siobhan, asking about justice for Deborah. What did she know? What had Siobhan found out? Siobhan had told her to hold on. She had to tell her that Angela's killer may never be brought up to justice in a court. The reach of the woman was too strong. Julian was involved because of that.

What they needed to do was to stop her. They were unsure of the depth of her talons, how far she'd clawed into society, into the social life around her. Was she in with the police? It wasn't unreasonable. Did they even know it? Did they think it was someone else that was playing them?

The wonder of what she'd set up was how far removed the whole idea of her was, and yet those at the top knew they were being manipulated by a coven. Throughout history, sometimes the true ideas of Eldridge horrors or witchcraft or whatever type of evil, sat in the minds of those at the top. Those at the bottom knew genuine fears.

They didn't believe something was coming for you in the middle of the night because they dreamt about it. It was because people close to them got killed. They feared real people. But those at the top, those who were removed from true violence in society, sometimes feared things that were in the imagination.

When you didn't have time to think because the danger was so real, you never had to imagine what was coming for you. Never had to imagine what could happen because the genuine horror was happening. In the middle of a war, you didn't worry about ghosts or spectres or aliens. You worried about the man with the gun pointed at you. There, they dreamed of what was going to save them. There, they imagined angels and saviours because they looked the horror in the face. What they didn't know was where their rescue would come from.

Siobhan switched off the engine and stepped out of the car, trying to push all of this from her mind. She needed to be on form. Walking up to the front door of the coven headquarters, she opened it with her key, and stepped inside to see Lorraine Campbell looking back at her.

'You're a full member now,' she said. 'You're part of us, so you need to wear your cloak when you're in here to respect our master.'

Mistress, she means, thought Siobhan, but knew this pretence of serving an evil deity had to be observed. A cloak was in the car, for Siobhan expected that something like this was coming. She brought it inside and changed in a small cloakroom. When she stepped back out, Eileen Quigley was there with Lorraine Campbell.

'It suits you,' said Eileen. 'I'm glad you're here. We've come to a bit of a crisis point and I need your expertise. We're going to take you over the next couple of days to see where all our money comes from. A large part of it is from drug running. A part of the master's plan, of course,' she said, 'but come on up the stairs. I've put out the full pieces of paper and my ideas. Not the carefully selected ones I had shown you previously. Come, sister.'

Siobhan walked, and Eileen Quigley put her arm around her, Lorraine Campbell joining from the other side. The three strode like they were graduating from school. They broke the formation to climb the wooden stairs up to the room with the desks. Siobhan was coming to think of it as the operations room. It had all the details. They never gave it a name.

As Siobhan entered, she realised that all the different papers had been changed. Eileen Quigley led her over to one desk where a lamp burned atop, illuminating the evil web of the empire. There were photographs of different men and women, details about who they were, where they lived, and what they did. Siobhan stood, scanning it all.

'Today, I want you to take this in,' said Eileen. 'I want you to learn the names. You'll meet them all over the next couple of days. We'll not tell them you are anyone important. In fact, we'll not let them know who you are. You'll send the likes of Lorraine here, or someone else in the coven, to deal with them. We'll keep you mysterious, that other figure.

'A lot of them believe that we have powers, and if they can't see a human face, it makes them wonder. I've got a rather nice attachment for the cloaks downstairs. It's a hood you can attach. You'll look like the Ghost of Christmas Future,' laughed Eileen. 'It'll be perfect, but learn these details today. Spend the next couple of hours in here and then you and I will go for dinner. I've got a pleasant restaurant in Newcastle that we run some business out of. Did you ever miss the scampi when you weren't here?'

She talked to Siobhan like they were a couple of work colleagues simply chewing the fat as the day was wearing on. It could have been anything before them. A chat held in any normal manufacturing company, or maybe a phone helpline. But the conversation was that of the working day, almost mundane. Yet here in front of Siobhan, was something so criminal, totally evil. Maybe a group of genuine witches would have been better than what she had here.

Regardless, Siobhan spent the day learning the details, memorising the web and the intrigue, but she also saw a problem. As it was coming towards dinnertime, Siobhan heard Eileen Quigley's steps coming up the wooden stairs.

As the woman entered in her robes, Siobhan turned to her, pointing to the map on the table.

'You don't control a lot of this part, do you? If you want to take it over. I think I know how to do it.'

'Good,' said Eileen. 'That's exactly why I want you in here. That'll be your job over the next while. I want it done in the next two weeks. There are some big shipments on their way.'

'I saw that. Columbia running some things in. How come you don't own the drug running in this part of the province?'

'The little enclaves in Northern Ireland can be tight, sometimes tough to break into. Some of them bite back. This one has bit back in a big way. You can see the man's name is John Carroll. He's making an absolute fortune from the drugs he's running in there. It's funny, based in the Antrim area, I never thought that would be a difficult one to get a hold of. Maybe I was just too focused around Belfast and some of the bigger areas.

'He runs it out of one of his farmhands. The difficulty has been establishing the coven's influence because a lot of the surrounding people don't prescribe to this witchcraft idea; this all-encompassing we can't be stopped because of the powers we have. I was thinking we need to make an example of him,' said Eileen. 'We need to leave him in a way that people know witches did their work on him.'

'Such as?' said Siobhan.

'It's very difficult for a person to be turned inside out, but you can do it and you can leave them that way.'

Siobhan went cold. *Turn a person inside out?*

'How?' she asked.

'We have people here who can do it. It's not pretty to say the least, but you leave the example of a person who is literally destroyed. There's also a great deal of pain with it, and if you can do it with his people watching, all the better.'

Siobhan almost hesitated, and she saw Eileen's face become a frown of worry. 'You have the stomach for this side of things?' asked Eileen.

Siobhan knew better than to lie. She knew better than to turn around and give the complete opposite to the truth that she felt.

'I don't do things like that. I'm quick and I'm clean normally,' said Siobhan. 'With Kylie, I just dispatched her in the night. Simple. When I make an example, I'm usually cold, and they're dead. People fear me coming when they don't expect it.'

'You'll have to adapt,' said Eileen. 'Will that be a problem?'

'No,' said Siobhan, 'but don't expect me to do the actual act. I've no ability to turn a person inside out.'

'Absolutely not. I told you that we have people who do that, and besides, you're a figure there to worry them. You can't be seen to be getting your hands dirty. Be the terror beyond what we show.'

'Terror beyond that?' said Siobhan. 'Really?'

'You will be surprised at what people can imagine, but let's worry about that tomorrow. Time for dinner. Part of me likes you, not just from a business point of view. You're tough like me. You're going to make it like me. It's not been easy being head of the coven. Most of the sisters with me are imbeciles. Oh yes, they can carry out tasks and threaten people, but they don't appreciate the finer overall control. Lorraine's not bad, but she's not up to your level.'

'She certainly doesn't have a lot of the skills that I learned,' said Siobhan. 'I remember taking her away from Kylie. It wasn't difficult.'

Eileen smiled. 'I knew you were something then. I'm so glad that you've chosen to come on board. Come on, let's eat some scampi. I can't get enough of it. You don't get the same thing anywhere else in the world. Do you know that?'

'I do,' said Siobhan. 'Portavogie scampi.'

Eileen turned away, and Siobhan fought to keep her face from breaking out into an angry scowl. The Service was never so brutal as to harm people in that way. When she'd worked for them abroad, everything was cold, quick, and clean. Then she stopped herself.

She was going to say they never tortured anyone, and she'd never been involved in that. There were always rumours, there was always talk, and if the Service needed to get something, they got it. Was Eileen Quigley any different? Was the Service different to her?

Siobhan parked the thought, just glad that she was no longer in it. Following Eileen down the wooden stairs to the lower level of the house, she got changed to go to dinner. As she sat that night, making small talk with Eileen over the excellent Portavogie scampi, Siobhan's mind was already working overtime.

How do we expose all of this? How do we bring something so big to bear that it couldn't be covered up? We have to get Eileen Quigley out of our wee country?

Chapter 29

Siobhan sat in her kitchen with all the curtains closed. Opposite her at the kitchen table was Julian. The man looked tired, but he had brought Declan with him. Their car wasn't outside. They'd walked in from a distance. Despite the cold, both of them looked sleepy as they arrived. However, once Siobhan told them why they were there, they woke up.

'She showed me how everything that works. More than that, I think there's a chance here. We need to bring down the coven. There's no point just getting bits and pieces. There's no point bringing them in to take care of them criminally. We need to do them in one sweep. There's a drug runner she's going to break and we can catch all the coven red-handed. I think you might need to come in as the Service, Julian.'

'That might be difficult to organise,' said Julian. 'How many people am I going to need?'

'You'll need a decent-sized squad. I'd say maybe twenty operatives. It's a large number so we can supervise everything else when the police come along afterwards, I would suspect. There's a man called John Carroll. He's currently running most of the drugs in the Antrim area. It all goes through a farm.

'Quigley wants us to step in and take that over. She wants him made an example of. To do this, we are to pull in all of his contacts, all of his network will come together. She wants it done soon because he's taking in a large shipment coming out of Colombia and working its passageway through. I've suggested that we can use the influence of the group to make sure his contacts are all there. I ensure Eileen Quigley is there as the head of the group to stand and do a brief explanation. She wants to turn him inside out in front of his people.'

'What does that mean?' asked Declan. 'Turn him inside out. Is that one of the terms you guys use? What, to show up who he is really or what?'

'No,' said Siobhan. 'She literally wants to turn him inside out in front of his group.'

Julian suddenly snapped into a much more concentrated mode. 'Really,' he said. 'Not just shoot him in front of everybody.'

'She literally said, "turn him inside out." What they did at the pillory is nothing. She's big on the witchcraft, making it look real. No doubt she'll do other things over his body. Gross, grotesque. She wants to leave people in no doubt that there is something truly evil behind it.'

'Sounds like she is the evil behind it, Mrs D.'

'You're right, Declan, but the way she operates, well, she's learnt it from here. It's terror. She makes it look like supernatural terror. It's not real. People think it's real. She controls them with their mind, with the fears they have there. Our fears usually control us. I think that's how she gets those who are higher up the tree to fall under a spell. They fear things much more like that than simply people with guns.

They have their own people with guns to deal with that. To see evil, that sort of evil, the clever bit is portraying it, making it look like it's real.'

'I can probably get twenty I can vouch for,' said Julian. 'Twenty good people that I can sign off. They'll be coming from all places. It'll take me a while.'

'She wants this done soon. I think we do it on a Sunday as well. That'll be part of her thing. Sunday. Lord's Day, and all that. It turns it around on its head. She'll make it an anti-sabbath, or a black sabbath, so to speak.'

'Where will you be?' asked Julian.

'Not there. I'm the planner, sitting over the top. I'm the one she doesn't want to be implicated. Nobody is ever to see my face. It's a joy because I won't have to extract myself. I won't have to hide. She'll be there. I'm going to pitch it that the rest of the coven needs to be there, too. Show of strength. If I end up there, I'll need to be covered. I can't be implicated. I need to be away from it.'

'The Service will probably know about you in the end. I mean, Kylie is going to come back to life.'

'We'll deal with that. The only people that know about Kylie are the coven.'

'Maybe you still have to move away after doing all of this,' warned Julian.

'It may be,' said Siobhan, testily. 'What choice do we have? We need to end it.'

Julian stood up, walked over to Siobhan, and put his hands on her shoulders, rubbing them. 'Easy,' he said. 'Easy.'

'You see what she's been doing? Angela Lynch lost her sister, just like that. This woman's operating as a . . . she's like a godfather. Except she's a godfather that isn't even being hunted by ourselves. She's everywhere. It needs to be shown that she can be taken down. The fear of others coming in, the fear of the law needs to be shown. We need to blow this myth, blow the idea of a witches' coven.'

'Send them back to the rule of the gun,' said Julian, a little too flippantly for Siobhan's liking. She knew what he was trying to do, trying to unwind the situation, trying to calm everything down.

'If I can get them to capture this big shipment. Convince Quigley that she needs to be there on the night of that's arrival. A night when his couriers and everybody will be there to pick up. If we round Carroll's men up and have Quigley display Carroll and his weakness in front of them. Then we have Service cover in there as well. We could all move in at once. You could take them down and whip them all out of the province.'

'It would be tight and difficult because I'd have to show their influence quickly after that. But beforehand, I'd have to keep it completely under cover because of this mole I've got. I still don't know who it is.'

'We won't have a better opportunity,' said Siobhan. 'I need reasons to have the coven altogether. The only other time you really see them all together is when they're doing their naked dance. How are you going to lift a load of people for doing a naked dance? It will not stand up.'

'If we did put it in the papers, all it would do would give even more credence to the rumour and the lie,' said Julian.

'Exactly. What do you want me to do, Mrs D?' asked Declan.

'Nothing at the moment. I will not be there. You don't need to be there either. Better if Julian does this because if it goes wrong, I'm still in the group. I might have to talk my way out of it, and it won't be easy, but it's doable.'

'I don't like that idea,' said Julian suddenly. 'You'd be compromised; you really would. This would be your setup, you're convincing on. She won't trust you after that. She's liable to just kill you.'

'I'm in this until we're out, until we get to the other side. We can't leave this woman in charge. How long will it take to get more people back into the group to get this close? I don't see anyone breaking into the ranks like I have.'

Julian looked at her. 'There's too much on the line to talk like that.'

'What do you mean?' asked Siobhan.

'I mean us.'

'There is no us yet. There is no us until we get this done.'

Julian looked somewhat disappointed. 'I thought there was us. I thought that's what you wanted.'

'Of course, it's what I want, but are you telling me you're going to walk away from this? Are you telling me you can let this happen?'

Julian stepped forward and kissed Siobhan on the lips. 'We do it well and we get out. I promise that when we get clear, when I see it all locked up, I walk. I will walk from the Service straight to you, but you promise me.'

'Promise you what?'

'That you pick up cases that don't involve so many nasty elements.'

'I promise you I will quit and retire,' said Siobhan. 'That I will become interested in painting, and walking, and doing whatever else with you.'

Julian put his finger up to Siobhan's lips. 'Don't make promises you can't keep.'

'And don't put promises up that take me out of a job,' said Declan. 'Kylie and I love doing this, and you know we can't do it without you. You're the brains. I'm just the brawn.'

'What does that make Kylie?' asked Siobhan.

'The good-looking one.'

'Cheers,' said Siobhan.

'Teenagers,' whispered Julian to Siobhan. 'They don't even understand what a woman is.'

'Hey,' said Declan. 'I'm not a teenager. I'm in my twenties.'

Julian went quiet again, and sat down. He was thinking. Siobhan knew that look. 'We do it, set it up, time, place everything to your plan. I'll start pulling my twenty in.'

'Good,' said Siobhan. 'We're agreed then.'

'Can you find your own way home, Declan?' asked Julian. The young man nodded and told them to have a good night as he left. When they heard the door shut, Julian stepped forward, taking Siobhan in his arms.

'What's the real matter? You used to be dispassionate. You used to . . .'

'That was when we weren't here. This is Northern Ireland, the province. This is where I live. She's doing it right where I live. Those Russian mobsters did it right where I live. I can't have that. I can't have this. You realise that I left because I couldn't sort out the problems here. Couldn't deal with my country's difficulties. I couldn't sort it, so I went and took part in sorting out other people's countries.

'I've come back, Julian, and we still have the issues. Oh, there are agreements. There are people up on the hill getting paid to do stuff and not doing stuff. We have still got all the issues. How do I come back and retire when the issues are still here?'

He tenderly held her, whispering in her ear. 'I know,' he said. 'I know you care,' he said. 'Maybe you care too much, but you care. That's why I said don't make promises you can't keep. You see yourself as a protector, as someone to look after the place.'

'I'm sorry,' she said. 'It should have got knocked out of me with my training, but it didn't. I can't be dispassionate about here.'

'Of course, you can't, Siobhan; it's why I love you and it's why I can't be dispassionate about you. Work it out. Tell me what we're doing—lead the way. I'm right with you; know that.'

Julian kissed her, and Siobhan didn't want it to stop. She held him, kissing back, feeling like they were school kids, with the excitement coursing through her body, but Julian broke off.

'I don't have all of you yet,' he said. 'I'll probably never get all of you. This land grabs you, but I'm happy to share you with the land. Let's get this done, then we can get more properly acquainted.'

'You really have to learn how to put things in a much sexier way,' said Siobhan. He kissed her on the forehead and left, leaving her standing in the kitchen. She tried to push away the feelings that were raging through her, the joy she felt about him. She needed to plan, she needed to scheme, and she needed to make this work. Everything depended on it. Her life ahead, Kylie's life, Declan's, Julian's, and also a little more cleanup for the land that she lived in.

Chapter 30

Siobhan donned her black cape and the inner black garments that combined for her coven outfit. She wrapped the cape up tight as she approached the house, opening the door with the key in her free hand, locking it behind her. It was standard practice, whoever was in, stopping any random callers popping in through the front door. As she locked the front door and turned into the hall, Lorraine Campbell was standing nearby. She looked rather suspiciously at Siobhan.

'Have you had any more thoughts about John Carroll?'

'Yes,' Siobhan said simply. 'I'm going to take them to Eileen. She'll be the one to give the go ahead.'

Siobhan felt like Lorraine was bothered that she had risen so fast and so quick. Eileen had said Lorraine wasn't that clever, but she was clearly more than just a foot soldier. Maybe she thought herself cleverer than she was and wasn't happy that Siobhan was stepping into her shoes. When you had ranks in organisations, people expected to climb, because if they weren't and other people were, it usually meant they were doing something wrong. However, they could see it also as someone rising too quick, getting past their grade, and not being worthy of that higher place. Lorraine seemed to have a problem with what was happening with Siobhan.

'Would you like to share any of it with me? I could run over it with you before you take it to Eileen.'

'No, thank you. If it's not going to be coven knowledge, it's better that only Eileen hears it. She may have her own reasons for not wanting it to go ahead. She does keep things to herself.'

'As the coven head, she's more than entitled to. I was just looking to assist you, sister.'

'Thank you,' said Siobhan. 'But it's not required.'

As Siobhan walked across the hallway, the soles of her shoes clipping the wooden floor, she could feel Lorraine's eyes staring at her. Siobhan walked to the small wooden stairs. Opening the door at the bottom, she climbed them to look at the tables of information. In that upper room, she pulled out a few local maps, arranged photographs of key players, and noted some timings. When she stood back, she gave a smile.

She was ready for this. As she looked at the detail in front of her, her eyes also saw people who weren't noted. Julian's people, where they would be, how they would intercept, how the drugs would be seized, and how, above all, Eileen would be held accountable. Just as she looked to commit that obscene act on John Carroll, just as she'd taken him to harm him, then Julian would step in. The drugs would be there, her attempted murder would be there, and he could film it all.

Siobhan gave another smile, turned, walked down the small wooden stairs, and locked the door at the bottom. As she crossed the building to where Eileen's personal office was, she saw Lorraine Campbell's eyes still following her. The woman's face looked like thunder, displaying a tight grimace.

Siobhan was wiser than to think of anyone as being nobody, but she didn't see Lorraine Campbell as a problem. Ignoring her, she turned the corner and rapped on Eileen Quigley's door. There was no answer, but Eileen was there. Siobhan stood back and waited. Two minutes later, Eileen opened the door and Siobhan could see that the desk behind her was clear.

'I was wondering if you'd come upstairs with me. I want to run you through a plan I've got.'

'Regarding what?' asked Eileen.

'John Carroll. I think I've got a way in which you can strike genuine fear into his people. I know you want to turn him inside out, but I think the way to do it will involve all his smaller people being there, too.'

Eileen turned without a word, locked her door behind her, and followed Siobhan to the upper room. Once there, Eileen stood looking at the various maps and photographs on the table.

'That's John Carroll,' said Siobhan. 'Normally, for a drop off of this size, he'll have scheduled in couriers. According to your intelligence reports, they come about fifteen minutes apart normally. The entire load is dropped off and then distributed quickly out to other smaller dealers he has throughout the Antrim area. I suggest we make this a showpiece event. We invite some of the current backers we have on our various estates.'

By this, Siobhan meant those already under the thumb of the coven, running drugs for the coven.

'We get them to wait outside and slowly capture each of the dealers as they arrive. Carroll is good at what he does, and he involves all of his people in doing it. In a short space of time, if we take them over, say, two hours, we would have all Carroll's dealers there. It also will show us if anyone else is onto him. If the Service or police step in, they'll either cause trouble for him, or they'll capture Carroll. If John Carroll's captured and taken out of the picture, it'll suit us. Similarly, if he's pestered by the police or the Service, it'll hurt his business. We need to be careful, obviously, just in case anyone is on to Carroll. Don't want to get caught up in that, ourselves. Always important to stay above things, Eileen.'

'I like the idea. Carroll will arrive and accept the first shipment from Colombia?'

'Yes,' said Siobhan. 'According to the intelligence that's been gathered, that will be round about eight o'clock. The last courier to take it away won't arrive until ten. That's the point at which we swoop. Each of the carriers will have been picked up leaving by our people. We give the drugs to our people as a thank you when they leave. Before we do, we bring all of them in, plus all of Carroll's workers. That's when you turn Carroll inside out.'

'I turn him inside out?' queried Eileen. 'Why me?'

'You're the head, the lead. You want me to be this shadowy presence, your hand. They need to know first and foremost, who the person is that I'm the hand of. You stand there and we bring the rest of the coven with you.'

'They'll have to all mask up, of course.'

'They will. You won't. They'll not speak about you, nor say anything. They won't trace any of it to you. We'll be in control of that barn. Nobody else. By the end, John Carroll will be no more. All of his people will be so terrified that they'll be desperate to work for you and not offend you. Our own people, working through all the other estates, well, they'll be heading home with some more gear to sell. They'll have been reminded of who's in charge and why they're working for you.'

Eileen stood for a moment, looking over the photographs and the maps. 'It's an excellent location, isn't it?' she said. 'It's out of the way. We can see quite far around as well. We should be able to pick them all. Coming and going. It could work very simply. I like it a lot. There's only one thing I don't like,' she said.

'What's that?' asked Siobhan.

'You not being there. It's not a good signal to the rest of the coven. When we appear as a group, we appear all as a group.'

'You said you didn't want me to be seen. You wanted me to be this mysterious hand.'

'I do, for two reasons. One, if anything happens to you, I can still keep that pretence up for somebody else. No offense to you, but these things happen. Two, it'll give confidence for the rest of our coven that you're in it with us.'

'But you said you didn't want me to be seen.'

'That's true. You'll wear a hood. Not just a mask, but a real hood. We'll not see your face.'

'As you wish,' said Siobhan.

'You don't like it?' asked Eileen.

'No, I don't see the requirement for me to be there, but if that's what it takes. If the rest of your group are incapable of understanding when somebody's working with them and needs to have some sort of camaraderie, well, then we'll do it. The money will be enough to cover my misgivings.'

'Good,' said Eileen. 'I've lifted you pretty quick to almost the top of the coven, but that's because I needed someone. Someone who knew what they were doing, someone who could help me take control of the coven more tightly. Beyonce had a lot of talent. Even Deborah had a mind. She acted incredibly dumb, but she was deeply involved in what we did. She just didn't like that we were more than just witches, more than people who were supernatural.

'When we did things with that in mind, she was quite happy. When not, well, she couldn't take it and had to be moved on. Pity. She gave a great air to the coven. A proper mystique. That's the thing that many people don't realise. When you despatch someone, when you move them on, it's because it needs to be done. There's nothing personal about it. Actually, losing them can quite affect you. I'm sure you know what I mean.'

She was hinting at Kylie. Siobhan knew it, and she simply gave a nod. 'Indeed.'

'We'll do that then. Your plan is good, but you'll be there.'

Siobhan watched Eileen descend the stairs and lock the door behind her. Remaining at the top, Siobhan looked around the room. So far, so good, except she was now going to be there. She'd have to get out of the way, must be clear, and she'd have to protect herself. Make sure that she didn't get seen. She would call Julian that night, explain the issue.

Siobhan remained upstairs for another three hours, thinking out the finer details of the plan. She checked over contacts that had been made, words that had been said, and confirmed all the times surrounding the drop.

It would happen in two days' time. She hoped it was enough time for Julian to get his troops together. Twenty of them. Twenty of them to capture these drug runners and coven. Siobhan licked her lips. She would look forward to that. A death avenged, and hopefully she could get into the clear. She didn't know.

Part of her thought she might be heading off to South America in the company of Declan and Kylie. Would Julian come with her? She hoped it wouldn't come to that, but if it did, she prayed he would. She'd been in foreign countries all her life, but she'd come home for a reason. It wouldn't be right that she was cast out of her province. Never to see the waters on the Irish Sea and outside of Belfast Lough, to not notice the Copelands from her window. Never again would she say to the man along the road, ''bout ye!'

A chill run up and down her, realising that the day was getting closer. This was coming to a head. Siobhan made her way down the wooden stairs, and as she closed the door behind her, locking it, she turned to see Lorraine Campbell standing there.

'Eileen said we'll be making a move soon. Told me to keep free in two days' time.'

'Did she?' said Siobhan.

'I hope you know what you're doing,' said Lorraine. 'Especially involving Eileen. All of us there? It sounds dangerous to me. Risky. Potentially expose the entire coven.'

'Indeed, but it's what Eileen has decreed, and if Eileen says it, it's what we do. You've been here longer than me. You understand that, don't you?'

'Of course, I do,' said Lorraine, casting a disparaging glance at Siobhan. 'But I hope you know what you're doing. I really do.'

'I do,' said Siobhan. 'I always do.'

Siobhan slept fitfully in her bed that night. Lorraine's look kept annoying her. She would turn over and over, but that same angry, almost worried look that was on Lorraine's face came back at her. What was the woman's problem? It was just the way things worked. Eileen had given the go ahead. Lorraine probably couldn't give a damn if Siobhan was caught out. Maybe Siobhan was in her way. She didn't know, but there was always a possibility.

Siobhan rang Julian that night, and he confirmed he had talked to his twenty people. He believed they would be good, but he'd also not informed any of them that any of the others were coming. He had contacted them one by one.

Siobhan passed on the detail of the location and what would be happening. She talked about the drug runners arriving, how Quigley's people would be gathering them all together. She told Julian to make a move once everyone was gathered in the barn and Quigley was about to turn John Carroll inside out.

Julian's demeanour cheered Siobhan somewhat, and she just wanted to get it over and done with. She sat up in bed thinking about the one thing she wanted, and then it clicked with her. She wanted to open that front door of hers and see Julian's face there with no agenda and no business to do. There simply for her, because he wanted to be.

Chapter 31

Siobhan spent the next couple of days trying to work out how she could change her plan to incorporate and escape for herself. She designed a mask inside of her hood that she could put up so she wouldn't be seen if she tried to escape.

There would never be definite proof who had betrayed the coven, who had got inside and broken up the business. But if she was there and wasn't taken away by the authorities and the rest were, it would be obvious it was her. She would leave, most probably with Kylie and Declan, on a plane for somewhere far away.

In truth, she couldn't work out how to get out of it. Eileen had called her bluff by putting her there. Maybe Eileen knew, or maybe she didn't. Siobhan didn't think so. She'd been so kind to Siobhan after she'd had to supposedly kill Kylie. She'd got close to Siobhan and cried with her. Everything that Eileen had done said that Siobhan had been taken in, but she now was part of them. Yes, she would be watched as anybody else was because allegiances and other things change over time, but Siobhan had only just arrived.

She didn't think that Eileen was suspicious. On the other

hand, Siobhan couldn't see her way out. Eileen was also deeply unsteady behind the figurative mask she had on. If Siobhan betrayed her, the woman would come. Julian would have to make sure that she went away for a long time. Even so, disappearing, becoming somebody else would be the wise option for Siobhan and her two employees. She only hoped that one day Julian would follow.

Declan was brought into the plan, and placed on the outskirts of the situation. He would sit in his car and await developments, and if Siobhan required him, he would come get her. Things were too serious for Declan to be too close. Siobhan didn't trust his ability, but she had told Julian that Declan would be there. Julian thought it a wise move. Certainly, when Julian made his move, Siobhan would have to step out and Declan would pick her up several fields away from the farm. Julian hadn't told his team about Siobhan, hadn't explained that she was the mole in the ranks. His team would pick her up the same as anyone else, so Siobhan would have to be quick on her feet.

She left the house that evening, the witch's cloak in the rear with the new hood attached to it. Inside of it, a new mask that the coven didn't know about was also there. Siobhan was nervous and she could feel it as she drove the road towards Belfast and then headed out towards Lisburn. Not far beyond Lisburn, she pulled off, parking her car up and awaited collection.

Eileen Quigley had said Siobhan would travel with her. They would wait as Eileen's foot soldiers watched the drug trafficking, collecting each of John Carroll's dealers. They would hold them before taking them back to the large barn that was being used for Carroll's activities that night. What

Quigley didn't know was that once Siobhan was in Quigley's car, Declan would move Siobhan's car, putting it out of sight to be picked up at another time. Siobhan would disappear in the chaos until it was decided what would happen with Declan, Kylie, and her.

As she got into Quigley's car, Siobhan tried to be calm, but her nerves jangled. At least, it wouldn't be unusual for nerves to be showing. She felt Eileen Quigley put her hand on her thigh.

'You get that way too,' she said. 'So do I, especially about turning someone inside out. It's been a while since I've done it. Had others do it for me a few times, but you don't lose the skill. But you're right, it really will look the part.'

The car rolled on before parking up in a small lay by, and Eileen Quigley sat looking at her watch. Her phone was in front of her, and the first text message came in.

'That's the first one grabbed,' she said.

Siobhan nodded and Quigley pulled out a small hip flask, offering Siobhan some. 'I usually do this when I'm going to carry out the more extreme work. Need a stiff drink to do it. You don't want to do it without one. You can end up throwing up. Always a shoddy look if you're causing such injuries to people, and then stand there being sick yourself, it isn't good.'

Siobhan shook her head and muttered, 'True,' and stared out of the window. The moon was out, and she could see its light falling down on the surrounding land. The green hues of day had faded to a myriad of blacks, the succulent land being stripped of its true lustre. Even now, looking around, this was home. But the Ard's peninsula was truly home. The arm-shaped spit of land hanging down around Strangford Lough—the gold coast as she called it.

It looked like she was saying goodbye to it tonight. It looked like it wouldn't be hers anymore. Would it be a goodbye to Julian as well? Her face, however, was expressionless, holding a calm resoluteness for the benefit of Eileen Quigley. Inside, Siobhan's stomach was churning as she feared losing the very thing she'd retired for.

One by one, the drug runners were caught by Quigley's people, and she advised Siobhan that they'd all been gathered. It was time for the coven to reveal themselves, for them to take over John Carroll's crew, and for John Carroll to be the sacrifice that installed discipline into the drug runners. They would now work for the coven.

The car rolled forward, driving down country lanes before turning off towards a large barn at one end of a farm. There were lights on inside and there were several cars parked there. Eileen Quigley's car pulled up and Siobhan got out, her hood wrapped up around her.

'Gather them all together,' said Eileen. 'I want you to talk to them all, instill some discipline. In twenty minutes' time, I'll come in. Build me up, tell them what I am, and then I'll come in, and do the deed. Make sure they're already trembling before I arrive.'

'I imagine they're already trembling, having been caught and not by the police,' said Siobhan. She prayed Julian was close by and watching, and would notice that Quigley's car was disappearing.

'I'll be there soon. I have a minor change to your plan,' said Quigley.

'Oh,' said Siobhan, 'I wasn't aware there was anything wrong with it.'

'I'm just activating an insurance policy. Nothing to worry

about. I'll be there soon enough.'

Siobhan walked up the side of the barn, noting that Quigley's car was now disappearing. She stepped inside the barn and found a large group of men on their knees, guns to their heads. Recognising their captors from photographs and the visits to the estates, she nodded at the men under the coven's thumb who had caught the drug runners. They would go away with some proceeds of the night's raid. Siobhan looked around her. There were no other coven members, none. She thought for a moment. *What's going on?*

'Where is she then?' asked one man. Siobhan turned, her mask now raised up inside her hood, so only her eyes could be seen at any point.

'Speak with a bit more respect. You could join tonight's entertainment,' said Siobhan. 'She'll be here when she's ready.'

'I don't wait for no one,' said the man.'

'Really? Two of our order didn't wait for her either,' said Siobhan, referencing those that have died in the pillory in Carrickfergus. The man backed down.

Siobhan walked up to the front of the barn. A few bales of hay had been placed for her to stand on to address them. She felt the vibration on her phone inside her outfit, and she reached in, looking around to make sure no one else could see. It was a text from Julian. It read, *My people are not here. No one. Someone called it off. Get out; get out now.*

Siobhan looked around her and then typed into the phone. *Declan, rendezvous point B now!*

As Siobhan finished sending the text, she heard something in the distance. It was the wail of police car sirens.

'What the hell is this?' shouted one man. *Siobhan's mind scrambled. What was going on? Had she been made? Why were the police coming now? Insurance policy. She was enacting an insurance policy.*

Siobhan's stomach sank. Quigley had made her. Somehow Quigley had made her, but she hadn't made her until after she'd opened all her secrets. The sirens were getting louder. The doors of the barn were opening. There was gunfire, men screaming.

Siobhan ran for the nearest door. As it opened, a policeman stepped in, but Siobhan kicked him hard, sending him backwards. She tore away from that door and over to another one, which was still unopened. Pushing it, she heard someone shout in the distance and rolled to the ground as gunfire erupted. She tore off into the nearest bush outside, jumping hard and half clattering through it. The thorns tore at the cloak, but it was thick and she was able to get through to the other side.

Declan would be half a mile away. Her feet ran through the muddy ground. It had been cold, so most of it was firm, but it had rained recently, hence the mud. She felt the cool night air, but it then gave way to heavy sweat inside her garments. The robes were heavy. She pulled down her mask briefly, trying to grab some air.

Looking quickly over her shoulder, she saw someone was following. Was that the police? There was a helicopter up above, a searchlight swinging here, there, and everywhere. She crossed two more fields, outrunning the person behind her, but as she reached the end of that one, she saw a car by a gate. *Be there, Declan! It had better be you!*

Siobhan saw Declan's car and slid inside the fast-opening passenger door, straight into the seat. The car tore off, and she barely got inside. Something that surprised her. Declan was usually very careful, making sure everyone was in, even when in a hurry. She glanced to her right and saw Julian in the driver's seat.

'What the hell is going on?'

'She's onto me. I think she's cutting and running. She always said she had enough. She could always get away. There was money in her bank accounts. I don't think she clocked me until after she told me everything. She's going to burn the house down.'

'Cutting and running?' said Declan from the rear seats.

'Yes, she's going to burn the house down and everyone else.'

'She's really going to go back there? To the Mournes?'

'Yes, Julian, everything about her is in there, everything that will convict her. All these people you catch, they're never going to talk about Eileen Quigley. They're going to be worried because she's going to be on the loose. She's going to disappear. She's got too much fear instilled in them, too much of an aura about her. If she cuts away the evidence, we'll never bring her in.'

'But if we don't get her, you'll have to leave if she's out in the open,' said Julian.

'I don't want to leave,' said Declan. 'Why would I ever want to leave?'

'The Mournes, fast as you can, Julian, fast as you can.'

Julian drove as hard as he could, but he had to be careful. They were leaving a busy crime scene. The police were everywhere. Julian controlled his speed when he saw police cars. Rounding away from a checkpoint, he took Siobhan down country roads she didn't know existed. It wasn't a quick trip either, the best part of an hour to arrive at the house. As they drove up the stony driveway, the flames were already burning the house down.

'Declan, 999; don't give a false name,' said Siobhan.

'She's been and gone,' said Julian. 'She's been and gone. I don't know what will be left in there by the time the fire engines get here.'

'But she's not clear. What's she going to do with a coven?' said Siobhan out loud. 'Julian, the coven still exists. Do they run together, or does she leave them?'

Chapter 32

Siobhan sat in the car, watching the burning house beneath the Mourne Mountains. The fire brigade had arrived and Julian pointed them to the building from the main road, saying that he'd just passed by and saw it on fire. As the fire crews attended it, he disappeared off in the car with Declan and Siobhan.

'Is that her away then, Mrs D?' said Declan. 'Can we get her? Can't you put something out? Can't you close down what she's doing? Find her in at an airport?'

'Somebody within my organisation is looking out for her,' said Julian. 'I can't go that wide and stop her. She'll know we've put things out. She'll . . .'

'Wait a minute,' said Siobhan. 'Insurance policy. If you want to be clear, if you truly want to be clear, you don't take everybody else along with you, do you?' She stared at Julian and saw the cogs working in the back of his mind.

'Don't get what you mean,' said Declan. 'You mean like kids; you don't take the kids with you if you want to have an enjoyable time.'

'No, Declan. She's just burnt the house down, and in the process of burning the evidence, who really knows what she did? Who could give proper testimony about her? The Coven. She said she was enacting an insurance policy.'

'I don't get that,' said Julian. 'Why did she want to tell you? We could have got here and stopped her. We could have . . .'

'No,' said Siobhan. 'She knew she'd beat me here, if I got away. She had more than a head start. She'll have a way and a means of closing everything down, burning it all, all the evidence gone. Taking the insurance policy,' thought Siobhan out loud. 'She needed to take out the insurance policy, not just this evidence, but everything, on everybody who could point towards her.

'The coven, Julian. She was going to implicate me because I knew all her plans. I had organised this. Everyone knew there that I was the one doing it. She left me in that barn. The police would have arrived. I was in charge. I was the mysterious one in the hood. She was dumping it on me because she had clocked who I was. Yet she couldn't let the other sisters find that out, so she just called it off for them. She just called it off and . . .'

'Did what?' asked Declan.

'She's going to end it all with them. She's going to gather them together, and she's going to end it with them.'

'How though?' asked Julian. 'Was she going to meet at a club or at one of the restaurants? Bring them to somebody's house.'

'No,' said Siobhan. 'The only time they all gather is when they dance, when they initiate, when they do their ceremonies. She'll have called it off and she will have brought a ceremony together. She'll kill them all at a ceremony.'

'Well, we know where the dance takes place. We just head for Greenisland,' said Julian.

'But she knows we know that. They must have other places. Must have . . .'

Siobhan suddenly remembered somewhere. She'd been taken by Angela Lynch.

'The Ballylone Road, there was a place there. I didn't know what it was for, but Deborah had been there. Must have been one of their other places. The Ballylone Road. Julian, the Ballylone Road. We need to go there now.' Julian put his foot down and sped off into the night. Meanwhile, in the backseat, Declan was stumped.

'But why the Ballylone Road? What are they going to do there?'

'Dance. Dance and what can you do when you dance? They must have ceremonies,' said Siobhan. They must do things that . . . Quickly, Julian,' she said. 'Quickly.'

Julian raced as quickly as he could in the car, but he was still going to take over half an hour to get there. Siobhan sat pensively in her seat, still dressed in her black outfit with cloak. As they got closer, Siobhan prayed they were in time. What would Quigley do to them? How would she go about it?

Quickly, Siobhan raced from the car as Julian pulled up close to the field at Ballylone. She could see a group of figures, all standing together in a circle beyond the lake.

'They're dancing,' said Declan. 'Like that time with Kylie, they're dancing. They've got nothing on and they're dancing.'

Siobhan wasn't waiting to confirm what was happening. Instead, she legged it down over to the ground where the women were performing what they believed to be a satanic and erotic dance. As she neared the group, several of them stopped and turned.

Siobhan noticed a cup was being passed around between

them and they were drinking. They all stopped suddenly and turned, looking at Siobhan in her witch's robes. She pulled the hood down and her dirty blonde hair was hung loosely behind her. Lorraine twisted round, looking at Eileen, standing in the altogether. Lorraine's face was bemused. She glanced back at Siobhan and then back to Eileen again.

'You said she betrayed us. Said she was dead. You had killed her.'

Siobhan noticed that the mouths of the women had red around their lips, not like a lipstick, but more like a damp sponge had been pressed against it with red paint on it.

'You said we drank her blood,' said Lorraine. 'You had caught her out and now we drank her blood. We blessed it to him, who we must obey.'

'You caught on then,' said Eileen. 'Did I overplay my hand? I guess I must have. I don't know quite how you're here, though.'

Suddenly, one witch to the right pitched to the ground. She was motionless, eyes staring straight ahead.

'What have you done?' screamed Lorraine. Siobhan noticed that Eileen Quigley was holding a goblet. It was silver.

'Did you all drink from that?' asked Siobhan.

Lorraine suddenly became extremely agitated. 'We passed it round. We passed it to . . . we pa . . .' Lorraine fell to the ground and her legs kicked briefly before she stopped moving for the last time. Others keeled over. One by one, before their eyes, each of the witches dropped dead to the ground.

'I couldn't help but gloat,' said Eileen Quigley. 'The insurance policy, but how did you get here? I never told you about here.'

'You were at the Mournes,' said Siobhan. 'You burnt the house down. All the evidence. The only people who knew it all and could incriminate you were the sisters of your coven. I thought you'd kill them all. We have to make sacrifices after all.'

'But how are you here?'

'Angela Lynch,' said Siobhan. 'Deborah was not the perfect witch. Deborah did tell Angela things. Although, it was spoken drunkenly out of turn. Angela was such a difficult witness, but I learnt from her about her sister, and what had happened, and she brought me here. I couldn't find much, but tonight I knew you would go to dance, but you couldn't go out there, not out to Greenisland. No, you knew I'd seen you out there. Kylie had seen you out there. Everyone would know about there.

'So, you came here. It wasn't quite a lucky guess, but an educated guess you'd come. This is the only other place I knew. You hadn't told me about any others. You hadn't told me about this,' said Siobhan. 'Angela Lynch told me about this place, and so I made my guess.'

'And you're too late,' said Eileen. She reached behind her and pulled up her robes from the ground, fastening them round her. What women seriously think you get places by dancing naked? They were sloppy overall. You weren't,' said Eileen.

'I actually thought that you might be worth it, but the problem was your friend doesn't judge his people that well. My contact said that he was coming to do an operation funnily enough, at the same time that we were taking out John Carroll. Coincidence? I don't believe in them, so I set you up there, but you seem to have escaped. Should have known that, really. I brought the girls here but I'm going to that beautiful beach. I'm going to find that boy who can keep me happy, or another one, or another one after that. Walking away from it, and in truth, it was probably you who did it for me. You with your idea, telling me you just wanted the money and to go. Well, you sold me on that one.'

'You won't get away,' said Siobhan. 'We're here now.'

A police car pulled up behind them on the road, and Siobhan turned, looking at the blue flashing lights. They were switched off, suddenly, and a single police officer walked across. The man pulled out a gun.

'What's the problem here? Something wrong, Mrs Quigley?'

Siobhan knew a stooge when she saw one. The man was in Quigley's pocket. Nobody would stop a police car, after all. He'd take her where she'd need to go.

'Where's the jet?' asked Siobhan. 'Aldergrove?'

'The handy thing about here,' said Quigley, 'is there's a lake. It'll be days before you'll be found if we weigh you down.'

As quick as a flash, Julian produced a gun from within his jacket. The police officer's weapon had been trained on Siobhan, and by the time he turned to fix his on Julian, he had one pointing straight back at him. It was a tense standoff. Julian watched the man closely, seeing if he would flinch, but neither man took their eyes off the other, guns pointed at heads.

'I think we're at a standoff,' said Siobhan. 'When you came to the graveside, you put your arm around me, with Kylie in the ground. You were genuine, weren't you?'

'You had me sold. All the way down the river and we brought you in. If it hadn't been for your friend calling his colleague to help him, you'd have gone right through with it. Of course, if you'd have brought the police in to round me up. I have enough of them so I could have got out of it. You must have thought yourself ever so lucky when John Carroll was bringing in those drugs. A chance to finish it all so quickly. Kudos to you though. Killing your friend to get in, that's impressive, even for the Service.'

Siobhan wanted to tell her that Kylie wasn't dead, but if this went south, she needed her to believe that Kylie was gone. If Kylie was out there to corroborate any story, it would be a long shot, but maybe they would still get Eileen if Siobhan was dead.

Siobhan stepped slowly to one side. The policeman with the gun looked at her, telling her not to move.

'Or you'll do what?'

'Steady,' said Eileen, 'she's baiting you. She's baiting you.'

'I'm just going sideways,' said Siobhan. 'Sideways.'

The police officer's eyes flicked to the right. The gun flickered for a moment to move towards Siobhan, and Julian shot the man clean between the eyes without hesitation. He tumbled backwards onto the ground, and Julian ran over, making sure he was dead, and taking the gun from the dead man's hand.

'I think you need to take her away,' Siobhan said to Julian, 'and use the police car. We'll need to get scarce.'

'I'll contact you. I hear Rio's nice at this time of year.'

'Why are we going to Rio though? He's got her,' asked Declan.

'Because she's alive, Declan. She can do a deal, a plea bargain, and then she'll come for us. I've betrayed her. I've gone into the deepest parts of her trust and blown it wide open. You can't forgive something like that, can you, Eileen?'

'No,' she said, as Julian told her to put her hands behind her head. He took the policeman's handcuffs and slapped them onto her wrists before pushing her towards the police car. Julian put Eileen into the back of it and then stepped into the front. He watched as Declan drove away with Siobhan in the car and he waited for five minutes for them to get clear.

He radioed he had Eileen Quigley in the rear of his vehicle to the police communications room. They asked who he was, and he gave his Service identity and asked them to contact the relevant authorities. Then he sat back in his seat, his eyes flicking to the rearview mirror where Eileen seemed to be asleep. He watched her chest; it didn't move.

Julian stepped out of the car, opened the rear door, and placed a hand up to the woman's neck. He saw the substance rolling out of her mouth; she was gone or bust, it seemed. She had decided it was a clean getaway tonight or she wouldn't make it anywhere ever again.

Julian stepped back into the front seat, called Quigley's death into the police station, and waited for the police cars to arrive. As he sat there, he smiled. Never before in his career had he smiled at so much death around him. There were eleven women out in that field. There was one in the back of the car, all dead. Twelve of the thirteen witches of the coven were no longer alive.

He smiled because one was alive and no longer would she need to go away. No longer was there anyone to come after her. There was no evidence either, all burnt through. This would be a Service job, wrapped up quietly. No one need ever know that Siobhan was even here. He had only one thing left to do: tidy up his mole. Julian put his hands on the steering wheel and smiled to himself. He could see retirement in the offing.

Chapter 33

Siobhan Duffy stood looking at the graveyard in front of her. She remembered the crunching path she'd walked along. She remembered the tears that she'd cried. False tears, but in some ways, they had been genuine. They were cried for the pain she'd put her employee through. In saying that, Kylie was becoming much more of a friend. Behind her in the car was Declan, and Siobhan waved him over. He opened up the boot of the car, lifting out a large sledgehammer.

'I thought she'd be here by now. You did manage to contact her, didn't you?' asked Declan.

'Course I did. I got the number from Julian. Julian told me to dig up the grave. Get rid of it. I thought the least I could do was start by doing the headstone. The digging up and removal of the coffin will have to be done a little more quietly. At least there's nobody here at the moment.'

Siobhan walked with Declan up to the grave and stared at the inscription in front of her. *Kylie, I'm sorry I let you down.*

'But you didn't let her down. You got us through it, didn't you?'

Siobhan went to speak, but there was a crunch from the stones over near the car park. A smaller woman than herself, and much younger, with black hair that ran down to her shoulders, was walking towards her, hands in the pockets of her jacket. There was a broad beam on her face, and as she came closer, Siobhan saw Declan's face light up. He tore off along the path, and Siobhan watched as the two of them embraced. She'd never seen him quite like that, never seen them so open about each other. Times had changed.

Once they'd calmed down, the two walked hand in hand over towards Siobhan. She had caught the sledgehammer as Declan dropped it when he ran over to Kylie, and then she held it up in front of Kylie.

'You want to knock it over?'

'It's kind of weird,' said Kylie, 'Looking at your own grave.'

'It's probably the worst thing you've seen in the last week,' said Declan.

'No, I've seen some rubbish TV,' said Kylie, smiling. She grabbed the sledgehammer and tried to swing it at the stone, but found it too heavy and almost lost her footing. Declan caught her as she fell, and Siobhan grabbed the sledgehammer.

'Maybe you want to do it, Declan,' said Siobhan.

'No,' he said. 'If you remember, I didn't put her here. You did.'

Siobhan gave him a sarky smile, took the sledgehammer, and brought it down hard on top of the stone. It cracked down the middle, and with repeated swings, she got the two halves to separate and fall flat.

'I am not carrying it back to the car and to the dump. That's your job. You're my gardener,' she said to Declan. He smiled and made two trips back and forward, loading up the car with the broken headstone.

As he did so, Kylie flung her arms around Siobhan. 'Is that

it?' she said. 'Are we in the clear?'

'Julian is coming to see me today,' said Siobhan. 'In fact, we'd better get back soon. He said two.'

'Do you want us to be there?'

'Well, you probably want to hear what he has to say.'

'You can text me. I'll take Declan up to the lodge. You can text me from yours. If Julian needs to talk to us, he's only fifty yards away.'

'Okay,' said Siobhan, 'that sounds good.'

The day was bitter, but the car was warm as they drove back out to Siobhan's house. The two youngsters couldn't wait to get out of the car, and they disappeared off to the lodge at the front of the driveway.

Siobhan didn't begrudge them. She'd put them in a terrible position, and she'd have to think about the future. If she was going to investigate, she was going to have to teach them. They were going to have to learn. Maybe be skilled in either espionage or computers, or something else because, at the moment, they weren't really skilled at all. She'd have to do a training programme. What was she thinking? They'd be getting trained soon enough. If things hadn't worked out right, they'd be on a plane by tonight.

She didn't go inside. Instead, she stood in her black coat in the garden. She looked around at the few flowers that were out because there weren't many. Declan had done such a good job with the garden. In the summer, she'd fancied sitting there enjoying it much more. She walked to the end, looking at the rocks that touched the sea at her garden's boundary. It wasn't a big place she had, but it was just right. She loved how the water lapped up. It was a wintry day, and she felt the chill, but everywhere here was beautiful. This was home. She didn't want to leave it. If it wasn't hers, she'd have to take it back one bit at a time.

She heard him creeping up. He was good. Very good. She had barely caught the sounds, but when she did, she didn't turn round. She didn't know that many people who were that good, and anyone who wanted to cause her harm would've caused it by now. There was his scent on the wind as well. His hand slipped around her, wrapping around her waist and pulling her close. She felt his breath in her ear.

'This is where I want to be,' she said. 'Everything I've got is right here. Everything I could ever want is right here. Tell me I can stay.'

'She died in the car,' said Julian. 'When you drove away, she was in the rear seat. Quigley killed herself. She couldn't face it and I couldn't have stopped her.

'The police arrived, and I showed them the eleven bodies in the field. I made my reports, and then I met with each of my twenty so-called collaborators who didn't turn up that night. It took me a while, but I found her. She was very promising, too. It's probably the saddest part of it. She's not with the Service anymore. In fact, I don't know where she is at all. I rather fancy that someone might have given her a headstone, but it wasn't my responsibility. Once I knew who it was, I reported it.'

Siobhan could feel a tingle in her stomach that ran down her arms. It wasn't his responsibility? The only way it couldn't be his responsibility was . . .

'And I told them,' said Julian, 'I told them right there and then I was out, so don't think you're going to get any more backup or help. You need to do something much quieter that pays the bills. You can't go through this sort of thing again. I paid Angela Lynch a visit, though. Felt she needed to know something. Of course, it was the Service version of the tale. But I don't think she's daft enough to think that's the whole truth.'

Siobhan smiled. She twisted her head round and let Julian kiss her. It was long, it was deep, and she didn't want it to stop. When he did, he simply held her as he looked out onto the water. 'Shall we go tell the other two?' asked Julian.

'I wouldn't. They're up in the lodge. They didn't go in that long ago, so I'd give them some time. I don't think they fully grasped what the consequences could have been, but I did. Thanks to my knight in shining armour, I don't have to go anywhere, so I'm not going to.'

'Are you not cold, standing here?' asked Julian.

'Not at all. I've got my jumper,' she said. 'I love this jumper. It comes right up to my neck. It's thick wool, it's lovely and warm, and I've got you.'

'Well, my hands are freezing,' he said. 'Good job you've got your jumper.'

Siobhan felt his hands suddenly go up the inside of her jumper and sit on her belly. They were cold, and she gave a shriek, but he was hanging on to her tightly. She pulled his hands close into her tummy, resting her hands outside her jumper.

'Now that's wicked,' said Siobhan.

'You're right about the jumper, though. So warm.'

'You still owe me something though,' said Siobhan, 'and I intend to collect on it.'

'What do you mean?' asked Julian. 'After all I've done for you, what could you possibly intend on collecting? Except for this.' He kissed her again. When they broke off, she shook her head.

'You've got to be having a laugh if you think you get it off that easy. I haven't forgotten.'

'Well, you better inform me,' he said.

'You saw me dance naked in a field on a chilly night. When we got out of this, you were going to let me see you dance that way. The bill's due tonight. We're going to be heading that way.'

He tickled her stomach, making her laughed. 'Deal,' he said, 'but we take a tent as well.'

'Like hell,' said Siobhan, 'we've got a perfectly suitable house here. We'll come back when you're done.'

With that, she pulled him tight again. For now, she was happy. He was here; she was here. Even the two up in the lodge seemed to be happy. Julian wanted a quieter life, did he? Well, that wasn't happening. She smiled. The wee country wasn't itself yet. There was still a long way to go.

Read on to discover the Patrick Smythe series!

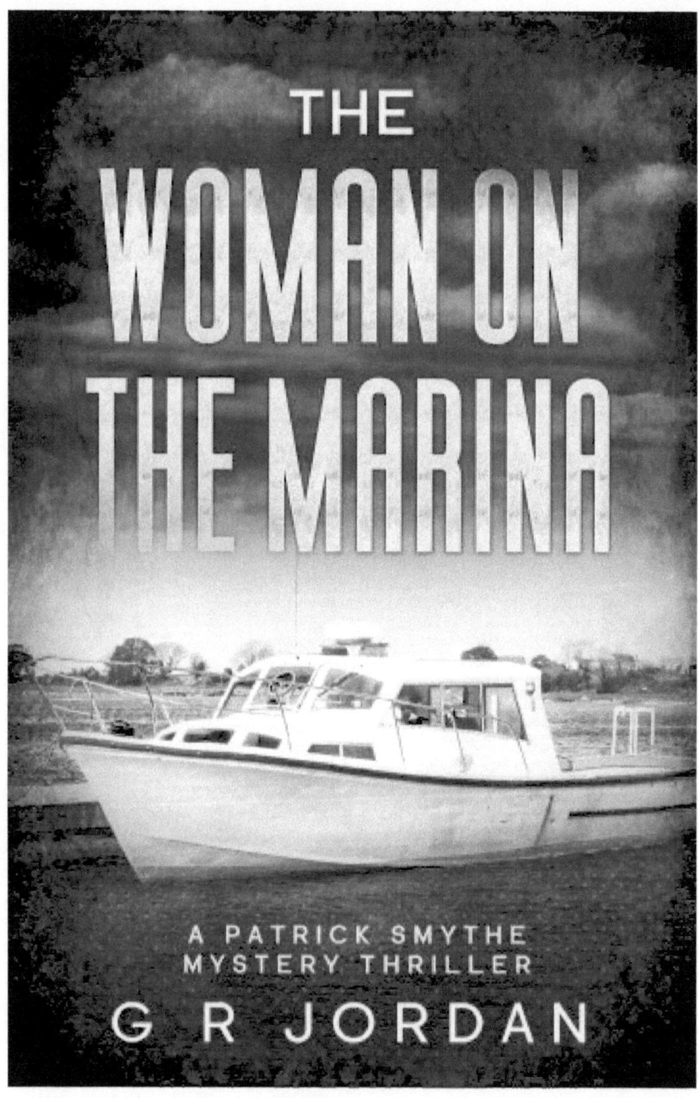

Patrick Smythe is a former Northern Irish policeman who after suffering an amputation after a bomb blast, takes to the sea between the west coast of Scotland and his homeland to ply his trade as a private investigator. Join Paddy as he tries to work to his own ethics while knowing how to bend the rules he once enforced. Working from his beloved motorboat 'Craigantlet', Paddy decides to rescue a drug mule in this short story from the pen of G R Jordan.

Join G R Jordan's monthly newsletter about forthcoming releases and special writings for his tribe of avid readers and then receive your free Patrick Smythe short story.

Go to https://bit.ly/PatrickSmythe for your Patrick Smythe journey to start!

About the Author

G R Jordan is a self-published author who finally decided at forty that in order to have an enjoyable lifestyle, his creative beast within would have to be unleashed. His books mirror that conflict in life where acts of decency contend with self-promotion, goodness stares in horror at evil, and kindness blindsides us when we at our worst. Corrupting our world with his parade of wondrous and horrific characters, he highlights everyday tensions with fresh eyes whilst taking his methodical, intelligent mainstays on a roller-coaster ride of dilemmas, all the while suffering the banter of their provocative sidekicks.

A graduate of Loughborough University where he masqueraded as a chemical engineer but ultimately played American football, Gary had worked at changing the shape of cereal flakes and pulled a pallet truck for a living. Watching vegetables freeze at -40'C was another career highlight and he was also one of the Scottish Highlands "blind" air traffic controllers. These days he has graduated to answering a telephone to people in trouble before telephoning other people to sort it out.

Having flirted with most places in the UK, he is now based in the Isle of Lewis in Scotland where his free time is spent between raising a young family with his wife, writing, figuring out how to work a loom and caring for a small flock of chickens. Luckily, his writing is influenced by his varied work and life experience as the chickens have not been the poetical inspiration he had hoped for!

You can connect with me on:

🌐 https://grjordan.com

f https://facebook.com/carpetlessleprechaun

Subscribe to my newsletter:

✉ https://bit.ly/PatrickSmythe

Also by G R Jordan

G R Jordan writes across multiple genres including crime, dark and action adventure fantasy, feel good fantasy, mystery thriller and horror fantasy. Below is a selection of his work. Whilst all books are available across online stores, signed copies are available at his personal shop.

The Bloodied Hands (Siobhan Duffy #3)
https://grjordan.com/product/the-bloodied-hands
Single hands posted to the local paper. Missing persons identified as the appendage owners. Can Siobhan Duffy find the link between those who have vanished before an even bloodier revenge is inflicted.

When a friend at the county's paper receives a hand in the post, Siobhan Duffy is dragged into a web of broken trust and bitter lies. After the intention to complete a horrific punishment is announced on completion of kidnapping the victims, Siobhan finds her investigation strapped for time. Can she unmask the perpetrator to bring home the innocent before Ulster runs red with their blood?

A betrayer of friends must understand the meaning of sacrifice!

Highlands and Islands Detective Thriller Series
https://grjordan.com/
product/waters-edge
Join stalwart DI Macleod and his burgeoning new DC McGrath as they look into the darker side of the stunningly scenic and wilder parts of the north of Scotland. From the Black Isle to Lewis, from Mull to Harris and across to the small Isles, the Uists and Barra, this mismatched pairing follow murders, thieves and vengeful victims in an effort to restore tranquillity to the remoter parts of the land.

Be part of this tale of a surprise partnership amidst the foulest deeds and darkest souls who stalk this peaceful and most beautiful of lands, and you'll never see the Highlands the same way again.

Kirsten Stewart Thrillers

https://grjordan.com/product/a-shot-at-democracy

Join Kirsten Stewart on a shadowy ride through the underbelly of the Highlands of Scotland where among the beauty and splendour of the majestic landscape lies corruption and intrigue to match any city. From murders to extortion, missing children to criminals operating above the law, the Highland former detective must learn a tougher edge to her work as she puts her own life on the line to protect those who cannot defend themselves.

Having left her beloved murder investigation team far behind, Kirsten has to battle personal tragedy and loss while adapting to a whole new way of executing her duties where your mistakes are your own. As Kirsten comes to terms with working with the new team, she often operates as the groups solo field agent, placing herself in danger and trouble to rescue those caught on the dark side of life. With action packed scenes and tense scenarios of murder and greed, the Kirsten Stewart thrillers will have you turning page after page to see your favourite Scottish lass home!

There's life after Macleod, but a whole new world of death!

Jac's Revenge (A Jack Moonshine Thriller #1)

https://grjordan.com/product/jacs-revenge

An unexpected hit makes Debbie a widow. The attention of her man's killer spawns a brutal yet classy alter ego. But how far can you play the game before it takes over your life?

All her life, Debbie Parlor lived in her man's shadow, knowing his work was never truly honest. She turned her head from news stories and rumours. But when he was disposed of for his smile to placate a rival crime lord, Jac Moonshine was born. And when Debbie is paid compensation for her loss like her car was written off, Jac decides that enough is enough.

Get on board with this tongue-in-cheek revenge thriller that will make you question how far you would go to avenge a loved one, and how much you would enjoy it!

www.ingramcontent.com/pod-product-compliance
Lightning Source LLC
Chambersburg PA
CBHW051248210726
48287CB00002B/399